THE VRIL AGENDA

AIRSHIP 27 PRODUCTIONS

The Vril Agenda
© 2014 Joshua Reynolds & Derrick Ferguson

Published by Airship 27 Productions
www.airship27.com
www.airship27hangar.com

Cover illustration © 2014 Adam Shaw
Interior illustrations © 2014 Rob Davis

Editor: Ron Fortier
Associate Editor: Charles Saunders
Production and design by Rob Davis.

ISBN-13: 978-0-692-02221-4 (Airship 27)
ISBN-10: 069202221X

Printed in the United States of America

10 9 8 7 6 5 4 3 2 1

THE VRIL AGENDA

BY JOSHUA REYNOLDS AND DERRICK FERGUSON

Part 1:
'THE POWER'

I.

The pedestrian traffic choking Fifth Avenue seemed even more hectic and bustling than usual to the tall young man who navigated his way through the horde of people who seemed hyper aware of their surroundings and oblivious of them at the same time. But that was New Yorkers for you. It was a strange set of survival skills the denizens of that great metropolis developed, one that the young man appreciated and found both fascinating and amusing. It had only been two years since he had been making his way in a world both alien and familiar to him. He found it simultaneously frightening and exhilarating.

His height and build were both exceptional. Standing at an easy six feet four, his impressive musculature drew more than an average share of admiring looks from women and a few men as well. It didn't hurt that he was also easy on the eye, with his high cheekbones and sparkling copper eyes under severe eyebrows. His dark skin seemed almost to glow with vitality and energy.

He dressed simply in well-worn jeans, battered high-top Billy Hoyle sneakers and a plain extra-large beige T-shirt. It was a little nippy that particular early spring morning but he didn't seem to notice or care. He'd suffered far worse cold during his training to the point where he could sleep naked in four feet of snow overnight with no discomfort.

He stopped in front of a building he'd come to know well over the past week. A wonderful example of Eighteenth century European domestic architecture, it was set back from the avenue proper by an elevated garden. It occupied the entire block, surrounded by a concrete wall twelve feet high on three sides with an ornate steel fence facing Fifth Avenue designed and constructed by the famous Israeli sculptor Abayev.

As he had done for the past week the young black man walked up to the front door. There was no name or plaque on the door identifying the building but such was not needed and hadn't been since the establishment of this edifice back in the 1930's. This was the New York chapter of the world famous and eminently prestigious Baltimore Gun Club. And the young black man had come here every day for a week to see one of its more famous members.

He rang the bell and no more than twenty seconds later it was opened by a footman who admitted him into the reception hall. As always, the footman allowed him to sit while Chamberlain Frick was summoned.

Chamberlain Frick arrived not more than a minute later. He supervised the activities of the staff and reigned over the building as if he were a feudal lord. As such, it was his purview to formally verify the business of visitors and personally escort them within.

Chamberlain Frick shook hands with the young man. "I must say that you are a most persistent young man, as well as punctual. You've been right on time at nine a.m. on the nose every morning."

"I don't mean to be a bother, sir."

"You're not bothering me, young man. But as I've told you every day for a week now, there is simply no way to anticipate when your party will be here. For as long as I've known him he's rarely come through that door like the other members. No one sees him come. He's simply here. No one sees him go. He's simply gone."

The young man's copper eyes gleamed with excitement. "Would you check to see if he's here?"

"I'll ask the kitchen to send you round coffee or tea if you'd like."

"Tea, please."

It had become their ritual. The young man would sit in the reception hall all day long. He only left at noontime for lunch and returned exactly one hour later at one o'clock. Frick would provide him with tea or water and newspapers to read. At five o'clock, the young man would leave, only to return the next day. Frick personally checked three or four times a day to see if the member the young man wanted to see had arrived and the staff had their orders that if they were to see that member they were to inform Frick immediately.

Chamberlain Frick moved through the large rooms of the first floor. It was his custom to make sweeps of the entire building at random moments just to keep the staff on their toes as well as to give whatever members were present that personal touch that was such a part of Frick's efficiency. But it wasn't just that. The Baltimore Gun Club had such an important and distinguished place in American history. Indeed, many events that had changed the course of history had their beginnings with the famous and infamous members of The Baltimore Gun Club and because of that Frick felt an almost fanatical devotion to preserve the dignity and prestige of the club.

The interior of the club was one of calm and serenity. Art and sculpture and period furniture lent an air of pure elegance. The long gallery leading to the library was lined on both sides with huge portraits of Baltimore Gun Club members both past and present. Many were men and women whose names had long ago become legend in all corners of the world.

Frick walked into the library. One of the finest collections in the country, all four walls were nothing but books from floor to ceiling. Huge picture windows allowed the strengthening morning sun to illuminate the huge room. Frick noted that the library appeared to be empty with no surprise. This early in the morning it usually was. It was after lunch that the room would be occupied and after dinner it would be positively packed with members having quiet discussion accompanied with fine cigars and even finer brandy.

Frick turned to leave and heard a slight motion from a huge high backed leather armchair placed near enough to a window that the occupant could look out onto Fifth Avenue. Frick quickly walked over, thinking that this was one of the twelve club members who resided in the club itself. Once he rounded the chair and looked at the man who sat in the chair, his leathery, wrinkled face brightened into a genuine smile of welcome. "I should have known it was you, sir," as indeed he should have. The only reason the man in the chair had made a sound was because he wished to be heard.

"A pleasure as always to see you, Frick. How have you been?"

"The back acts up from time to time, sir, but nothing more than a nuisance. And yourself?"

A shrug of shoulders that were still fairly brawny despite the advanced age of the man in the chair. "Mostly consulting work. It takes up a fair amount of my time."

"It's been far too long since you've visited us, sir."

"I've been meaning to come here for some time now. My decision was accelerated by the word I've been hearing of this young man who's been asking for me."

Frick nodded. "He's been here for seven days in a row, sir. He sits in the reception hall all day long, hoping that you will show."

"Hostile?" The man asked with a smile. He was teasing. Frick wouldn't have been the Chamberlain of the New York branch of The Baltimore Gun Club if he weren't able to spot an enemy five seconds after clapping eyes upon him.

"Hardly, sir. But he is a most serious, and if I dare say, troubled young man. Life weighs heavily on him. There is no smile in his eyes. And there is something else as well. But I think that will be obvious when you see him."

The man gestured. "Bring him to me, then. He obviously needs to see me very badly. Let's find out why. And would you see that some tea is sent round to me?"

"But of course, sir."

Frick left the library briefly stopping to give instructions to the footman whose post was just outside the library doors. Then Frick quickly walked back to where he left the young black man who got to his feet anxiously as Frick approached.

"You are indeed a child of fortune, young sir. The member you seek is here. He has consented to see you."

The young man gestured at his clothes. "I hope I'm okay dressed like this...I don't have a lot of clothes."

Frick smiled slightly. "I think we can overlook the dress code this once. And I'll show you the reason why. Come with me."

Frick and the young man walked down the long gallery until stopping at one of the portraits. It depicted a woman in her twenties. Such was the skill of the artist that the youth, the strength, the vitality of the woman reached out from the paint and canvas and struck the eye with much the same effect as this woman had once had in life. A classical beauty with high cheekbones not unlike those of the young man who gazed upon the portrait with reverence. Oil black hair fell to her graceful shoulders. An eye patch covered her right eye.

"Your mother, I believe," Frick said quietly. "Right from the first day you came here I saw the resemblance."

The young man turned to the Chamberlain. "Why is her picture here?"

"Your mother was an honored member of The Baltimore Gun Club, young sir. Why else do you think I allowed you to sit inside the club every day? It is a courtesy I extended to you in honor of your mother's membership."

"Does that mean I'm a member as well?"

"Membership in The Baltimore Gun Club is not hereditary, young sir. It must be earned. If you are truly interested in becoming a member, please let me know and I myself would be most pleased to sponsor you."

"You knew my mother?"

"I did indeed, young sir. She was both a lady and a warrior in every sense of both those words."

The young man reached out a trembling hand to stroke the portrait's cheek. "She's dead."

"My condolences and sincere regrets. I have long thought she was. Otherwise she would have returned to the club at some time. I will make arraignments for the Gunnery Sacrament. It is a special ritual performed when a member of The Baltimore Gun Club dies. I will naturally accord you privileged dispensation to attend the ritual."

The young man smiled. It was an odd smile. Frick got the impression that the young man spent long hours in front of the mirror practicing how to smile. It was as if he were unsure of how big to make the smile, how many teeth to show or if he should show any teeth at all.

"Young sir? Please come with me."

The young man followed Frick into the library. The footman had not only brought the man in the armchair his tea but another chair, a twin to the one the man sat in. Frick motioned for him to sit down and the young man did so, letting his amazed copper eyes freely examine the man sitting across from him.

He could have been anywhere between seventy and eighty with curly pure platinum silver hair that looked cotton soft cut so close that the young man could see his scalp. His skin was dark. Not as dark as the young man's. No, this man's skin was akin to the texture of aged wood, as if he were drying out like leather left in the strong southwestern sun. The unseen scars on his arms, chest and legs bespoke of a life of wild adventure and battles too numerous to count.

On any other man the three-day stubble covering his cheeks and chin would have seemed like an affected fashion accessory but not on him. He dressed simply in a plain white cotton crew neck shirt with baggy linen trousers. Instead of shoes he wore black slippers greatly resembling Japanese *uwabaki*. His only concession to popular fashion was the crisp looking, unfussy graphite Daniel Meade designer sport coat.

The silver-haired man sized up the younger man, not saying anything.

Finally, the young man spoke in a hesitant voice. "You're Jim Anthony. They called you the Super Detective back in the 30's and 40's."

"It was the newspapers who hung that label on me. Even the ones I owned." He grinned wryly.

The young man continued. "You hunted criminals. Technological terrorists—"

"—we called them mad scientists back then—"

"—monsters, killers, gangsters, spies, lunatics—"

Jim Anthony held up a dark, scarred hand, palm outwards. "I know who I am, boy. And I know what I did. The question is who are you and what do you want?"

"My name, sir, is Dillon. I want you to teach me how to hunt men and how to stay alive while doing so."

Z.

Dillon had said that with no youthful bombast or unnecessary drama. He had said it with certainty that Jim Anthony had heard from men far older and far more world-weary than this boy. Whoever he was, wherever he came from, this Dillon had packed a lot of years into his short life.

Frick bent down and whispered something in Jim's ear. Jim's eyes flickered briefly to Dillon's face, probing every square inch in the time it took for a fly to blink. Jim looked back at Frick and nodded.

"Would you mind leaving us alone, Frick? I have a feeling our young master Dillon has a lot he wants to talk about."

"Certainly, sir. But if there is anything you require, do not hesitate to summon me."

Dillon watched him go. "I like him."

"You should. Frick's a good man to be on the right side of. You'd be surprised at who he has the ear of and who seeks him out for advice. Many powerful men who steered the destiny of this country and were members of this club have benefited from Frick's advice." Jim put his china cup down. "But let's get back to you. Frick told you your mother was a member of the club?"

"He did, sir. Did you know her?"

"I had long retired by the time she joined. I met her at one of the club ceremonies and functions that I still attend occasionally. The one time I spoke to her in depth we traded stories about a mythical place that I knew as Xembala but your mother called Shamballah."

Dillon smiled. "The City Eternal has many names. Shamballah is the one I know it as."

"Fascinating. Are you telling me that you've been there?"

"My mother gave her life to see that I reached Shamballah safely. I was raised and taught by The Warmasters of Liguria for seven years. When I turned nineteen I left Shamballah to make my way back to the world. That was two years ago."

"You're being awfully free with this information it seems to me."

Dillon shrugged. "Why not? I will probably never see Shamballah again. It was a miracle that my mother found her way back. She was the first person in five hundred years, man or woman to find their way to

Shamballah a second time. And my teachers believe that she did so because of her overwhelming desire to see that I was safe. We were being pursued by…" Dillon's throat tightened with a surge of emotion. Jim didn't push.

Dillon got himself under control with a visible effort and continued. "And I realize that if you're going to help me then I need to trust you and you need to trust me as well. And if everything I've heard and read about you is true then I've got nothing to fear by telling you about Shamballah."

Jim motioned for the footman at the door to bring them more tea. To Dillon he said, "have you breakfasted yet?"

"Just some scrambled eggs and toast in the Howard Johnson's I'm staying at on 8th Avenue."

"You need more than that to get you going. You're a big guy. For maximum efficiency your metabolism needs a protein boost in the morning. You'll have breakfast with me while we talk."

"Does this mean you'll teach me?"

"Don't rush me, youngster. I said we'll talk and that's all we'll do. I'm retired and have been for a long time. I've come to enjoy my retirement. Besides, I don't know a thing about you."

Dillon's obvious disappointment dimmed the sparkle in his copper eyes as he said, "I just told you who I was and you said you knew my mother."

"To be precise I said that I *met* your mother. That's a long way from knowing her. And I've just met you and you've told me a yarn about having been raised in a mythical lost city by an equally mythical group of master martial artists. No, I cannot say with any sort of confidence that I know you at all."

And now Dillon's eyes changed. The anger rising in him at Jim's calm but firm words produced a remarkable effect in the eyes under those severe eyebrows that became even more severe. The friendly, sparkling copper of Dillon's eyes were no longer sparkling or friendly.

Dillon rose to his feet. "I'm sorry to have wasted your time, then. I'll take my leave and bid you good day, sir."

Jim sighed and waved for him to sit back down. "Take it easy, youngster. You'll live longer if you don't get mad so quickly. I said we'd talk. That's what you wanted, wasn't it?"

"I want you to train me!"

"Baby steps, boy. Baby steps. You've gotten an invitation to have breakfast with me. Isn't that more than what you had an hour ago?"

Dillon mulled that over for about twelve seconds. "I suppose it is."

"I want you to train me!"

"Then there's no telling what you'll have in another hour if you exercise a little patience, is there?"

Slowly, Dillon resumed his seat. "No, I suppose there isn't."

"Excellent. Then let's retire to the dining room and have a proper breakfast while we continue our talk."

The dining room was easily as luxurious and elegant as the rest of the mansion, a spacious room with rich oak paneling and reeded moldings. The vaulted, arched ceiling rose so high over their heads that the dining room actually took up two floors. Jim and Dillon sat across from each other in hand carved Adam style chairs, eating under the watchful, intense gaze of the life sized portrait of Impey Barbicane, the first president of The Baltimore Gun Club, which hung over the fireplace. A replica of this portrait hung in every dining room of every branch of the club while the original, quite rightly, hung in the main branch of the club located in Baltimore.

"How's your steak?" Jim asked, while cutting into his own.

"Just fine, sir. Thank you." And indeed, the young man appeared to have the appetite of a thoroughbred racehorse. Jim had a more than healthy appetite himself but even he was impressed by the way Dillon shoveled in the grub.

Dillon looked around the dining room. Six other men were also taking their breakfast. Jim had nodded to them as he had entered and had even gone over to shake hands and quietly converse with two of them while the waiters set the table and served the food.

"The first thing I'm curious about is how you made your way to America. What did you use for money?"

Dillon swallowed a mouthful of food and washed it down with a gulp of apple juice before answering; "I remembered a lot of how the world works before Mother took me to Shamballah so I had a general idea of where to go and what to do. When I left Shamballah I was given a leather bag full of precious gems, mostly emeralds, rubies, and a couple of diamonds. I journeyed to Lhasa where I was able to barter and trade some of my jewels for currency. From there I worked passage on tramp steamers to Australia and from there to Africa. I wanted to travel, get reacquainted with the world. I sold the rest of my jewels and opened up bank accounts in several cities around the world, including New York. I worked odd jobs here and there while drifting north, making my way up to London."

"What did you do there?"

"Believe it or not I went to school." Dillon laughed and for the first time Jim felt that his laugh was genuine. "Most of my formal education came from my father, you see."

"He was a teacher?"

"He was a genius," Dillon replied simply. He abruptly switched back to the story he had been telling. "It was in London that I decided that I needed training. My enemies are still out there. The enemies that killed my mother and my father. They destroyed my people and my home. The Warmasters taught me a lot. But I need to know more. A lot more if I'm to find them. If I'm to survive until I find them."

Dillon reached in his pocket and took out a square of folded paper from a well-worn leather wallet. He passed it over to Jim.

Jim unfolded it and scanned the list of two-dozen names. His eyes opened slightly wider. "You've just earned a couple more checks in your win column, young sir. I know the names on here. Either personally or I've heard of them."

"Do you think they'll help me? That they would consent to teach me?"

Jim reached into an inside jacket pocket for a silver pen and smoothed out the paper on the table. He drew lines through some names, put a star next to others and passed the paper back.

Dillon studied the list for a minute. He turned the paper around and pointed at a name that had a line through it. Dillon's disappointment was obvious. "Why wouldn't he help me? Of all the people on this list I would imagine that he'd be the last to turn me down."

"He no longer lives in New York. Or even in this country. Last I heard he was living down in Central America. Supposedly he's built quite a remarkable research complex down there. It's also said he married a Mayan princess and has two daughters he's training to continue his work." Jim frowned slightly. "I met him a few times but we never worked together. Still, for some odd reason I never understood, some people mistook me for him on occasion. "

Dillon pointed at another name. "And him?"

"He's reclusive. Won't see anybody. He bought a small island off the coast of Maine, built a modest house and lives there very simply, despite his wealth. I've tried a few times to see him but he refuses to talk with me or anybody else from the old days. He never remarried or had children. But the children of his associates still carry on his work. His corporation operates on a global scale now."

"And him?" Dillon pointed at another name which was also had a line through it.

"Leave him alone. Oh, he's still active. I don't think he'll ever stop until somebody kills him. That's if he *can* be killed. I worked with him two or three times and quite sincerely I have my doubts. But he's someone you most certainly should stay away from. He's..." Jim appeared to be at a loss for words. He finally, waved his hand as if trying to dismiss unwanted memories. "Just leave him alone. Trust me."

Dillon pointed at still another name, also with a line through it. "And him?"

"He's insane. Obsessed. Downright fanatical, if he's still alive. Nobody knows for sure."

Dillon sighed as he refolded the paper and put it away. "You're not being very encouraging."

"Look, there are a lot of other good people on your list and they can teach you a lot. And you'll run across others."

"But what about you? You haven't said yet if you'll teach me."

Jim sighed and picked up his tea cup, then sipped before answering. "You want some advice?"

"Of course."

"Go back to school. Get a degree. Become a doctor or an architect or a teacher. You obviously are a young man with exceptional intelligence and an amazing degree of confidence and resourcefulness. Go put those talents to use in a profession where you can immediately see the good that you're doing. Your life will have infinitely more satisfaction that way."

Dillon cocked his head to the side, detecting the note of weary resignation in the older man's voice. "And what about your life? I read up on your career as well as the career of the others on my list. You've done an awful lot of good. There's no way to count how many people owe their lives to you."

Jim munched thoughtfully on buttered toast, thinking of his response before he answered. "I don't regret the life I've lived and I'm proud of the work I've done. And still am doing. But my career hasn't exactly been all glorious fun and excitement. I know that what you read about me and those others makes it seem as if our lives were just one long wonderful adventure. That wasn't always the case. And we had loved ones to think of as well. Families. Such a life takes a toll on everybody involved."

"I don't have a family, or friends, for that matter. There's nobody I have to worry about."

"That will change." Jim sat back, folding his hands across his still concrete hard stomach. "What exactly is it you want from me, young man?"

"They called you the Super Detective. You were known as a murderist of international renown and expertise. Teach me what you know. It's that simple."

"Suppose I do. To what end will you put these skills?"

"As I told you: I intend to find those who killed my mother and father. I have to because they still want to kill me. I have to defend myself. I have to stay alive. The more I learn, the more I know, the better chance I have."

"Who exactly are these people?"

Dillon's voice dropped slightly as he said; "In your career have you ever run across Thahali, She Who Wears The Dress of Seven Sorrows?"

And now Dillon did have Jim's full and undivided attention. "Fascinating. Back in 1956 I had a run in with some of her servants in San Francisco. I had some help from a private eye named George Valentine. We barely survived. Those are some very bad people you've gotten mixed up with, son."

"I have no idea how. All I know is that my parents were her enemies. She destroyed their life's work and a lot of innocent people. Then she came after them. And I have no doubt that she will come after me."

Jim fell silent as he turned his gaze to look out the nearest window. Outside that window was a world he had spent fifty years of his life to defend, protect and preserve. It wasn't a perfect world or even a peaceful one. But it was one worth keeping. He liked his life as it was. But he had to admit: retirement was pretty damn boring at times. And this wouldn't be getting back into the game. Just passing on some of what he knew. And Jim had to admit that this young man with his stories of Shamballah and his as yet unexplained ties to Thahali intrigued him to no end. But there was no reason to tell all that just yet.

"You have anything planned for today?" Jim asked.

"Me? No! Not a thing! Does this mean—"

Jim held up a hand in that firm commanding gesture that stopped Dillon's gush of words as effectively as if a huge cork had been shoved in his mouth. "It doesn't mean anything. I'm still thinking about it. But there's no reason why you can't come with me while I'm still thinking."

"Where are we going?"

"There's someplace I check on whenever I'm in New York. Just let me have a word with Frick and we'll be on our way."

❦ ❦ ❦

The two men in the black SUV hadn't been on watch long. They'd just relieved the previous two lookouts that used a similar SUV. They parked across the street from the Gun Club. Whenever a traffic cop charged at them, waving a ticket book, the man on the passenger side would simply flip open his wallet. Whatever it was the traffic cop saw satisfied them as to the legitimacy of their right to park there and they went on their way.

Both men had a disturbing similarity in their features. They were alike enough to pass for brothers with their very blond hair, chiseled features and impressive musculature. Even sitting at rest in their car they gave off the air that they could explode into furious action at any moment.

The driver nudged his partner. "Looks like we're the lucky ones, eh?"

The passenger nodded and smiled. He picked up a cell phone from the cup holder he had placed it in. He flipped it open. It automatically dialed the number and a strong, vibrant female voice on the other end said; "Report."

"We have a confirmed visual on Jim Anthony. He's standing in front of the Gun Club right now. Looks as if he's waiting for one of the footmen to bring his car round to him."

"Is he alone?"

"No. There's a black man with him. Young. Dressed extremely casually. I would say that he's a janitor or kitchen help from the Gun Club Anthony has engaged to help him do some work."

"Follow Anthony. Report his every move. Where he goes. Who he speaks to."

"Understood."

The two men continued to watch as a black Ford Crown Victoria drove up to the front of the club from the garage. The Baltimore Gun Club kept a variety of vehicles that were at the disposal of the membership when needed. The two men watched Jim and Dillon climb into the car, Jim behind the wheel. The Crown Victoria crunched along the driveway. The gate smoothly drew aside to allow the car to merge into traffic.

The driver started up the SUV and they followed.

3.

Dillon powered down the window and looked out onto the throngs of pedestrians on the street and the river of automobiles they were now a part of.

"Have you ever been in Manhattan before?" Jim asked.

Dillon nodded. "I must have been here with my parents when I was little. When I first got here I took a couple of days just walking around. Every once in a while I'd get a flash of memory...my mother and father talking and laughing...them pointing at something...eating a hot dog..." Dillon stopped and chuckled. "Funny how memory works, isn't it? I bought a hot dog and while eating it, it was as if I was back being a kid again, standing on a corner with my parents eating a hot dog. It was a wild feeling."

"Taste and smell are powerful memory triggers," Jim agreed. "I can smell something once and never forget it. My sense of smell has saved my life more times than I can count."

Dillon sat up straighter. "How so?"

"Surely The Warmasters must have taught you that. People smell differently according to their dietary and toiletry habits. Once I was able to turn the tables on a hired killer tracking me in the Pacific Northwest because he was a cigarette smoker. The nicotine was so ingrained in his system I could smell him from three city blocks away when the wind was right."

"The Warmasters focused mainly on developing hearing and sight."

Jim nodded in sudden understanding. "Being in a closed society where everyone ate and drank the same food and water and probably had the same toiletry habits there wouldn't have been much variation in smell to matter. And then again, they never anticipated you leaving, either."

They were now on Park Avenue and Jim pulled into the garage of a tremendous eighty-six story Art Deco hotel. Jim used a keycard to gain access and parked the car in a slot boasting a simple brass plaque: RESERVED FOR MR. ANTHONY.

Jim and Dillon got out of the car and took an elevator up to the lobby. "I used to have a private garage and elevator that took me directly to my rooms upstairs but I had those sealed off long ago when I stopped living here."

"Why did you stop living here?"

Before Jim could answer, the doors opened and they stepped into a magnificently opulent lobby. Despite it being completely windowless, the sheer power of the antique French crystal chandeliers created the illusion that it was flooded with sunlight. The walls were paneled in genuine Oregon maple.

Dillon was plainly amazed and impressed. "I've seen pictures of this! This is—"

He was cut off by a short, graceful man who hurried over to them without seeming to hurry and said in a hushed, indignant tone; "You know full well that tradesmen are not to come through the lobby where the guests are!"

"If you'll give me a minute to explain—"

"I know, I know, you're in a hurry. But this is The Waldorf-Anthony and we have standards to maintain. I'll excuse you this time, but—"

"Mr. Anthony! My word, why didn't you let me know you were in town? I'd have had your rooms cleaned and aired out!"

The new voice belonged to a wiry, balding man nearly as tall as Dillon with bright, friendly eyes and a mouth that looked as if he spent a goodly amount of his time using it.

Jim shook hands with him. "Hello, Terrence. Good to see you again. You're keeping the place looking splendid as always."

"I try, sir. I try." Terrence turned to the other man. "What seems to be the problem, Matthews?"

Dillon had to stifle a grin as he watched Matthews. You could almost see the gears in the poor fellow's brain switching as it tried to process this new bit of intelligence. "I beg your pardon, Mr. Terwilliger...but you...am I to understand you know this man? Personally, I mean?"

"I should say I do! And you should as well! This man pays your salary and everybody else who works here! This is Mr. Anthony!"

Matthews looked as if he had just been ordered to stick his arm up to the elbow into a backed-up toilet bowl in order to unclog it. "Mr. Anthony? The owner of the hotel?"

Terrence Terwilliger, General Manager of The Waldorf-Anthony turned back to Jim. "I deeply apologize, Mr. Anthony. Matthews is our new concierge. He came highly recommended and I hired him only five weeks ago." Terrence swiveled his head to glare at the stone-faced Matthews. "But that's still no excuse for not knowing what the man whose name is on the hotel looks like!"

Jim placed a hand on Terrence's shoulder. "Oh, that's okay. In fact, I applaud Mr. Matthews for his diligence. It was an honest misunderstanding, given the way my young friend and I are dressed."

"Mr. Anthony, any friend of yours can wear whatever they like and if anybody has a problem with it, they'll deal with me. How have you been, sir?"

"Quite well, thank you. How's the family?"

"They're just dandy, sir. Thanks for asking. My oldest daughter got married back in March and my oldest boy graduated from the FBI just three weeks ago."

"My God...seems like he just graduated high school."

"Top ten percent of his class at Quantico. And thank you again for your letter of recommendation, Mr. Anthony. It meant the world to him."

"My pleasure. I'm going upstairs for a bit to poke around. May I have the keys?"

"Certainly, sir. If you'll just come with me to the office..."

The two men following Jim looked at the fabulous exterior of The Waldorf-Anthony as they sized up the situation. The driver gestured to the cell phone. "Best report in and get orders."

"Let's not be so hasty. This could be an excellent opportunity for us." The driver's partner smiled. "Why not take Anthony ourselves? I can call up a strike team, have them here in twenty minutes."

The driver looked dubious. "We're supposed to report."

"We have an opportunity to rise up in the organization, show our initiative and gain favor with *der Meister*."

"We also have an opportunity to be disciplined."

"What have we to fear? It's only an old man and a *schvartzer*! Surely we can take them with a strike team backing us up. Think of the rewards that will be heaped upon us when we bring Anthony ourselves to *der Meister*! Do you want to spend the rest of your life in stupid, meaningless surveillance details such as this one? Do you want the snake bitch to continually get the credit for our hard work?"

The driver drummed the fingers of his left hand on the steering wheel. What his partner said made much sense. The two of them were part of a special detail permanently stationed in New York to keep track of Anthony when he made his very infrequent trips to New York. It didn't make for very exciting work. He made a decision.

"Call up the strike team and tell them to report immediately. We'll take Anthony ourselves."

The elevator doors opened with the barest whisper of sound, despite the fact that it had been a couple of years since they had to do so. Jim and his young guest stepped out and directly into the entrance gallery of the penthouse brilliantly lit by the early afternoon sun. Due to there being no drapes or curtains on the windows or furniture to help absorb sound, their steps echoed cavernously. Dillon looked up and around in amazement. The vaulted ceiling had to be at least fifteen feet above their heads. The windows were nearly as tall but narrower than the standard. They continued on into what had once been the library. Inside there were still some chairs and a writing desk. The room smelled warmly of rosewood.

Most of the books in the floor-to-ceiling bookcases were gone. But there were still some impressive looking volumes here and there. Dillon examined them curiously. Mostly they were law books.

"After I retired I went back to studying law for a time," Jim said from where he sat at an antique Winslow writing desk. He waved for Dillon to take a seat.

"Why'd you leave the books here?"

Jim shrugged. "Why did I leave some of the furniture here? Further on in the penthouse there's the master bedroom with everything still there and my laboratory has some equipment. Mostly obsolete now, I'm afraid. But I can't bear to get rid of it. Just sentiment, I suppose. From time to time I have business in the city and I stay here. Admittedly I haven't been back for about two years now but when I do visit, I stay here."

Dillon slowly lowered himself into an armchair. "It's wonderful."

"For many years this was my home and my base of operations." Jim looked around the library with its mostly empty shelves and through the windows at the city beyond. "I thought it more fitting that we continue our talk here, rather back at the club. After all, this is where the Jim Anthony you know truly lives."

"You say you don't stay here anymore? Where do you live?"

"That's not your concern. I didn't invite you up here to tell you my secrets. I invited you up here so you could tell me yours." Jim leaned forward, elbows on his knees. "I think you're a very sincere and earnest young man. I think you've been honest and truthful with me about what you want."

"Then I don't see the problem," Dillon frowned slightly.

Jim smiled. "Dillon, what exactly do you want to do with your life?"

"I told you: I intend to find out why my parents were killed by Thahali and why she hated them. And why she hates me."

Jim nodded, sunlight highlighting his silver hair. "I got that part. But it's going to take you time. What do you intend to do with the time in-between?"

"I have skills, talents...I can use them to help people, help the authorities..."

Jim chuckled.

Dillon frowned. "I don't think I like being laughed at, Mr. Anthony. And I don't think I appreciate being toyed with. I came to you in good faith to ask you if you would teach me what you know. If it's a matter of money—"

"Money isn't an issue. Trust me when I say that I'd need another two lifetimes to spend the money I have."

"Then I don't understand what the problem is!"

Jim sighed. "Maybe it's because I want you to take a good hard look at what you're proposing. You want to devote your life to following a pursuit of enemies you have no idea where to find or even who they actually are. You say you want to help people. Fine. You say you want to help the authorities. Fine. But you should know what you're getting into and I don't think you have a real conception of what this life is.

"It's not about revenge for whatever injustice or dirty deal you think life has handed you. It's about fighting for those who can't fight for themselves. It's about putting yourself, your very life between those innocents and madmen who desire nothing but power for themselves. And it won't be just one. You vanquish one enemy and before you can get a good night's sleep, there's another one and then another. And you'll collect more enemies while you do so. Enemies who will do nothing but dream and plot to do nothing but destroy you. It's not just a life of glorious, grand adventure. It's a war. Is this truly the path you want to walk?"

Dillon looked as if he were struggling within himself not to say or do something he'd regret. Finally he said, "I don't know."

Jim nodded in approval. "Good. You just passed your first test."

Dillon's face immediately lost its angry cast as his eyes opened wide and his mouth formed a shocked O. It took him more than a while to get himself under control enough to say something. And even then it wasn't very articulate. "Say what-?"

"If you'd said anything except 'I don't know' I'd have turned you down. But you were open and honest enough to admit you didn't know. I like that."

"It's just as simple as that? You like what I said?"

"As you get older, boy, you'll find that most things in this life are simple. It's people who make them complicated." Jim smiled as he sat back in his chair. "A good friend told me that a long time ago. Took me an even longer time to realize he was right. What you need to start thinking about is a network."

"Network?"

"I didn't accomplish everything I did on my own. Nobody who worked back then in the old days did. I had an entire network that I could rely on. If you want to make this your work then you'll have to develop one of your own. And that is just as valuable a skill as anything else I'll teach you."

Dillon couldn't help but smile. Those last fourteen words were the best he had heard in a long time.

Like most luxury hotels, The Waldorf-Anthony boasted its own parking garage for the guests and residents of the establishment. But below that one there was another parking garage, one that did not appear on any official blueprints or plans of the hotel. That was because it had been used exclusively by Jim Anthony and his associates during his active career. At one time Jim had kept an entire fleet of cars and trucks here, various customized vehicles that he used in his work.

But that had been years ago. When he stopped residing in The Penthouse, Jim himself had supervised the sealing up of his private garage. He had been confident that no one knew of its existence.

Inside the dark garage, a section of one of the walls appeared to be melting. The bricks oozed like melted chocolate as a perfectly round hole appeared as if by magic. Six men stepped through the hole, one by one. Trained soldiers, every one of them. Tried by combat and expert in their business. All dressed in black with body armor, they carried KM2000 combat knives, Heckler & Koch P8 semi-automatic pistols and H&K MP7 sub-machine guns with suppressors.

The leader carefully placed on the ground the ceramic canister that had been filled with the corrosive agent that had eaten through the bricks. On the other side of the wall was a long-forgotten side-track of the New York City subway system. The track had been used when a subway stop right under the Waldorf-Anthony had been constructed back in the forties. It had been used up until the early 70's when city budget cuts had forced the Transit Authority to close down numerous subway stations including the one under the Waldorf-Anthony. The subway stop had been sealed up and Jim secretly had motion activated sensors installed so that he would be alerted if anyone tried to break into the building via that route.

But the strike team knew about the sensors and so they had come in through the wall, directly though the garage. The leader looked at his watch. If things were going on schedule…

He silently motioned to his men, hand signals conveying instructions as plainly as if he had spoken instead. They fell into single file. Three of them headed for the staircase while the other three marched over to the sealed private elevator.

Jim lifted his head, turning it slightly. Dillon could almost swear that the man's ears slightly twitched, making him think of a wolf fixing onto the prey by using hearing alone. Jim got up from his chair in one easy, smooth motion. Dillon stood up as well. He could tell from Jim's body language that their situation had changed, and not necessarily for the better. "What's wrong?"

"The elevator. It's coming up. First of all, it wasn't supposed to go back down and if it did, I'm supposed to be notified that it did so. There are certain protocols I have in place that Terrence follows to the letter."

"Maybe it's him?"

"No. Terrence wouldn't come up to The Penthouse or send somebody up here without calling and checking with me first. Come on." Jim left the library with long strides easily matched by Dillon. "Somebody overrode the elevator's control system, dropped it down to a lower floor, boarded it and now they're on their way back up. You got any enemies that followed you here, boy?"

"Here? No!"

They reached the laboratory. The door was a blast proof metal door that greatly resembled a submarine hatch. Next to the handle was a circular punch plate with five regularly spaced grooves, barely big enough for the tip of a finger. Jim placed the fingers of his right hand in those grooves and the muscles in his right arm from wrist to shoulder flexed as he gave the plate a half-twist. He laid hold of the circular handle and twirled it to the left. Then he laid both hands on it and yanked. The hermetically sealed door hissed as it swung open wide. "Inside, quickly."

Dillon obeyed without question, followed by Jim who closed the door behind them, twirled the inside handle. "That'll buy us some time. Unless they've brought a bazooka with them, they'll never breach that." He turned to face the perplexed younger man. "Who are they?"

"How would I know?"

"I hardly think it a coincidence that the same day I meet you and come to my old home that all of a sudden strangers are coming up in my elevator."

"I have no idea who's in your elevator. How do you know that they're not old enemies of yours?"

Jim had to smile at that. "God knows I've collected my share in my day. Okay." He clapped Dillon on the shoulder. "I hope your vaunted Warmasters trained you well."

"Why?"

"We're going to go on the offensive and attack them."

"Don't you have another way out of here?"

"I do but I'd like to find out who they are and what they want with me. Or you. And secondly, this is my home. I don't run from any man in my own home."

"You have any weapons here?" Dillon asked.

"No. I used to have quite a sizeable arsenal here but all the guns were long since removed." Jim gestured at the laboratory. "But if you give me a hand, I think we can whip up something that will give us an edge."

Dillon looked around the huge room and didn't see how anything in here could help them. There had to be at least a dozen long benches, most of them covered up but some still had pieces of equipment that were arcane to Dillon's eyes. Numerous cabinets lined the walls but most of those were empty as well. Jim walked swiftly over to one cabinet that still contained jars, beakers and reagent bottles. He motioned for Dillon to come over. Jim swiftly filled the younger man's arms with the beakers and indicated that he should place them on one of the uncovered workbenches.

☥ ☥ ☥

The elevator door opened and five armed men emerged. Three of them were members of the strike team. The other two men were the pair that had followed Jim and Dillon from The Baltimore Gun Club here. One of them looked at the other. "Where are they, Gustav?"

Agitated, Gustav snapped back, "How should I know? They came up here!"

Gustav's partner sighed. "Maybe Anthony somehow detected us? Left by another way?"

Gustav shook his head. "He's here." He gestured with his gun at the three members of the strike team. "Search the other rooms. He and the black are up here somewhere. Look in the bedroom. Who knows what degenerate practices those mongrels might be performing—"

From the doorway that led deeper into the suite of rooms, two large beakers arced through the air. Filled with dark liquid, the beakers were stoppered to prevent the liquid from spilling out as the beakers tumbled through the air to smash on the polished floor. Almost immediately, thick white smoke billowed from the rapidly evaporating liquid, filling the huge room with thick impenetrable fog.

Dillon and Jim Anthony moved as soon as the beakers hit the floor. Jim had discarded his designer sport jacket and Japanese slippers. Even though Dillon still wore his battered sneakers he did not make any more sound that Jim did. Without a word, the two men moved through the thick fog, flanking their prey. The fog would not last long but this fight wouldn't last long either.

One of the strike team members panicked, fired blindly. Bad mistake. Dillon targeted him and came in with a solid punch straight to the man's stomach that lifted him up and off his feet. His weapon clattered to the floor as he flew backwards.

Jim held in his two sinewy hands a belt whose buckle split apart to make two weighted ends. Swiftly, he crept up in back of another assassin and with one deft motion, wrapped the belt around the man's neck and with one seemingly effortless motion, yanked the belt hard enough to instantly crush the man's windpipe. He died without a sound. The belt, made from woven, shaped fibers from a rare and exotic South American vine had long ago proven itself to be the most reliable and versatile weapon in Jim's arsenal for fifty years and he never went anywhere without it.

The strike team were well trained men and immediately spread out. No one yelled out or fired another shot. Much like Jim and Dillon, they depended on their ears to pinpoint their targets.

The fog thinned out. In another minute or so it would be gone entirely. But there was no help for it. Jim had concocted that formula years ago and designed it to be absolutely impenetrable but also to dissipate quickly.

Dillon crept up on a third man who heard Dillon at the last minute, whipped around, attempted to train the weapon on Dillon. The barrel slapped into Dillon's palm and he held it away from his body as he delivered a crushing back fist to the man's cheek, breaking it. The man howled but held onto his weapon, squeezed the trigger.

Dillon let go of it, dropped and executed a leg sweep takedown. The man held onto his weapon, squeezing the trigger reflexively and the random spray of bullets took out Gustav's partner. Dillon put him out completely with another blow.

Jim whipped his belt over his head, twirled it around and around rapidly and let fly. Due to the weighted ends, the belt acted just like a bola, wrapping around Gustav's knees, bringing him crashing painfully down to the floor.

The fog had cleared away by now. Dillon surveyed the damage. Two men dead, two unconscious and one captured. Jim stood about ten feet away from Gustav who eyed his gun where it had landed when he had fallen. The gun was closer to Gustav than Jim was to him. Gustav's eyes flickered from the weapon to Jim's face. He licked his lips, obviously trying to estimate if it was worth the risk to go after the gun.

Jim had seen that same look on the faces of many men in years past. "I know what you're thinking. You're thinking I'm an old man long past his prime and there's no way that I can get to you before you get the gun and put a bullet into me." Jim smiled and it was by no means a friendly smile. "If you truly believe that then you go right ahead and make your play."

Gustav licked his lips again, looked at Dillon.

"Don't look at him! I'm talking to you!" Jim's voice whip cracked in Gustav's ears, causing him to snap his head back around to look at Jim. "The boy's got nothing to do with this. It's between you and me. So you've got a decision to make. Are you faster than than this old man? Well? Are you?"

Gustav's trembling hand trembled even more. He weighed the odds one last time and made his choice. He let the gun stay where it was and lifted his hands in surrender.

"Smart choice. Dillon, would you—"

Machine gun bullets ripped into the bodies lying on the floor. Dillon and Jim Anthony moved as one, diving for the floor, rolling out of the path of the line of machine gun fire as they chewed up the floor and walls as they sought their new targets.

Dillon charged for the laboratory, Jim right behind him. They got behind the door and inside the lab but didn't close it so that they could listen to what their new assailants were up to.

"Where did they come from?" Dillon demanded.

"There's a staircase that stops three floor below this one. After that there's a small private staircase that lets you out into a utility closet in the foyer. Somehow they must have found out about it since it's not on any of the blueprints."

"Quiet out there," Dillon said. "I think they're gone."

"Only one way to find out." Jim lead the way on bare feet back into the entrance gallery. The bodies were gone, along with their weapons, leaving only grisly splashes and broad trails of blood to indicate that they had ever been there. The air smelled of cordite and death.

Dillon wrinkled his nose. "Where did the bodies go?"

"They took them."

"And who are 'they'?"

Jim shrugged brawny shoulders. "That's why *they* killed their own men and then took the bodies away. So that we couldn't discover who *they* were."

"Aren't we going after them?"

"No. We're not armed. And I'm guessing they came in from the lower levels I had sealed off years ago down where the subway used to run. No telling if they have more men down there. We'd be worse than foolish to pursue such a well-armed force of men without weapons."

"Seems like a waste of time to kill their own men. As quickly as they moved they could have just taken them away."

Jim sighed. "You do have a lot to learn. First of all, they killed them because they messed up the mission, which I'm guessing was to kill or capture me. They couldn't leave the bodies behind because they obviously know me and know that my examining the bodies of the dead men and their clothes would have told me more than they could have with words."

"You don't seem very worried."

"Oh, but I am. But wringing my hands and wailing would just be a waste of time and energy. Come on, let's get out of here." Jim swiftly recovered his jacket and slippers. They went to the elevator and were soon dropping down to the lobby while Jim put the slippers and jacket back on.

"How are we going to explain this to the police?" Dillon wanted to know.

"Explain *what* to the police, boy?"

Dillon blinked perplexed copper eyes.

"The gunfight upstairs! The whole hotel must have heard it!"

Jim shook his head. "The entire Penthouse is completely and totally soundproof. They could have detonated a bunker buster up there and nobody would have heard a thing."

"But...there were men killed up there! We've got to report it to somebody!"

Jim sighed. Took in a deep breath and said slowly and quietly; "And report what, exactly? We have no bodies, just blood and bullets in the walls. Yes, we could show the police the blood and let them dig the bullets out of the walls and run their forensic tests and while they did so we would be detained until they finished their investigation. Do you want that?"

"It just doesn't seem right to walk away from all that and not do anything, is all."

"We are doing something. It's just not what you think we should be doing." Jim said as the elevator doors opened into the bustling, busy lobby of The Waldorf-Anthony. As before, Matthews fixed on them like a heat seeking missile but this time his attitude was quite different.

"Mr. Anthony, I'm glad to have an opportunity to apologize for my boorish behavior earlier."

"Nothing to apologize for, Matthews. I appreciate your diligence."

"Is there anything you or your friend require? Something I can help you with?"

"Yes you can. Find Mr. Terwilliger and tell him this message word for word. Tell him that the bathroom faucet is clogged."

Matthews blinked. "I can send Maintenance up right away, Mr. Anthony—"

"No. You do as I say. Go tell Mr. Terwilliger that the bathroom faucet is clogged. No more than that. He'll know what to do."

Matthews was no fool. He caught on and simply said, "At once, Mr. Anthony." He turned and walked away rapidly in the direction of Terwilliger's office.

Jim motioned for Dillon to follow him as he said, "That was a code phrase. Terwilliger will do what needs to be done. By this time tomorrow you'd never know that there was a gun battle up there or that men were killed."

"It still doesn't seem right, Mr. Anthony. Men were killed. We should make a report of it to the proper authorities."

"Dillon, if I still had the influence and reputation I once enjoyed with the authorities I would call them myself. But I don't. Hell, to most people in the city I'm a half-remembered celebrity. You're simply going to have to trust me on this."

"So what do we do now? Where do we go?"

"First things first: we'll go to your hotel and get your stuff and then we'll head for the airport. We've got to get out of the city as soon as possible."

"But where are we going?"

Jim looked at Dillon with a such a warm smile that Dillon couldn't help but smile back. "You know I'm Comanche on my mother's side, right?"

"Yes."

"And where do Indians live?" Jim's smile widened into a grin at Dillon's look of consternation.

"I give up, Mr. Anthony."

"Why, they live in teepees, youngster. And that's where we're going. To The Teepee."

4.

The two black SUVs drove easily and smoothly through the traffic crowded Manhattan streets. The drivers stayed in their lanes, not switching from one to the other or blasting through yellow lights like most other drivers. They followed each other close but not too close. The whole point was not to bring attention to themselves. There had already been enough of that. Their section leader would not be happy at all. The first SUV held the bodies of the strike team members that had been killed during the ill-advised raid, driven by one of the team members who had come up the stairs. In the second SUV, the other two surviving members sat in the front with a tied-up Gustav in the back.

"Why do you have me tied up?" Gustav yelled for probably the twentieth time. Neither man had spoken to him since they stormed Jim Anthony's Penthouse and recovered the dead and injured members of the strike team. They had themselves killed their injured comrades but left Gustav alive. He assumed that it was because they needed him to give orders. Such apparently was not the case. "Are we going to the safe house?"

Finally, an answer. From the soldier in the passenger seat. The driver said nothing. "No. We have been instructed to bring you directly to the section leader."

Gustav's mouth suddenly went dry as extra coarse sandpaper. "The section leader? You…you informed her of our raid?"

"Of course. But she was not at the residence. By the time she returned and we got in contact with her, it was too late. The raid was not sanctioned by her. She is not happy that you took it upon yourself to attack Anthony."

Gustav said nothing. It was better he save his breath and spend what few minutes he had before they arrived at their destination coming up with an explanation that would save him from broken bones. Or worse.

They drove in silence until arriving at an address on Eleventh Avenue and Forty-Fourth Street. The SUVs drove straight into the private garage attached to the house. They left the dead bodies and brought Gustav with them, taking the elevator up to the fifth floor.

The elevator doors opened into a room that had nothing of comfort anywhere. Long tables against the walls and laptop computers manned by technicians who did not look up. Monitor screens illuminated the face of the woman who sat behind a desk at the far end of the room. Gustav's captors marched him through the room toward the desk. The woman rose from her seat with a movement as elegant as that of a snake.

Tall and slender, she possessed a breathtaking beauty that quickened the pulse of every man in the room, even though they feared her as well. She was well aware of her effect on men and had used it many, many a time to her advantage in her long life and she had lived so very long thanks to the Elixir of Life. She wore a pale green sari that looked deceptively light. All of her saris were woven from spider web silk and as such were virtually bulletproof. She stopped in front of Gustav. "Untie his hands," she commanded in a husky yet seductive voice. "Gustav is not an enemy."

The plastic binders around Gustav's wrists were cut. He shook the circulation back into his hands as the Indian woman regarded him silently. He had known and served Ashanti Garuda for twelve years now loyally and faithfully. He hoped that she would take that into account.

"You called in a strike team and attacked Jim Anthony. You did this without my authorization. You will explain."

Gustav knew better than to try and lay the blame on his dead partner. "It was a risk, yes. But it's been two years since Jim Anthony was in the city. Romberg and I thought we should capture him as who knows when would be the next time he would be back?"

"That was not your decision to make. Your instructions were simply to watch Anthony whenever he came to the city and monitor his movements. That was all. Now you have alerted him that he is being watched. He will be vigilant."

"But Anthony is an old man!"

Shani smiled. "That old man survived your attack, did he not? Were he blind, deaf and in a wheelchair, Jim Anthony would be still a formidable opponent. The only thing you accomplished was to put him on his guard." Shani paused, lifting a slim and deceptively delicate looking hand to her ear. Her fingers lightly stroked something that glittered in her ear. She appeared to be listening to a voice only she could hear.

After about half a minute she turned her full attention back to Gustav and the situation at hand.

"Count yourself fortunate, Gustav. I had decided to punish you severely for your error but things have changed and I am going to need every man I have. Chances are that you will die anyway."

Gustav had no shame about letting his relief show on his face. He had seen Shani punish men before. It wasn't fun to watch. "Have our orders changed?"

"Yes. Go prepare all strike teams. Once I have a location we will be leaving immediately." The men turned and moved away to carry out her orders.

But Shani spoke once more, "Gustav."

He turned back to face her. "Yes?"

"There was a young man with Anthony?"

"Yes. A black man. We thought that he worked for The Baltimore Gun Club. A menial."

"But the report was that he helped Anthony take down your strike team. That does not sound like kitchen help to me."

"No, it does not. Obviously this young man must be a new Anthony aide. Perhaps one he's trained himself to act as a bodyguard. That is the only way I can explain his combat prowess."

Shani appeared to think that over for a bit. "Hm. Interesting. In any case I trust that when we catch up to Anthony you will not underestimate this young man again?"

Gustav's voice thickened with hate as he replied, "I most certainly will not. My word on it."

"Then go and get ready." Shani watched Gustav as he strode away quickly. No doubt delighted beyond words to be able to do so on two unbroken legs. Shani watched him go with a slight smile on her long, beautiful face.

The device in her ear tingled slightly as it activated by voice. A voice that spoke in Shani's ear. It was the voice of a man who she served and worshipped as a god on Earth. "You grow merciful in your old age, Shani. I remember a time not so long ago when you would have killed that man. And I told you that you could dispose of him as you see fit."

"Getting old has nothing to do with it. We have a wild card in the deck. This young man with Anthony. Nothing in the previous surveillance reports indicate that Anthony has been recruiting a new team of assistants. So who is this boy? And where did he acquire the skills to hold his own against one of our strike teams? He is an unknown quantity. Who is to say there will not be more of them? Gustav dying at my hands serves no purpose ."

"Jim Anthony is, as always, a man full of surprises."

Shani cocked her head in amusement. "Do I detect a note of admiration?"

"Respect. You would do well to cultivate it. The day you stop respecting Jim Anthony as a foe is the day you will die at his hand."

Shani sniffed dismissively. She changed the subject. "Why did you want me to prepare all strike teams?"

"Because it is time. The confluence will be in alignment soon and I must have a piece of equipment that Anthony has in his possession. You know what it is."

"I do."

"Then get it for me. Now."

"I've got my people on foot at all the airports. Anthony will most likely leave the city. We've known for some time now that he has an upstate residence but we've never been able to find out exactly where. I suspect that Anthony has been using technological methods to keep it hidden. But I will find it. And then I myself will lead the raid and recover your property."

"Excellent. And Shani?"

"Yes?"

"Give him a clean death. He has earned that from us."

Jim reflected that for the first time that day he saw a grin on Dillon's face that truly looked authentically happy. The youth's obvious delight was infectious and Jim found himself grinning right back. That was always the blessing the young bestowed on the old: the ability to see familiar things through their new eyes. "You've never flown in a helicopter before?" Jim asked.

"Never!" Dillon shouted back, unable to take his eyes off the gorgeous foliage beneath them. Before them stretched low, tree-covered mountains that appeared to go on to the horizon and back. Dillon could hardly believe that such beauty existed a scarce thirty minutes from the hot, noisy city they had just left.

They flew in Jim's Sikorsky helicopter. He'd bought it at the very tail end of his career back in the early '60's. It had been a strictly impulse buy. Just a way for him to keep his flying skills honed as the Sikorsky was perfect for him to make short hops. Sometimes he took it up just for fun. Once in a while when he went to Washington at the request of whatever law enforcement agencies requested his aid he flew the helicopter. And when he flew it he thought of his good friend Tom Gentry. Tom would have loved the Sikorsky.

Jim reached out a hand to tune in a special frequency on the radio. "I'm going to speak in Comanche for the next few minutes just to relay instruction to my staff at The Teepee."

Dillon blinked. "Why tell me?"

"Because some people who only speak English get very nervous, offended and even insulted if somebody is speaking in a language they don't understand while they're present."

Dillon frowned and shrugged at the same time, as if not quite sure which response was the appropriate one so he just did them both. "Why?"

"Because they think that if you're talking in a language they can't understand, you must be talking about them."

"But why would they think that?"

Jim laughed. "You know, Dillon, in all the excitement I completely forgot you weren't raised in this country. It's as if you truly do come from another world. We'll have to discuss the racial issues of this country another time. Right now I need to talk to my people."

Dillon nodded and turned back to look out the window at the ocean of trees passing under them. Jim found his frequency, adjusted the microphone attached to his headset and spoke rapidly for about two minutes. When done with his instructions he turned his attention back to the young man.

"You ever flown at all?" Jim said.

"Two times," Dillon said. "That's it. This is my third time."

"Like it?"

"Sure!"

"Think you might want to learn to fly one of these things?"

"I think I should…shouldn't I?"

"Here's your first official lesson; learn everything and anything you can. No matter how silly or how esoteric or banal that skill may seem to be. Because you'll never know what will save your life or the lives of others. It may be something as simple as knowing how to make a soufflé or as complicated as defusing a cobalt bomb. But whatever it is you want to learn, make sure you find the best to learn from."

"That's why I came to you, Mr. Anthony. I spent time in the libraries in London and read up on some of your cases that took you to Europe. You're the best when it comes to tracking men."

Jim said nothing. He had already told Dillon he would teach him what he knew but now there was a new element added. Someone was after Jim and he had no idea of who it was or why they were after him. *This boy came looking for Jim Anthony, Super Detective. But I haven't been that Jim Anthony for longer than I care to remember. If worse comes to worse, can I be that Jim Anthony again?*

And then he remembered just a few hours ago how his blood sang and felt like liquid fire in his veins during the combat. How his hearing, his sense of smell, his sight, all were sharper...how every single cell in his body felt as if it were exploding with energy.

He smiled at his reflection in the helicopter's windshield. *Maybe I can't be that Jim Anthony again...but I'm close enough!*

"Are we there yet?" Dillon asked.

In answer, Jim manipulated the controls and the helicopter hovered over the dense carpet of trees blanketing the land below them. Jim jerked his chin to indicate that Dillon should look below. "See anything?"

"Just trees."

"No place to land, right?"

Dillon looked again, harder and longer. But for the life of him he couldn't see anything but trees. He looked back at Jim. "I'm not sure what it is I'm supposed to be looking for, Mr. Anthony."

"I'll show you."

Jim again worked the controls and the helicopter dropped toward the ground, apparently Jim's intention being to crash the machine right into the trees below them. But the Sikorsky dropped past the top of the trees and continued on, coming to land in an amazingly large clearing.

While Jim powered down the Sikorsky, Dillon scrambled out of the helicopter, wildly curious as to how such a feat of what had to be magic had been performed. Dillon stood next to the helicopter and peered upwards, looking at the clear sky above them. The trees had been cleared in a perfectly square landing area. But why couldn't he see the clearing from above? Dillon looked down and then he got it.

By now, Jim had joined him. "Caught on yet?"

Dillon pointed down at the thick carpet of leaves under their feet. Even the backwash of the helicopter's blade had only blown the leaves around but hadn't cleared them away completely. And the leaves were the exact same color as the surrounding trees. "It's a natural optical illusion. The leaves blend in with the trees, providing a natural camouflage. Unless you know what you're looking for, you'll fly right over it."

"Exactly. The way the trees are cut helps as well. My staff here maintains this, keeps the leaves down here on the ground the same colors as the leaves on the trees. Ah, here they come."

"I'll show you."

A dozen men had seemingly appeared out of nowhere, jogging toward Jim and Dillon. They stopped some distance away, reached down and lifted up camouflage netting of natural colors just like the leaves and trees around them.

"Come on," Jim said. "They'll take care of the 'copter. When they're done placing the netting over it, it'll be invisible from the air."

"I can't believe it's just that simple," Dillon said.

"Whenever possible, take advantage of what nature gives you to work with. If you know the terrain and know how to use it, you can hide in plain sight. Look right there. What do you see?"

Once again Dillon looked right at where Jim was pointing but all he could see was trees.

"You have to develop the trick of looking slightly out of focus," Jim said. "Once you do, it's something you'll always be able to do. I'm guessing there weren't many forests like this in Shamballah?"

"No, there weren't." Dillon turned his head slightly from side to side. "Matter of fact there was just-Hey!" He thrust out a long arm. "I see it! I see it!"

Jim clapped him on the shoulder. "Welcome to The Teepee."

The two of them walked the long path toward the building that had seemed to just materialize into existence right in front of Dillon's eyes. Now that he could see it, it was as if he couldn't *unsee* it. Concealed among the tall pines and maple trees, its log exterior had merged right in with them. And now, once he had seen it, he couldn't un-see it. Dillon was frankly flabbergasted. He looked up through the trees at the late afternoon sun. Hard to believe that so much had happened since he had met Mr. Anthony this morning. And now here he was in-

"Mr. Anthony, where are we, anyway?"

"You're in the Catskill Mountains, north of New York City. It doesn't take long by car to get here. And you saw how fast we got here by air. It's famous as a scenic tourist attraction. A lot of New Yorkers also have weekend and vacation homes here. A short drive from the city and you're in a wilderness. I built The Teepee back in the 1930's. It's been one of my homes away from home. The other is in the southwest. You'll see that in a few weeks."

As they drew closer, and Dillon's sight became more acclimated to what he was seeing, he could take in more and more of the exterior of The Teepee. From the outside it looked to Dillon to be a one story hunting lodge built of pine and maple logs. Jim opened the front door and they

stepped into a wonderfully rustic entrance hall well illuminated by rope chandeliers. The log motif of the outside continued on the inside as well. A fountain made of Moroccan marble stood in the center of the room. A young woman dressed simply in a long white dress stood just off to the left of the door and greeted them with a bow. Her deep set chestnut eyes rested on Dillon briefly with calm competence before turning to Jim. Dillon ran his own eyes over her athletic build and neck length straight black hair.

Jim smiled and returned her bow with one of his own. "Hello, Martha. Everything well?"

"Yes, Mr. Anthony. You did receive a telephone call you might like to return from Senator Ruskin."

"Oh, yes. I did some research for him last week. I need to fax him the information. Martha, this is Dillon. He's going to be staying with us for a while. Please show him to a room and see to his needs." Jim turned to Dillon. "Martha's in charge of my staff that works and maintains The Teepee. You'll see them around but unless you ask them a direct question they won't say anything or even look at you. I tell you this so that you won't think them rude. Best thing to do is if you need anything, just ask Martha."

"Sure. Where are you going?"

"My office. Don't worry, we're safe up here. I'll meet you in the dining room for dinner. Martha, tell Albert I expect something special in honor of our guest." Abruptly he turned and walked away.

Martha smiled gently. "This way, sir."

As he walked with her, Dillon said, "You don't have to call me 'sir.' I feel odd when people do."

"And why shouldn't you be called 'sir.'? It is a sign of respect. You don't think you deserve respect?"

"Well…yes. It's just that…" Dillon trailed off, waved his hands helplessly. "I just would rather you call me Dillon, is all. That's it."

"I could call you Mr. Dillon," Martha laughed, a delightfully musical laugh that seemed to dance merrily in the air. Her laughter made Dillon laugh as well.

"Why are we laughing?" he finally asked.

"I don't know why you're laughing but I'm laughing because I don't look anything like Dennis Weaver."

"Who?"

Martha linked her slim arm in his muscular one. "Come. I'll take you to your room. You can have a shower and change clothes. And then while you're resting, through the magic of Blu-Ray I'll introduce you to 'Gunsmoke' and then you'll get the joke."

Dillon still had no idea whatsoever what she was talking about but if it meant he could hear her laugh once again, it didn't matter.

Jim walked swiftly to his office located in the west wing of The Teepee. He passed by various staff members who bowed and nodded in respectful greeting as he passed. The Teepee had been built on sixty acres of land and Jim kept a permanent staff of seventy that lived on the property to maintain the land and The Teepee. Back in the 1940's and 50's Jim had rented or loaned out The Teepee to friends of his who for one reason or another needed solitude or wanted to do some hunting and fishing. But once he'd retired for good and made this his primary residence he'd taken great pains to wipe The Teepee's existence from all official records. He'd also spent a small fortune reinforcing and rebuilding so that now The Teepee was as much a fortress as a home.

Jim opened the door to his office. Anybody who had visited Jim's Penthouse office in The Waldorf-Anthony would have recognized much of the furniture and works of art adorning the walls. He loved the familiar feelings that flowed through him as he sat behind the familiar old oak pedestal desk that he had bought brand new back in 1930 for $400. Today if he ever decided to sell it he could easily get ten times that much. He rummaged through the stacks of folders and papers, looking for his phone.

Jim really didn't have to call Senator Ruskin. That bit of playacting had been for Dillon's benefit. When Jim had spoken to Martha on the radio he had outlined the situation for her. He instructed her to alert the staff, make sure that the The Teepee was secure and then make a security sweep of the acreage. No one was to talk to the young man Jim was bringing with him and Jim asked Martha to keep him busy for a couple of hours while Jim made some calls.

He opened a desk drawer, removed his reading glasses and put them on. He picked up the phone's receiver, dialed a number.

Three rings later a warm voice which still had a distinct Midwestern tang said, "Jim Anthony! I'll be damned! To what do I owe the honor? You're not working on anything for us now, are you?"

"No, Dan. Actually, I called to ask you for a favor."

"Anything you need from the F.B.I. you just ask, Jim." Dan Fowler, Director of The Federal Bureau of Investigation replied with genuine feeling. He and Jim Anthony went back a long way. They'd first met in 1938 while investigating what looked to be a series of bank robberies. The case quickly turned into something more bizarre and far reaching. But they'd solved it and so began their friendship. In fact, it was Dan Fowler who had started Jim on his retirement career of consulting. Dan had called Jim in to assist with a number of high profile cases ten years ago. Jim's success on that case had caused him to be brought in for consultation by a number of other government agencies and ever since then the two men had renewed their professional and personal relationship.

"I was attacked today, Dan. A well-armed squad of highly trained men hit my old headquarters at The Waldorf-Anthony. If I didn't have help I don't think I would have been able to take them all. I got lucky today and I don't mind telling you that."

"You want us to find out who they were? Send a Cleaner over to your place?"

"No. My people there will clean up. I don't think this situation is over and in any case, I've got resources of my own to try and find out who they are. But what I need from you is to find out if my name is being spoken of in the ears of certain people."

"I understand perfectly, my friend. Let me ask you something; you think this might have something to do with one of the cases you worked for us?"

"Dan, at this point I don't know what it's all about. I was approached by a young man today who claims he wants me to teach him what I know and as soon as he shows up I've got men pointing guns at me."

Dan chuckled. "You sound almost happy."

"I do?"

"You do. Might be you're glad for the excitement."

"If I want excitement I'm perfectly capable of finding it on my own. I'd also like you to see if you can find out anything for me about this young man."

"Is he dangerous?"

"Judging by the way I saw him take down two men armed with automatic weapons with nothing but his bare hands I'd have to say that he's extremely dangerous."

"Sounds like somebody we should know about. I'll put the NSB to work on him. Give me a thumbnail description and I'll have them pull his picture off the security cameras at the Waldorf-Anthony."

"He'll be the black man standing next to me. He tends to stand out. Dillon is the only name I have for him. I'd appreciate a deep check."

"No problem. And I'll post some men at the Waldorf-Anthony just in case your friends decide to return."

"I don't think that will be necessary, Dan. If they're as good as I think they are then they know already that I've already left town."

"Still, it won't hurt to put half a dozen agents on surveillance just to watch the place to be sure that your playmates don't blow it up just for fun or to draw you back to the city. Hey, you've done a lot of favors for me, Jim. Give me a chance to pay you back."

Jim laughed. "If it'll make you feel better and you don't mind paying the overtime, go right ahead."

"Anything else I can do for you, Jim?"

"That's all I can think of for now, Dan. If anything else comes to mind, you'll hear from me."

"You just watch your back and be careful. And don't be too proud to ask for help if you need it."

"Yes, mother."

Dan Fowler chuckled. "I get the point. Okay, I got another call I have to take. You keep me in the loop as to what's going on and next time you come to Washington, dinner's on me."

Jim hung up and sat back in the leather tilt swivel office chair that was as old as the desk and looked up at the ceiling for about thirty seconds before reaching for the phone again. He dialed another number. This phone was answered halfway through the first ring and a young woman's voice said with some irritation; "Who is this?"

"My name is Mr. Anthony. Is Mr. Brown at home?"

"Yes, yes he is. You're not going to be on the phone long with him, are you?"

"I can't say, miss."

"Because I lost my cell phone day before yesterday and all my calls are coming through on this phone so I need to have it free."

"I understand, miss. If I could speak to Mr. Brown—"

"I just need to get my calls is all. I'd really appreciate it if you wouldn't tie up the phone too long. I—" Suddenly the young woman's voice was gone and Jim could hear an older, male voice promising grief and woe of Biblical proportions if the young woman ever answered his phone again in such a manner. Then his voice was in Jim's ear. "Brown speaking. Sorry about that. To whom am I speaking?"

"How are you, Alcatraz?"

"Jim? Jim Anthony? Well, paint me green and call me a pickle! Jim Anthony! I haven't seen you since we both were at that Baltimore Gun Club dinner, what was it, three years ago? Two?"

"Something like that. How have you been, old friend?"

The man on the other end grunted. "That was my granddaughter who answered the phone. She's having some kinda problem with her husband 'cause they lost their house in Florida so she left him and came to stay with me. Brought her three kids with her. I love 'em all to death but she's working my last nerve and I lost that in Saigon back in '75. Kids are smart as hell but she's dumb as a loaf of bread."

Jim laughed out loud and the rich laughter of Otis 'Alcatraz' Brown joined him. When they settled down, Jim said, "I wish this was a social call, Alcatraz. I need your help."

"Jim, I haven't been called 'Alcatraz' in twenty five years. I'm just plain Otis Brown these days and I like it like that. I'm too old and too set in my ways to go back to slaying dragons. And aren't you retired as well? Last time we talked you said you were just doing consulting work is all."

"Still am. But somebody tried to kill me today. Don't know who, don't know why."

"Damn. You still in one piece?"

"Yes. I'm okay. But I need you to ask around for me."

"Jim, you got way more resources than I do. I been out the game for twenty-five years. I don't know nothing about nobody no more."

"That's not what Van Loan told me. Few years ago we found ourselves attending the same function at the Metropolitan Museum of Art and went out for drinks afterwards. You know the drill. We spent the next five hours trading information and playing catch-up."

Jim heard Alcatraz suck his teeth in annoyance. "Y'know, he never could keep his mouth shut about other folks' business. You won't hear him telling his, though. Look, I pretty much do the same thing you do but in a way more informal basis. People call me, ask me to pass on information to other people. From time to time I get people driving black SUVs, dressed like Will Smith and Tommy Lee Jones come by my house. They come in, they ask me to look at some files and give them my opinion on what's in those files. That's about it."

"What outfits?"

"The Machine, ComTeg, Humanidyne Institute, F.L.A.G., a couple others."

"Can you make some phone calls? Find out if I'm on somebody's radar for some reason?"

Alcatraz sighed heavily. "Yeah, man. Sure. You know you ever need a favor you got it. I just want you to know that I'm not as much in the loop as you might think and anything I may come up with—"

"Hey, they didn't call you The Magician for nothing, my friend."

Alcatraz Brown laughed again before saying, "Stay by the phone. I'll make those calls. Keep your head down in the meantime."

Jim hung up the phone. Picked up a pencil and tapped it against his chin while he thought. There was one more call he could make but was reluctant to do so. But he needed all bases covered just in case the F.B.I. and Alcatraz Brown turned up nothing. Not that he actually thought that would happen. But still…he had always been a cautious man. Which was what had enabled him to live so long and he fully intended to live even longer. He picked up the phone again, dialed a number. It was answered on the third ring.

"I've been expecting you to call me." The female voice was full of humor. "You have had a very busy day, old man."

"You don't know the half of it. And why am I not surprised you know about it?"

"Why wouldn't I? You keep track of me, I keep track of you. That's how it's always been. Are you all right?" Even though she tried to keep her voice light there was a distinct note of concern in her voice.

"Yes. I feel pretty good, in fact. Haven't had a decent workout like that in years."

The woman on the other end laughed merrily. "Does this mean that the Super Detective is once more going to sally forth against the forces of evil?"

"This means that Jim Anthony is going to figure out a way to keep himself from getting killed. I need a favor from you."

"I'm listening."

"I've got a couple of friends making inquiries to find out who hit The Penthouse today and why they're after me. But one is limited by the law and the other by age."

"Meaning you need someone out there in the field who can crack heads and break bones if necessary to get you the answers you need. I'm your girl."

"Where are you now?"

"Qingdao."

"What in the world are you…no. Wait. Stop. Never mind. I don't think

I want to know."

"Better if you don't."

"You working a job there?"

"Not anymore. I just quit."

"Vera—"

"Hush. It's not often you ask for help and if you are you're more worried than you'd ever admit out loud. I'll start my inquiries and let you know what I find out."

"Thank you, Vera. I mean that."

"I know you do. So, are you going to tell me the whole story now?"

Jim sighed. "You sure you have time for this?"

"You never did tell me bedtime stories when I was a child. Here's your chance to make up for it."

"Very well. It all starts with this rather curious and odd young man named Dillon…"

5.

Jim watched Dillon spar with the chunky Rubio. He wasn't the only observer. Four or five other members of The Teepee staff stood around the boxing ring, making bets with each other and shouting encouragement to either Rubio or Dillon. Both men wore ten ounce sparring gloves and boxing trunks but no shoes. A foot shorter but insanely muscled, Rubio was more than a good match for Dillon. The two men circled each other in the boxing ring, eyeing each other carefully. One of the onlookers rang a bell and the match was on.

A full equipped gym was just one of the amenities of The Teepee. Jim sat on the bleacher seats with Martha, both of them watching as Dillon and Rubio warily continued to circle each other. This was Dillon's fourth sparring partner of the day. Jim was impressed at how apparently Dillon showed no signs of fatigue or of slowing down.

"How is he doing so far?" Martha asked. She had just joined Jim perhaps ten minutes ago, bringing him a turkey and Swiss cheese sandwich and a bottle of chilled water.

"He's good. Even better than I thought. His martial art style is one I've never seen before but it has elements of Tibetan and Western Chinese martial arts. Very fluid and evasive but still powerful. Emphasizes speed and efficiency. I like it."

Martha nodded as she watched Dillon and Rubio continue to spar. Rubio snapped in a couple of hooks that slammed into Dillon's left side. Rubio looked as if he were enjoying himself while Dillon had a serious look of the utmost concentration on his face. "Has he checked out okay?"

Jim swallowed, took a sip of water before answering. "Dan Fowler said that our young friend apparently has quite the reputation in London. He attended the University of West London for a time using the name Jasper Dillon. At the same time he became known in the underground street fighting club circuit as Jake Dillon. Made quite a bit of money before suddenly leaving."

"Why?"

Jim shrugged, took another sip of water. "He told me that in the two years since he left Shamballah he's been making his way across Asia,

Africa and then he came to England. Apparently he spent the last eight months there."

"How and where did he get the necessary paperwork to allow him to study at a university?"

Again Jim shrugged. "Damned if I know. But I do know that the more I find out about this young man's activities before he came to me the more my respect for his resourcefulness increases. According to Dan, the NSB can't find a single bit of information on Dillon before he showed up in London. Naturally there are numerous video images of him there and Dan himself made some calls to some contacts he has over there and they've put together an embarrassingly skimpy file on Dillon. And apparently that's because he seems to have just materialized out of thin air."

"Is such a thing possible?" Martha's eyes followed Dillon as he threw a straight punch at Rubio. The wily Rubio nimbly turned the blow aside with a forearm block, stepped in, twisted and with one fluid move, hip-flipped Dillon through the air. Dillon twisted like a giant lynx in mid-air and came down in a three-point landing, grinning in delight at his own agility.

"Even in this age of digital footprints and constant surveillance there are ways of hiding one's identity if one truly does not want one's identity known." Jim took another bite of sandwich, spoke around it as he chewed. "And Dan says that as far as he can find out, nobody is after me. Otis confirms the same thing."

"So maybe they *were* after Dillon?" Martha said. Dillon was now on the offensive, peppering Rubio's shoulders and head with quick, sharp jabs.

"Maybe. I really don't know." It had been four days since the attack on The Penthouse. Since then Jim had kept Dillon busy with physical exercises and reading. Dillon had never read Sun Tzu's "The Art of War" which as far as Jim was concerned was unforgiveable. He also had never read "The Laws of Human History" by Karstev or "The Principles of Private Detection" by Clovis Anderson. Jim had loaded him up with the books, ordered him to read them and when he had done so they would discuss them.

"I'm going to be taking him to The Pueblo in about another week or so. Would you like to come along?" Jim asked.

"Me? Why?"

"I think he'd take very well to Isuna Nika," Jim said. He had mastered that Comanche martial art before he was ten years old. And he had trained Martha in that art. "You could train him in that while I concentrated on teaching him the science and art of tracking. And it hasn't escaped my notice that you and he have become quite the good friends in the past three days." Jim smiled slightly.

Martha blushed slightly. "Ah, it's nothing like what you're thinking, Mr. Anthony—" she paused as they both heard a boom from the ring. Rubio was flat on his back, having taken a solid shot from Dillon's uppercut. The onlookers grumbled as money changed hands and a couple of them climbed in to help the dazed Rubio up. "—he's a very nice boy, yes. But—"

"But what?" Jim had a reason for making sure that Martha and Dillon spent time together. Being a woman she would pick up on things that he, as a man would overlook. "Speak your mind, Martha. If I'm going to train him I need to know everything about him."

Martha jerked her chin at Dillon who was shadow boxing in his corner of the ring, waiting for another opponent. Rubio had been propped up on a stool with cool water being splashed on his face. "Him you will never know everything about. I ask him certain questions and I can actually see walls going up in his eyes as he shuts down his memories. And there's something else as well…"

"Go on."

"Sometimes he will react to something that's said to him or he sees. And he reacts…well, the only way I can describe it as I get the distinct impression that he's not reacting as he truly wishes to react but as he *thinks* he should react. If that makes any sense."

"It does. And it confirms my own theory that he may have suffered some form of emotional abuse in his past that has caused him to become detached from his emotional responses to a degree. It doesn't appear to be interfering with his handling himself socially as he's been making his way in various societal situations for two years now. But it's apparently the residue of some form of psychological trauma."

"Can you do anything to help him?"

Jim didn't answer. Instead he clapped his hands for attention. It sounded like a pair of two by fours being whacked together. "That's it for today. Dillon, you keep on knocking out my men I won't have anybody to work the place."

Dillon stopped his shadow boxing and grinned at Jim. "I just barely tapped them, Mr. Anthony. Promise."

"Hit the showers and have your lunch. Come to my office in two hours."

"Sure, Mr. Anthony." Dillon walked over to Rubio's corner, taking off his gloves as he did so. Rubio had regained consciousness and he hugged

Dillon fiercely, with genuine affection and no hard feelings at all.

"Mr. Anthony? Maybe I'm speaking out of turn here," Martha said. "But you didn't answer my question. Can you help him?"

Jim handed her the empty plate and bottle of water. "Until I find out who is after either him or me and why they're trying to kill one or the other, it's not a case of helping anybody. It's a case of staying alive."

Martha walked on over to the guest wing of The Teepee to collect Dillon and bring him to Jim's office. Not that Dillon would be late for a meeting by a minute. Martha had noticed that even though he never seemed to look at a clock or wore a watch he always knew what time it was. As she approached his room she could hear singing and music coming from inside, thanks to the half open door.

Martha pushed open the door slightly to see Dillon spinning around the room, dancing with himself or at least she hoped it was dancing. One might have taken it for some sort of controlled total body cramp set to music. The spacious living room gave Dillon plenty of room to do his thing. Exactly what that thing was...well, that was an entirely different matter.

Dillon spun around, fingers snapping and saw her through half closed eyes. "Oh, hey!" His head bobbed as his feet stamped gracelessly. "You ever heard this? It's great!"

Martha cocked her head to the side in disbelief. "You've never heard Marvin Gaye before?"

"Is that who it is? He can sing, can't he?" Dillon continued popping his fingers as he did the best he could to keep time. Martha couldn't help but smile. Even though he was dancing about as well as a pregnant hippopotamus he was having such a good time and was so unselfconscious about it, it was fun to watch.

"You're going to tell me you've never heard Marvin Gaye before?"

"I don't know if Mr. Anthony told you this or not, but I was raised in a very remote part of the world. Been away from everything for years."

"They didn't have radios? TVs? Computers?"

Dillon spun around again. "No. No. And no. And most of the day was about training. When I wasn't training I was reading. When I wasn't training or reading I was cleaning. When I wasn't training, reading or cleaning I was practicing. When I—"

"I get it. I get it. Look, if you're going to dance, do it right. Here, let me show you." Martha walked over to the in-wall digital stereo and pressed a button to start that track again from the beginning. Then she stepped over to Dillon. "Watch my feet, okay?"

Dillon nodded, excited. Marvin Gaye started singing "I'll Be Doggone," again, his carefree, rapturous voice coming from the ceiling speakers and filling the room.

"Okay, let's start by taking three steps to the right...take it slow and just listen to the music...good! Now three steps to the left...follow me...that's it! Swing your arms, like you were before, but in time, like me....three to the right...three to the left...again! Good! That's it, c'mon!"

Dillon's arms were going up and back as he enthusiastically fell into it, a huge grin spreading across his face. A genuine grin, Martha couldn't help but notice. He actually had quite the infectious grin when it was real and coming from that remote emotional core that he worked so hard to keep hidden.

"Now that you've got that, let's put a little rock step on it. Here we go... left three times...right three times...one step back with your left foot... now bring it back, yeah! Again!"

Dillon truly did have it, his hips and arms moving in smooth rhythm, easily matching Martha's movements as they continued dancing, just enjoying the music and the movement of their bodies. Dillon even got confident enough to improvise a couple of steps that made Martha clap her hands in approval.

Marvin Gaye's voice faded away and Dillon kept on moving. "C'mon, show me another step!"

"You've got your meeting with Mr. Anthony, remember? But later on, I'll show you a few more steps. You're a quick learner, aren't you?"

"I like to learn," Dillon said as he followed her out of his quarters. "There was no dancing like that where I came from. Ceremonial dancing is all, not for fun."

"When you were in London you never went clubbing?"

"I went to clubs but just watched. It was like I was on a different planet... the people, the music, the way they just threw themselves into their dancing...but I could never do that. You have to lose control of yourself to have fun like that."

"Would that be such a bad thing? Sometimes it's fun to lose control of yourself and just let go."

"No it isn't." Dillon said firmly in a voice that let Martha know that once again those walls had gone up, carefully keeping whatever Dillon felt secure. Not for the first time the thought went through Martha's mind;

Who ARE you, Dillon? Where did you come from? What happened to you to make you so afraid of your own feelings?

The line of vehicles made their way up the back road at a steady, even thirty miles an hour. The engines barely made a whisper of sound. They were modified to operate that way. Eight trucks in all. Led by a black Humvee. The convoy came to a halt in a small clearing just outside the boundaries of Jim Anthony's property. The passenger side of the Humvee opened and the gracefully slim form of Ashanti Garuda emerged. Her blood-red sari matched the equally crimson tikala mark on her forehead. A golden bracelet in the form of a cobra encircled her right forearm. Unlike the heavily armed men who climbed down from the backs of the trucks, she carried no weapon. She had no need. If there were any person walking the earth today who deserved to be termed a living weapon, Ashanti Garuda was that person.

Each truck contained ten men in all, secured in body armor and with similar armaments that the men who had assaulted Jim Anthony's penthouse had carried. One man from each truck left their fellows and walked over to where Shani stood with her driver and Gustav. He held a tablet computer for her to see as they both studied the map displayed on the device.

The team leaders arrayed themselves in a semi-circle and stood at attention as Shani issued her final orders; "You've all been briefed on the target as much as possible. The interior design of the structure may have been changed as our source of information had not been there in twenty years. So we must be prepared for that. We also must be prepared for Anthony's people to put up stiff resistance."

Shani's eyes locked on the eyes of each individual team leader as she continued. "Our primary mission is to acquire a piece of equipment Jim Anthony has that we must secure for our master and that above all else is our goal. Under no circumstances must Jim Anthony be killed. You all have been given a precise description of Anthony so you cannot mistake him for anybody else. He must be taken alive at all costs. And gentlemen, I mean exactly that. When you have a twenty on Anthony notify me immediately." Shani's eyes communicated quite well the penalty should that order be disobeyed.

"You know the terrain. Deploy your men into Attack Pattern Ceti Alpha Five and execute the plan. Go!"

Dillon knocked on the door of Jim's office and was rewarded with a "Come!" Dillon came on in and sat in the seat Jim waved him to. Jim sat behind his desk, his reading glasses perched precariously on the end of his nose as he read through some faxed papers that had just been sent to him.

"I'm not interrupting, am I?"

"Not at all. Just getting more useless information that serves no purpose and just wastes paper." Jim sighed, took off his glasses and threw them on his desk. "How'd you like to start your training in earnest tomorrow?"

"Really?"

"Really. I've been observing you these past four days. Physically you're more than up to what I want to put you through. Your stamina is amazing. It's as if you never get tired. I was wondering if you'd permit me to take some blood samples from you to analyze?"

"Is that necessary?"

"No. Not at all. Just want to indulge my scientific curiosity is all. And in any case, a full medical examination wouldn't hurt. I should have done that first thing. Have you ever been examined by a doctor since you came back to the world?"

Dillon shook his head. "No."

"Ever been sick?"

Dillon thought about that for about twenty seconds. "Not that I can remember."

"Not even so much as a cold? Had your tonsils taken out? Measles? Chicken pox? Still got all your teeth?"

"No, no, no, no and yes."

"Hm. If you'd rather not give me a blood sample, that's your right, of course. But I wish you would. And I still want you to have a cursory physical examination."

"Hey, it's no problem," Dillon shrugged. "You want blood you can have it. You've been so generous with your time and you've shown me nothing but friendship. And the medical examination is fine."

"I don't want to pressure you into anything or for you to do something you don't want to do just because you think you owe me. I—" Jim looked up in surprised annoyance as his office door flew open. One of his people stood there, a wiry middle-aged horse wrangler named George cradling a Winchester pump-action shotgun. "What's the problem?" Jim asked.

"Trouble. We got visitors."

Jim came around his desk and followed George out into the hallway, both of them jogging, closely followed by Dillon. They stopped at the armory where a dozen of Jim's people, men and women alike were arming themselves. Martha spoke rapidly as she checked and loaded a Glock.

"Got a routine report from our scouts. There's a large force of heavily armed men converging on The Teepee."

"How large?" Jim asked, picking a modified lever action Winchester 1892 rifle with an enlarged hand guard, sawed down stock and barrel.

"Forty, maybe fifty." Martha tossed Dillon the Glock. He caught it, looked at it as if she had thrown him a snail.

"What do you expect me to do with this?" Dillon demanded.

"Don't you know how to shoot?" Martha asked.

"Why would I know how to use one of these noisy things?" Dillon snapped. He threw it back to her. "I'll be fine with my hands. You have knives here? Swords?"

Jim took the gun from Martha and gave it back to Dillon. "Take it and stay with me," he ordered. "Looks like you'll have to learn by doing. These men aren't going to fight hand-to-hand. They'd rather put a bullet in your brain and not work up a sweat. You'll use a gun."

Dillon didn't give him any more argument. Jim watched as his people spread out, going to their defensive positions inside The Teepee. "You come with me," he said and began walking to the entrance, Dillon right behind him.

"How did your people know they were coming? Motion detectors? Heat sensors?"

"The best motion detector is a Comanche warrior," Jim said. "Technology is fine but never to be solely relied upon. My people regularly patrol the grounds. Nobody can get within five miles of The Teepee without them knowing about it and alerting us." Jim paused as a headset was passed to him by Martha. He slipped it over his right ear, adjusted it and said, "talk to me."

Dillon stood off to one side and just watched as Jim's staff effectively went about their jobs. Steel shutters were pulled out of recessed slots to cover the windows. Lights were extinguished. Headsets were passed out so that everybody could stay in communication at all times.

Jim motioned to Dillon. "No matter what, you stay with me. Here, give me that gun. Let me give you a quick tutorial. Here's the safety, you click it on and off like so. Got it? The magazine holds seventeen shots so make sure you count them off. Hold the gun like *this* and squeeze the trigger, don't yank on it. Point it at whatever isn't one of my people and fire. Even if you don't hit anything you'll keep the opposition at bay and that's enough. Get a couple of spare magazines from Martha and come right back here." Jim listened to his headset for a few seconds. "And hurry. They're here."

Shani crouched down next to her driver and Gustav. They had come up independently of the other squads as she wanted to swing round wide, looking for an airstrip. They had found the helicopter and quickly disabled it. The strike teams were all in position and Shani eyed The Teepee carefully. If she hadn't seen it with her own eyes she wouldn't have believed it. She herself was no slouch when it came to disguise and deception but Jim Anthony had raised the art to another level. If one didn't know what to look for, one could walk right past The Teepee not knowing it was in plain sight. But the man she had tortured for two days until breaking him at last had told the secret of Jim Anthony's camouflage.

Everything was absolutely still and quiet. Which in itself made her suspicious. As well as their handheld scanning devices had not picked up any kind of alarm system or motion detectors. Anthony was far too cautious a man to not some sort of early warning system. Supposedly Anthony had a sizeable staff living and working here but they had not seen a soul since arriving. In the middle of the day there should be somebody moving around. "They know we're here," Shani snarled. "Very well. Attack! Attack!"

6.

The strike teams on the west and east sides of The Teepee opened fire first. There was another team at the rear but they would not fire or attack unless somebody tried to escape from that route. Shani and her two men were in the front with another team backing them up but she didn't want them to fire either. She wanted to get an idea of what kind of firepower Jim and his people had. And she suspected that The Teepee wouldn't be that easy to charge.

A veritable hail of bullets from twenty H&K MP7 machine guns tore into the walls of The Teepee. The reinforced walls held up against the onslaught but inside it sounded as if boulders were slamming against the building. Wood chips flew through the air as if they were being savaged by buzz saws. So fast and so sharp were the chips that they sliced through leaves and small branches like miniature shuriken.

Jim slid back a slot on the shutters covering a window and stuck his Winchester out, smashing a hole in the window. He blasted away. It was a scene reproduced all throughout The Teepee as Jim's people fired back with precision and accuracy. Dillon stayed down behind a couch. He didn't think he'd be able to hit a thing unless it was standing right in front of him so he judged it was best for him to stay out of the way of those who could shoot. He snuck a look at Jim's face. The old man didn't look so old all of sudden.

Outside, Shani's teams were taking casualties. Jim's people were all excellent shots and using armor piercing bullets. And they aimed for arms and legs. If they hit, good and well because that man was down. And if they hit his armored torso, he still was down because even if the round didn't penetrate the armor all the way through, he was still knocked down and chances were he'd stay that way for a while, due to cracked ribs.

Gustav turned to Shani. "We should bring up reinforcements, rush the building before we lose more men."

"No, you idiot," Shani said calmly. "We have to get inside and find Anthony. They've got the advantage as long as they can keep us outside." Shani held out her hand to her driver who placed a satellite phone in it. She spoke into the device quietly. "Drop two."

About a thousand yards away, the three man crew manning the M224 mortar went to work. They had targeted in The Teepee minutes ago, just waiting for Shani's word. In seconds, an explosive shell whooshed through the air in an arc, coming down right on top on The Teepee.

"They surely can't be planning on just staying out there and shooting at us?" Rubio joined Jim, Dillon and Martha, a smoking AR-15 with a hundred round ammo drum in his big hands. "We can hold them off all day long like this." He peered through a slit in a window, looking for a new target.

"Maybe they're waiting for night?" Dillon wondered aloud.

Suddenly Jim yelled, "Incoming!" With one thrust of his big body he slammed into Rubio, knocking him and Martha to the floor next to Dillon and throwing himself on top of them.

The explosion seemed to fill Dillon's head as a huge chunk of The Teepee's ceiling collapsed inward as if the foot of a giant had suddenly stomped on the building. Cries of shock, surprise and pain mixed with the cacophony of massive ceiling beams cracked in half by the explosive shockwave smashing to the floor.

The first explosion was followed by another one almost immediately, completing the destruction of the ceiling and adding to the chaos and confusion. Jim shouted orders in Comanche so that they would not be understood by the armed men who now charged The Teepee.

Some of Jim's people resumed their places and began firing back, covering the others who gave assistance to the injured and wounded. Jim continued issuing orders Dillon did not understand. He scrambled to his feet and got to a window, looked out the slot. Even though Jim's people were doing their best to hold them back, their attackers stormed up the short flight of steps and through the barred door, snapping the thick plank of wood as though it were a matchstick and charged into the entrance hall of The Teepee.

Dillon lifted his Glock in both hands just as Jim had showed him and the first man that burst through the door got a bullet right in his forehead. He fell backwards, impeding the progress of the men following him. Dillon advanced coolly, calmly, continuing firing at the attackers. The second man caught a bullet in his throat. He fell to the ground, a mist of blood spraying into the air in a wide crimson fan that drenched the men crowding behind him. The third man caught his bullet on his helmet but that was enough to drive him backwards. Dillon reached down, grabbed the harness of the first man he'd killed, dragged him inside. Dillon kicked the door shut and put his back to it keeping them out, feeling bullets thud against the reinforced door.

A raking burst of multiple machine gun fire caused one window to explode inward, taking the steel shutters off the hinges and shredding two of Jim's people to ribbons, bullets slashing through them with devastating force at such a close range.

Rubio let out a blood freezing war cry as he lifted his AR15 and held down the trigger, moving the weapon back and forth as if it were a fire hose on full aimed at a burning building and the results were just about the same. The bullets chewed through the three or four men standing right outside the window. Their bodies jiggled madly, bullets punching right through their body armor, blood geysering from the golf ball sized exit wounds.

Dillon heard yells from further on inside The Teepee. Even though he spoke no Comanche he could guess what they were saying. Jim confirmed it for him. "They're inside."

Martha and Rubio were at the window with no shutters, returning fire, keeping Shani's forces at bay. "Can we get out the back?" Dillon asked.

Jim shook his head. "No way. There's a large armed force at the rear." Jim reached down and picked up a couch all by himself, lifting it as if weighed no more than a loaf of bread. "Get away from there," he said to Dillon, who scrambled out of the way. Jim jammed the couch up against the door. "That won't keep them back for long but it'll give us some time. Come."

By now, the smoke from fires inside the building had spread throughout. Jim barked more orders into his headset. He motioned for Dillon to come with him. Martha and Rubio brought up the rear.

Jim's people were pulling out, withdrawing from the windows, laying down covering fire as they did so.

The strike teams were indeed inside The Teepee. Two bulky forms emerged from the smoke. Jim whipped up his Winchester, fired twice and the men dropped. From the sounds of gunfire outside Jim could tell that the strike teams were enveloping The Teepee in a crossfire, pouring bullets into the building from three angles so they they would not hit their fellows. It was a solid, tried and true military strategy that Jim would have done himself if he'd been in charge of this raid.

More gunfire, more yelling and cursing. Dillon wiped his streaming eyes and followed Jim through the smoky corridor. Jim fired twice more, both bullets taking down their targets. Occasionally Dillon could hear Rubio's AR-15 behind him as he covered their escape.

A door to their left whipped open and a man leaped from within, right at Martha. Taken by surprise she wasn't able to get her weapon up in time to fire. Both of them slammed into the far wall. Dillon turned around, tried to train his gun on the man but he himself caught the butt of a machine gun in the small of his back. The impact was enough to make him lose all strength in his legs and collapse to his knees.

Jim Anthony came up behind Dillon's attacker, jammed his Winchester right up against the man's spine, just below his bulletproof vest and pulled the trigger, blowing his spine out through this stomach. Jim kicked the body away and turned to shoot at another man coming through the same door. The body kicked back from the impact of the bullets.

Martha rolled smoothly out of her attacker's grasp. She had dropped her gun but she didn't need it. With deceptively slim hands she gripped her attacker's head at the back and by the chin. She twisted hard and the crack of his neck breaking cleanly was somehow louder than any other sounds of combat Dillon had heard that day.

Rubio helped Dillon to his feet and they again started their run down the corridor.

Shani stepped through the shattered entrance door of The Teepee, surveying the blood-splashed floor and walls of the entrance hall. Most of them were her men she noted. Whoever had been in here defending the doors was good. "Anthony was right here," she said to Gustav. "I want him found."

Gustav had his hand to his left ear, cupping it so that he could hear the reports coming through his headset more clearly. "Nobody's seen Anthony as yet. But they report that gradually, resistance is easing up."

"They're leaving," Shani said. "Probably through secret tunnels. Call our reinforcements. Have them sweep the perimeter. They must be coming out of exits in the woods. Tell them I want captives, not bodies." Shani gestured to Gustav. "Search the place. Anthony must have an office, personal quarters. Find them. I'll supervise from here."

Gustav gulped. "I'll take three men with me—"

"You will go yourself."

Gustav saw the expression on Shani's face and decided not to press the issue. He left her and walked down the smoky corridor into The Teepee.

They made it to Jim's office. He closed the door behind them and walked swiftly over to his desk. He pressed a concealed switch and a series of iron bars, thick as his thumb slid upwards from recessed holes in the floor to help reinforce the door, which itself was solid steel, cunningly designed to look like wood.

Jim walked over to the bookcase and with a swipe of one arm, cleared a shelf of books. He opened a panel, stuck his hand in and yanked. A section of the bookcase swung outwards, revealing a corridor. "In," Jim commanded.

"What about you?" Dillon asked. "You're not going to try and hold them off by yourself?"

"No, I'm not. Go with Martha and Rubio. Now." Jim's voice had none of the warmth and friendliness Dillon had become used to. It was now as unfeeling as granite.

Martha tugged on Dillon's arm. "We have to go."

"But, I don't—"

"He's going to activate the self-destruct! There's a couple hundred pounds of TNT buried under The Teepee! He's going to blow it up!"

Dillon gave no more argument. He joined Martha and Rubio, running along the well-lit corridor.

Jim went over to his computer which he always kept on. He typed in a code. All the information on his computer was now being sent to two other computers. One in Washington, DC in The J. Edgar Hoover Building. It was located in a small office Dan had set aside for him to work in when on a consulting job for The Bureau. The other computer belonged to someone he trusted. Jim opened a panel on his desk and pressed a large red button. Warning klaxons blared, giving his people notice that he was about to blow up The Teepee. He wished that there was a way he could have blown up the place with his enemies in it but there wasn't and that was all there was to it. He wouldn't have his people sacrificing their lives anymore for him. Whoever these new enemies were, he'd deal with them. And he knew where to start. Above the red button was a timer. Jim set it for five minutes. He took a last look around his office. Furniture and works of art that he had owned since the 1930's were about to be destroyed forever. The Teepee, which had been his home ever since his retirement was about to be destroyed forever.

Somebody would have to pay for that.

Jim Anthony turned and ran into the corridor, the relentless clicking of the timer counting down sounding like gunshots in his ears.

Shani listened to the reports from her strike teams scurrying through the various rooms of The Teepee. All resistance inside had ceased. But she heard gunshots coming from outside. Anthony's people were emerging from escape tunnels and disappearing into the woods. Night was coming on and the Comanche knew this region better than anybody else. They could find secure hidden places and pick off her men.

What of the valuable item her master needed? Did Anthony have it? Was it here in this place? Shani ground her teeth in anger. She should have planned better, perhaps infiltrated Anthony's home on her own and secured the item. She had vastly underrated Anthony. But who could have known that Anthony would maintain such a well-armed force? She'd expected to have just found Anthony, his new bodyguard and maybe a few others. The information she'd gotten had been deliberately misleading. Shani was impressed. The old man had held out for two days under torture before talking and he'd still had the presence of mind to mislead her. Her master would not be pleased by this.

The air filled with the shrieking of a warning klaxon going off and Shani knew it could mean only one thing. She touched her headset, activating it. "Everybody pull out and get clear. The building is going to explode. Get out and get clear."

Gustav approached her, running flat out for the door. Shani's long arm came out straight and direct as a spear, taking Gustav in the throat. He hit the floor as if he'd been struck with a sledgehammer and did not move. Shani left him where he lay. Yes, it was somewhat petty of her to take out her momentary lapse into anger on Gustav but even after all the years she had lived and all the horrors she had experienced and inflicted on others, she was still human.

Shani left the burning building.

Dillon turned as he heard Jim emerging from the hidden entrance of the escape tunnel. They stood on a high ridge overlooking The Teepee which was half consumed in flames. The surrounding trees had caught fire as well. The makings of a devastating forest fire was beginning down there. They could see the attackers withdrawing, running away from the conflagration.

"Damn!" Jim snarled.

"What's wrong?" Rubio asked. He and Martha stood nearby, looking at the destruction of what had been their home in stunned disbelief.

Jim leveled an arm, finger pointing at a slim, female form emerging from the Teepee and walking away from it. "I can't make her out and I didn't think to bring any binoculars. Can you—"

The Teepee exploded with such force that it knocked down trees for a thousand yards in all directions. Even from where they stood the four of them felt the shock wave through their feet and the hot wind on their faces.

The Teepee was gone. Totally obliterated. Nothing of it remained except for a blackened, flaming hole in the ground.

Dillon could only stare in astonishment. It was hard for him to believe what he had just seen. He had seen explosions, sure. But nothing like this. He turned to Jim, "Mr. Anthony-AWK!"

Jim had covered the ground between himself and Dillon in a blur of movement. His left forearm thrust into the younger man's neck, slamming his body against the trunk of a tree with such force that for a few seconds Dillon actually thought his back had broken. But if such was the case he wouldn't be feeling the excruciating agony he felt as Jim's other hand gripped Dillon's right wrist with such force that he dropped the gun as Dillon suddenly had no strength in that hand. He tried to strike back but Jim let go of his wrist and his fingers sank into vital pressure points on Dillon's body and just that simple, Dillon was numb all over. He couldn't breathe. His vision faded and all he could hear was the bloodthirsty growl of Jim Anthony in his ears.

"No more games, damn you. Who are you, really? Who sent you?"

"Mr. Anthony! Mr. Anthony! Let him go!" Martha screamed. "You're killing him!" She yanked on the arm that firmly kept Dillon pinned to the tree but it didn't budge a millimeter. She looked at Rubio. He stood a few feet away, looking on dispassionately. "Help me!"

Dillon again tried to struggle but his arms felt cold and heavy. He simply couldn't move them. And again, Jim Anthony's voice spoke softly; "What do you think I was doing the past three days when I had you in the ring sparring? I watched every move you made. Just in case of a situation just like this. There isn't a move you make I can't counter. Now. Answer me. Who are you and what do you want?"

Dillon tried to answer but his tongue had gone as numb as his arms. Everything was going away in a dark mist and he couldn't draw in a decent breath to answer Jim.

"Mr. Anthony! Jim! Let him GO! You're killing him!" Martha shrieked again, kicking and punching at Jim's back. She might as well have been punching a marble statue. She turned again to Rubio. "For God's sake, why won't you help me?"

"Mr. Anthony's the boss. He knows what he's doing! If that kid helped kill our people—"

"POPPA!"

The voice slashed through the air with a level of command that caused everybody, including Jim Anthony to whirl about as if they were trained soldiers. Jim let Dillon go and he fell heavily to the ground, drawing in great whooping breaths, filling his lungs with air that tasted sweeter than anything he could remember in recent memory.

The astoundingly lovely woman standing ten feet away on top of a moss covered boulder facing Jim was tall and her slender, acrobatic build made her seem even taller. The helmet bob of her dark hair shone like polished metal. Her black jumpsuit fitted her like a second skin. Holstered under each slim arm were gleaming stainless steel Coonan Classic .357 Magnums. She also toted an A-91 bull pup assault rifle with grenade launcher, the butt resting on her hip.

Jim spoke, his voice soft. The bloodlust that had totally consumed him gone as quickly as it had risen. "You startled me."

The tall woman grinned. "It was supposed to. Been a long time since I had to use the command voice you taught me. But I didn't think anything short of me shooting you in the back would cease your enthusiastic strangling of that strapping young man lying there on the ground."

"You learned well. And once I get the answers I need from him, I intend to resume killing him."

The woman lightly jumped down from the boulder and walked closer to Jim, slipped her slim white hand into Jim's sun-bronzed one and lifted that hand gently to her cheek. "He's not to blame, Poppa. He didn't bring those men here."

"Then who did?"

"Ashanti Garuda."

Jim stepped back, lower jaw sagging, eyes opening wide in an expression that worried both Martha and Rubio as in all the time they'd worked for Jim Anthony they'd never seen that expression on his face. It was fear. Total, unrefined, naked fear. The woman gripped his hand tightly, not letting him pull away from her. Her voice was pure silk and steel as she murmured; "Steady, Poppa. Steady."

"Are you sure?"

She nodded firmly. "I've been tracking her for the past couple of days. I didn't catch up to her but I found one of her safe houses. And I found something else. You remember Jimmy Holm?"

He nodded, his eyes blank of feeling, as he knew what was coming next.

"Ashanti had him tortured. That's how she found out where The Teepee was. She's been trying to get hold of your old friends who have been to The Teepee and knew where it was. Most of them I was able to warn via The DarkNet, The Two Tin Cans and The Grooveline. But I didn't know where Holm was until it was too late.

"He was living in a nursing home in Kentucky. She just walked in without resistance and walked out with him. She brought him to her Manhattan safe house and went to work on him. The poor old man was barely alive when we got there but he was able to tell us what we needed to know. I'm only sorry we got there too late." The woman smiled and uncannily looked like Jim Anthony at that moment as she continued; "But we took care of the men she left behind to watch him and guard the house. They won't be torturing any more old men. I saw to that."

"Holm?"

The smile vanished as the woman again lifted his hand to her cheek. "There wasn't much left of him, Poppa. They'd been working on him for a whole day, maybe two. I did him an act of kindness."

Jim nodded, leaned forward and brushed aside her hair to kiss the woman's forehead. She at last let his hand go and he walked away, back to where he could look at where The Teepee had been.

The woman walked past the bewildered Martha and Rubio to where Dillon still lay. She offered her hand. "And you must be The Boy Wonder

I've heard so much about. Come on, get up. You aren't hurt."

Dillon took her hand and she yanked him to his feet with a strength he wouldn't have believed could be contained in such a slim body. Dillon rubbed his sore, bruised throat. "He tried to kill me."

"Twaddle. If Poppa really wanted to kill you, you'd be dead."

"Why do you keep calling Mr. Anthony 'Poppa?'"

"Because he's my father, silly. My name is Vera Gemini."

Dillon stopped rubbing his throat. "Your father? He didn't say anything about having a daughter."

"And why would he mention that to someone he just met a few days ago? Excuse me." Vera Gemini placed her pinkies in the corners of her mouth. A series of sharp, high notes, followed by murky low ones filled the air. And then Dillon jumped in surprise as a dozen ebony clad forms seemed to appear out of nowhere. The black suits they wore covered them completely from head to toe. Insectile crimson and yellow lenses covered their eyes. They crept along the ground like crabs or loped along like apes. Some even swung in the surrounding trees like monkeys. The backpacks attached to their suits looked cumbersome to Dillon and he would have thought were too bulky for such movements but the packs didn't seem to impede them in the slightest.

"What the hell—" Dillon began.

Vera Gemini removed her pinkies. "That's how *Les Vampires* communicate with each other in the field. They don't use words while working."

"And what the hell are *Les Vampires*?"

Vera jerked a chin at the black clad forms that spread out through the forest. "Them. They work for me."

"I see," Dillon said slowly. But he actually didn't. "Thanks for stopping your...father from killing me."

Vera shrugged. "Don't thank me yet, Boy Wonder. We're still not out of danger. As long as Ashanti Garuda is above ground and drawing breath, none of us are safe." Abruptly, Vera turned and walked over to where Jim Anthony stood. Dillon followed, but hung back a bit.

Vera touched Jim's brawny shoulder. "Poppa?"

Jim's turned his head, smiled down at her. "I'm fine now, Vera. It's just a shock, that's all. If Shanti is here that means *he's* back as well. We've got to get out of here."

"My Vampires are scouring the forest, looking for your people. They'll bring them here. I've got a C-130 two miles east from here in the Christopher Clearing."

"Come on, get up. You aren't hurt."

Jim nodded. "Thank you, Vera." Jim looked at Dillon. "My deepest apologies, young man. I allowed my emotions to overcome me. It's a problem I've had in the past. I thought I had overcome it years ago." Jim smiled somewhat ruefully. "I suppose I haven't."

"I think it should have been pretty obvious I wasn't with those people since they were trying to kill me right along with you," Dillon said. "And I can't say I appreciate somebody I was beginning to think of as a friend trying to kill me either."

"I've apologized. You can either accept it or not. That's up to you. But you can't stay here. Vera will fly us out of here. I strongly advise you to come with us. Once we've reached safety you can do whatever you want."

"Who were those people? Who's Ashanti Garuda? Why does she want to kill you?"

"She didn't want to kill me. She wants something I have. She couldn't kill me until she has it because the man she worships needs it."

"Worships? What do you mean?"

"I mean exactly what I said. She doesn't work for him. She worships him as if he were her god. She's committed unspeakable acts in his name. I prayed I would never hear either her name or his again in my life. I suppose that deep down I knew that was just a way of me not having to deal with it. I always knew that one day he would resurface."

Dillon looked from the solemn faced Jim Anthony to Vera Gemini, who pretended to be looking for her Vampires. Martha and Rubio stood off to the side, both looking uncomfortable and sad.

"Who are we talking about, Mr. Anthony?"

Jim's voice was as remote as if he were speaking from the dark side of The Moon as he said two simple words. And even though Dillon had never heard them before, his limbs trembled as if someone had just walked over his grave.

"Sun Koh."

Dillon sat in the cargo section of the Hercules C-130 transport plane. He looked around at the exhausted faces of the painfully few survivors of the attack on The Teepee. Jim moved among them, speaking softly to each and every one. Martha passed out sandwiches and bottles of water while Rubio took care of their immediate medical needs. Sitting a respectable distance away from Jim's people were *Les Vampires*. They sat ramrod straight, hands on their knees, looking straight ahead. Not talking. Not breathing. They might have been onyx statues.

Vera strode up the ramp into the plane. She had been the last one to board. She gestured to Dillon. "Come on up front with me, Boy Wonder."

As he followed her, Dillon asked, "Why do you keep calling me that? My name is Dillon."

"I know full well what your name is but you walk around with such a serious look on your face I'm afraid it's going to stay like that forever. Don't you ever smile?"

"There hasn't been much to smile about today."

They entered the cockpit and Vera settled herself into the pilot's chair while indicating Dillon should take the co-pilot's seat.

"Ah, but that's where you're wrong, my grim young paladin. It's when things are at the worst and their blackest that you should grin and laugh." Vera displayed her own marvelous smile as she started her pre-flight check. "Because it may just be your last."

Jim stuck his head into the cockpit. "We going?"

"We going. The Pueblo?"

"Yes." Jim withdrew his head and Vera flicked a switch. Music filled the cockpit.

"Who's this?" Dillon asked.

"Are you for real? You don't know Booker T and The MG's?"

Dillon shook his head. "Who are they?"

"The band we're listening to, silly. It's 'Time Is Tight'. Kinda appropriate considering our situation.'"

"It's loud."

"But good, right?"

And Vera was truly amazed to see Dillon smile. "Matter of fact it is."

"Word of advice. Always travel with music."

The big cargo plane started down the clearing which made a natural runway. It lifted into the thickening darkness of the sky and headed west.

7.

Dillon awoke without that period of grogginess that most people did where they had to transition between the periods of sleep and consciousness. Once his eyes were open he was immediately awake, aware of his surroundings, ready for action. He swung his bare legs off the cot and stood up, walked to the window, opened it and looked out. He leaned on the windowsill as dawn came up over the American Southwest.

Dillon occupied one of a number of adobe buildings grouped around an oasis in a huge crescent. This was The Pueblo, another one of Jim Anthony's retreats. When they had landed here yesterday, Dillon had remarked to Vera Gemini that they looked like children's blocks stacked together. Everyone had been exhausted and helped by Jim and Martha had been shown to their quarters. Dillon had no idea where *Les Vampires* had slept the night or even if they slept. Once disembarking from the plane they had disappeared into the night. Dillon and Jim hadn't spoken much. It was Martha who had shown Dillon to his lodgings and she herself didn't want to talk much, either. Dillon had taken off his clothes and went right to sleep, compartmentalizing the horror of the day's death and bloodshed to a remote corner of his mind where it would not interfere with his rest.

As he continued to watch, he saw Vera herself come out another one of the buildings and walk down to the oasis. She wore a flowing blood-red robe that billowed behind her like a cape. She reached the edge of the the water and with one sweep of her arms threw the robe off, revealing her splendid body naked to the rising sun.

Dillon gulped.

Vera dived in, barely causing a splash. She surfaced and swam with clean strokes and kicks, looking as if she was barely exerting herself. But before Dillon could draw more than a few breaths, she was already to the other side of the pool of crystal blue water. She turned around and backstroked her way back to where she had started.

In all this time, Dillon had stayed where he was, transfixed by her elegant grace and power. Vera emerged from the water and retrieved her robe. Wrapping it around her body she headed in the direction of Dillon's quarters.

He hastily got his pants and shirt on before she got to the door. She knocked politely and Dillon opened the door. "Good morning. You're up early."

Vera breezed into the room. "Don't play innocent with me. I saw you looking at me swimming."

"Ah. Yeah...about that...look, I'm not a pervert or anything like that..."

Vera walked through the living room and dropped into a comfortable chair. "What's the matter, you don't like looking at naked girls?"

"Of course I do. But it's different with you. You're Mr. Anthony's daughter."

Vera sighed. "Trust me when I say that Poppa would be the last man to criticize you for looking at me naked. He's looked at more than his share of other men's daughters naked, let me assure you. How are you this morning?"

"Ready to find out what is going on around here and who this Sun Koh is. Who's Ashanti Garuda? Why did she attack The Teepee? I didn't want to bother anybody about this last night but it's a new day and a day for questions to be answered."

"Aren't you feisty? But that's okay. I like feist." Vera pulled up delightfully slim, yet muscular legs and wrapped her arms around them, resting her pointed chin in the small gap between her dimpled knees. "And you're right. This is a day for answers but they won't come from me. It's for Poppa to tell you. But that doesn't mean I don't have anything to say."

Dillon wasn't sure he liked the sound of that. "What do you mean?"

"Just this: I'll have my people take you anywhere you want to to go in the world. They'll make sure you get there safely. Trust me when I say that when you have the protection of *Les Vampires* you truly are protected. I'll also give you a hundred thousand dollars for your trouble."

"So you think I'm a threat to your father!"

"What? No! No, not at all. You idiot, I'm trying to save your life!"

Dillon blinked, totally perplexed. "I don't understand you people at all. Trying to save my life? How?"

"Because anybody who gets in between Poppa and Sun Koh is going to get killed and that's truth. Poppa's told me about you. He likes you a lot and therefore, so do I. He wouldn't want to see you hurt or killed—"

"—he made an excellent try at it yesterday!"

Vera grunted that away. "Poppa was upset and can you blame him? The Teepee was his home for years before either of us were born. The people who were killed just weren't employees. They were friends. Some he had known ever since they were babies."

Dillon subsided. "I'm really sorry about that."

"You're not a sorry person, Dillon. Never say you're sorry. Always say 'I apologize.'"

Dillon smiled slightly. "I apologize. But I'm not running out on your father. Seems to me he can use as much help as he can get now."

"And your loyalty is admirable but you can't do anything but get yourself killed. The people Sun Koh has working for him are skilled on a level you can't even imagine. And they've been doing this work for going on seventy years now. They've got years of experience beyond anything you've ever encountered. Best to leave this to me and Poppa."

"You? You don't look much older than me!"

"Trust me when I say that I wear my age well. I'm a tad older than you think. But just a tad, mind you."

"I'm not running."

Vera shrugged. "Don't say I didn't warn you. Before this is all over you may wish you'd taken me up on my offer."

"I'm not a coward, Vera."

Vera Gemini's inky eyes looked deep into Dillon's sparkling copper ones. "No. No, I don't think you are."

"Where is your father?"

"Apparently I should have been here keeping an eye on you two." Jim Anthony said from the doorway. He only wore trousers, his torso and feet bare. Dirt crusting his feet and arms up to the elbow testified to the hard digging he had been doing. In his hands he held an iron box that had been welded shut. Even though his words were accusatory, his eyes said that he had just been joking with them.

"Poppa! Where have you been? You were up before dawn!" Vera bounded from her seat and ran over to Jim, stood on her tiptoes to give him a kiss on his unshaven cheek.

"Had to dig this up," Jim hefted the iron box. "I buried it in the tunnels under The Pueblo."

"What is it?" Dillon asked.

"Get dressed then meet me in my quarters. Bring Martha and Rubio with you. I'll explain while we eat. We've got plans to make."

❦ ❦ ❦

The smells of cooking food filled the common room of Jim's quarters with tantalizingly delicious odors that made Dillon's stomach rumble. The cool, calm interior of the building amazed Dillon with its hominess. Comanche artwork decorated the walls. Thick bear hide throw rugs on the hardwood floor. Martha and Rubio had just finished setting the table. Vera Gemini sat at the table, once more wearing her black jumpsuit along with her holstered guns.

Jim Anthony emerged from the bedroom. He'd showered, shaved and dressed in a fresh pair of white linen pants, linen collarless Irish Grandad shirt with his indispensable belt around his waist. When he walked on bare feet as he did now he moved with absolutely no sound at all.

Three Comanche women, survivors of the attack the night before came out of the kitchen carrying bowls and trays. Jim motioned for Dillon to sit and he did so himself while the women served the food. Everybody dug into the broiled steak, baked chicken, mixed vegetables and freshly baked bread with a will. For the next half hour there was no sound except for that of food being heartily chewed, knives and forks clinking on the plates, water, orange juice and iced tea being drunk.

Jim sat back, pushing his empty plate away. He spoke in Comanche to the young women who nodded and went into his bedroom. They came back in a minute carrying the great iron box. One woman handed Jim a well-worn hardcover book. They sat it next to Jim's feet then made themselves scarce. Jim looked around the table and said, "Well, I guess it's time I clarified a few things." He looked directly at Dillon. "Vera knows all this while Martha and Rubio know bits and pieces of the story. You, of course, know none of it."

Dillon wiped his mouth with a silk napkin. "I'm listening."

"You should know that it's not too late for you to get clear of this. Ashanti probably doesn't know who you are. Vera can get you away from here and you don't have to be involved."

"I'm no coward, Mr. Anthony. I've explained that to your daughter. I'm not running."

Jim's eyes shone with admiration but his voice held a different tone as he replied; "You may wish you had. Sun Koh is probably the most dangerous man I've ever faced. And he has a worldwide organization that easily equals the one I used to have. From time to time I checked up on The Thule Society just out of curiosity. It always appeared to me that they were now regarded as little more than crackpots and proponents of a long out-of-date belief. Obviously such is not the case. Those men Shani brought with her were Thule Society soldiers." Jim sighed. "If it were a snake it would have bit me. Remember how they took all the bodies in my penthouse after the failed attack?"

Dillon nodded.

"Because they knew that once I got a good look at the bodies and examined them I'd have identified them as Thule Society soldiers. Here" Jim slid the book he'd been given across the table to Dillon. "That's *Bulwer-Lytton's* 'The Coming Race.' If you're serious about wanting in on this, you need to read that. It'll fill in a lot of the gaps in the story that I'm about to tell you."

Dillon picked up the book and examined it carefully. He opened it, saw on many of the pages there were notes in the margins, presumably written in Jim's handwriting.

"Make yourselves comfortable. This story is going to take some time." Jim sat back in his seat and he seemed to be looking beyond the room he sat in as he began: "This story begins in 1937...an old friend of mine who was also a brilliant scientist had asked me for help. Professor Helmut Spengler has discovered a secret that could rock the very foundations of the world and he desperately needed my help..."

Part 2:
'THE COMING RACE'

I.

It was 1937 and Professor Helmut Spengler was boiling in his own fear. Wrapped in a heavy coat, he descended the steps of the airplane, head bowed, eyes cutting from side to side. A chill wind rolled off the Hudson, ruffling the untidy mop of prematurely silver hair that covered his narrow head, and he jammed his hand into his pocket, clutching the folded over shape of the telegram resting there.

A porter handed Spengler his bags, two bulky duffels left over from his term of service in the army of the Kaiser, and he maneuvered them away from the plane and the stink of the diesel engines. The wind cut through him, despite his coat, and he felt it dance along the lines of old wounds. He'd found himself tangled in barbed wire not two weeks after reporting to the Western Front, and he still carried the marks of that youthful foolishness.

The sound of birds made him turn, and he caught sight of the New York skyline for the first time. He let out a soft breath and looked around.

Newark Airport was situated near a section of thriving marsh, and the smell of life grown wild competed with the farts of exhaust given off by the plane. On the whole, Spengler preferred the former to the latter. He pulled a pocketwatch out of his threadbare waist-coat and opened it. He closed it a few seconds later, without having really examined it.

The watch had been a gift from his wife, dead these past six years. He closed his eyes and rubbed his brow, trying not to think of her. To think of what he'd lost, or why he'd started down the path he now found himself inextricably bound to.

A sob bobbed in his throat, threatening to burst free. Her face floated before his eyes, and he recalled the way she wore her hair and the smell of her perfume. Then, he thought of the shriek of the generator and the harsh smell of electricity as it caressed unprotected flesh.

His hand clenched, and the edges of the watch bit into his palm. His eyes opened and he took a shuddery breath. He looked at the line of people still climbing off the plane, his eyes dissecting their faces for any trace of familiarity.

Who would they send? He had heard the names, but never seen the faces of those who served the man he was running from. Ghostly titles for spectral figures, flitting about the edges of the Reich. Spengler swallowed, fighting the bile that burned his throat. Fear replaced sadness.

He looked at the watch again, rubbing a calloused thumb over the engraved surface. In a way, it was her fault. He grunted, gripped by a sudden grim humor. In an entirely more logical and rational way, it was most certainly his, however. Spengler sighed and put the pocket watch away. His hands were shaking, though not as bad as they had been. He looked at the river, and began to rummage in his pockets for his cigarettes.

He found the telegram instead, and pulled it out, reading it for the fiftieth time. Or maybe the hundredth. He'd lost count of the times he'd tried to squeeze additional meaning out of the trio of brisk lines inviting him to New York. It was better than he'd hoped, but not as much as he'd wished.

"Jimmy," he muttered, remembering the young man he'd first seen slinking towards him through the crooked bowels of a trench, a bone-handled knife held between his teeth.

Spengler could almost smell the trenches; that bouquet of industrial effluvium and human excretion. He could hear the creak of the wire in the rain, and feel the barbs digging through the stiff wool of his uniform, biting into the wet flesh below.

No matter how much he struggled, he'd been unable to pull himself free. The splash of feet through the water that submerged the bottom of the trench had sent a thrill of panic through him.

A dim, dark shape, inhuman, came loping through the trench, cloaked in terror. Long arms and legs, moving with feline grace. The apparition had bare hands and feet wrapped in muddy rags, and wore a tattered ruin of a uniform bearing neither insignia nor badge. He could have been English or German or Russian. Lightning glinted off the metal of the knife trapped between his teeth, and Spengler had almost died then and there.

Instead of flesh, however, the knife had cut the wire. Spengler had tumbled free, falling into the filthy water of the trench. Sputtering, unable to believe his good fortune, he'd looked up into the face of a young man. Dark eyes had examined him for a moment, then, "*Guten abend, mein freund.*"

That was his first memory of Jim Anthony.

The telegram crumpled in his hand, and he hunched against the wind rolling off of the river. A sense of self-disgust blossomed momentarily within him. Was this what it had come to? Running for help to a former enemy?

But what else could he do? A shiver cut through him, and he shook his head slightly. He was not a soldier anymore, and in truth, he'd never been much of one, even in his younger days. He lacked the steel.

No, he was a scientist. A thinker. But now his thoughts were being put towards foul purposes. His life, his work, both were in danger. And that danger was what had propelled him across the Atlantic, to accept the invitation of a man who had once spared his life on a muddy battlefield.

It all seemed so far away, now. As if he'd left it all behind, left everything bad back in Vienna. Pulling out the leather wallet that held his cigarettes, he extricated one with trembling fingers and stuffed it between his lips. But the fear wasn't receding. If anything, distance only made it worse. Only made the threat more menacing.

They could kill him as easily as he might swat a fly. In Berlin, or Vienna, or here, it made little difference to them. He could feel their eyes on him. They had been watching him as he boarded the plane at Aspern, and they were watching him now.

The sole of a shoe scraped on the tarmac. Spengler's heart stuttered, and he nearly swallowed his cigarette.

"Professor Spengler?"

The accent was American, but with a trace of a Gaelic brogue. Spengler turned. The man was broad, though not tall, and wearing a leather aviator's jacket. A wide, open face peeked out from beneath a mop of shaggy, straw-colored hair and the hand he extended was burnt brown by the sun. "You're Spengler, right? *Sprechen sie Englisch?*"

"*Ja, Ja,*" Spengler said, nodding rapidly. "I am Spengler."

"My name's Gentry. Tom Gentry," the man said. "Jimmy-Jim-Mr. Anthony-sent me to pick you up, Professor Spengler."

"*Gut.* Good, I mean," Spengler said, taking Gentry's hand gingerly. The man was bigger than he looked at first glance, and his grip was like iron. Thin scars decorated his craggy features, attesting to a life lived hard.

Spengler felt relief at first, then suspicion. What was to stop them from having someone waiting for him, from intercepting his telegrams and setting an ambush? He tensed as Gentry bent to take one of his bags. The big man noticed, and stepped back, raising his hands.

"Easy Professor; Jimmy said you might be feeling a bit paranoid-"

"Paranoid? Is that what he thinks?" Spengler barked. He shook his head. "It is not paranoia. Merely caution."

"Yeah? Better safe than sorry, right?" Gentry said. "Look, Jimmy said you might feel that way, so he said to remind you that you still owed him an-ah-*Amneris…*"

Spengler blinked, then relaxed. "*Ja. Ja, Amneris. Gut.* Gentry, you said?"

"Jimmy never mentioned me?" Gentry said, making a face. "All them letters you two exchanged and I don't even rate a mention?"

"I-ah-" Spengler hesitated, bewildered.

"Ah, I'm just kidding you Professor," Gentry said, waving his hand. "Don't look so worried. By the way, what's an amnah-amneri-whatever it was?"

"A cigarette. Austrian brand. Before the War," Spengler said, and decided to change the subject. "You are carrying a weapon."

"That a question, or a suggestion?" Gentry said, grinning. He patted a bulge in the pocket of his jacket. "Either way, the answer is yes. Why?"

Spengler nodded again. "I think I was followed."

"Yeah?" Gentry's eyes narrowed. He stiffened slightly, recognizably alert now. "How many?"

"I don't know. It's just a feeling." Spengler looked at him. "You believe me?"

"People usually got a good reason for feelings, Professor, in my experience." Gentry hefted the duffel bags without apparent strain. "Come on. You'll feel better when we're moving."

"Where are we-?"

"You got a room waiting for you at the Waldorf-Anthony," Gentry interjected, leading him towards a black Rolls-Royce which sat catty-corner to the tarmac. "Free of charge, courtesy of Mr. Anthony."

"That is generous," Spengler said. "He is well, then?"

"Who, Jimmy? Fit as the proverbial fiddle," Gentry said, depositing Spengler's luggage in the trunk of the Rolls. "Hop in, Professor."

Spengler slid in to the back of the Rolls, and Gentry shut his door for him. He banged a big fist on the roof. "Won't take us too long, depending on traffic."

"*Gut, gut.*" Spengler nodded. Then, he rubbed his eyes. A flash of something had caught them. A wink of light from the top of one of the nearby aerodromes...

"*Nein!*" he yelped, reaching for the door. Gentry looked at him, puzzled, then, eyes flashing with a sudden realization, spun. His hand clawed for the pistol in his coat, but too late.

A rifle spoke, once, sharply.

And as Spengler watched in horrified silence, Tom Gentry toppled forward to lay unmoving on the tarmac!

Z.

The sound of Gentry's body hitting the ground seemed to echo through the interior of the Rolls. Spengler froze, mouth open, his brilliant mind brought to a crashing halt. He replayed the events of the last few seconds over and over again as he scrabbled at the door handle.

So close. He'd been so close to freedom. He felt a stab of pity for the dead man on the ground. Gentry had seemed like a decent enough fellow. Hardly deserving of his fate. Just as Greta had been undeserving of hers.

Greta...

Gentry hadn't had time to scream, but Greta had. Spengler could still hear her, when he closed his eyes.

No. Not Greta. Not this time. Spengler's eyes opened. His fellow passengers were scattering, screaming, flinging luggage aside in their haste to get away from the unseen assassin.

Well, all but one of them. Spengler's eyes caught him out, the way the eyes of a gazelle caught the swish of a lion's tail through the tall grass. He was innocuous, dressed in a cheap suit and a small-brimmed hat. Cigarette smoke curled around his head in a hazy halo as he trotted towards the Rolls, his hands in his pockets, his coat over his arm.

He'd been sitting two rows back on the plane. He had, in fact, already been seated when Spengler had climbed aboard, huffing and puffing.

They'd known, even then. They'd planned for it, in fact. All a trap and he'd walked right into it, even as he'd tumbled into the barbed wire.

Why had they let him get this far? Just to toy with him? To show him that he couldn't escape?

He glared at the approaching man. Spengler didn't recognize him, but he knew him all the same. He could see what he was. He could tell by the easy walk, the nonchalance. There was an automatic under that coat, Spengler knew. He had to get out, to get away.

He rammed his shoulder against the door and jerked on the handle. The rifle, wherever it was, spoke again, and Spengler jerked back as the window rattled and a spider-web of cracks spread across the surface. He reached out to touch the glass with tentative fingers and felt that it was unusually thick.

"Armored, *ja*?" The man in the cheap suit stopped a few feet away. He took the cigarette out of his mouth and flicked ash off of the end. "Mr.

Anthony's dossier mentioned that he had enemies. Stands to reason he'd ride in an armored vehicle."

Spengler looked at him. He had a tough looking face that could have belonged to an Italian or a German or even an Englishman, and he spoke English with a fluency that far outclassed Spengler's own. "Smart, really. Not smart enough, though." He glanced down at Gentry's body and shook his head. "Poor fellow; you should have warned him what he was getting into, Professor."

Spengler didn't reply. Had the shot been intended to kill him, or merely to warn him?

The man in the hat shifted and stepped past the body. "Get out of the car slowly, *Herr* Spengler."

Spengler didn't move. His heart was beating wildly, his limbs trembling in panic-induced adrenalin. That they wanted him alive was no guarantee that they wouldn't shoot him. He had to think.

"Out, I said." The coat twitched, and Spengler heard a muffled click. Would the man really shoot him? Seeing the hard glint in his eye, Spengler thought perhaps he would. This was a man who did not seem inclined to follow orders.

"*Nein.* I will not go back with you!" Spengler shouted.

"You act as if you have another option," the gunman snapped. "There are no more choices, Professor. Not now. Not for you."

"Who says? You? The devil you serve?"

"Me, myself and I."

"Kill me then," Spengler said, swallowing. "Better to die than to help your master."

The gunman frowned and shook his head. "I do not have all day, *mein herr*," he said, pushing the brim of his hat back with his thumb and tossing aside his coat. He raised a bulky automatic and aimed at the Rolls.

Spengler flinched as the pistol snarled. The man cursed. "Even the locks? *Scheisse…*"

"Especially the locks, you mook."

Spengler's eyes bulged as the gunman spun to confront the shape of Tom Gentry, rising to his feet!

"*Mein Gott-*" The pistol cracked again, but Gentry stepped aside with surprising speed and drove two pile-driver blows into his opponent's gut, picking him up off of the pavement. The pistol snapped around, catching Gentry on the side of the head and he stumbled.

A rifle shot plucked at the tarmac, and Gentry hit the ground, rolling desperately. The gunman tracked him, obviously intending to finish the job in a more permanent fashion.

Spengler reacted without thinking, sitting back and kicking up the door of the Rolls. It swung out, smashing into the gunman's hip. He slewed sideways with a yelp, but didn't let go of his weapon. The automatic belched a third and a fourth time as Spengler cowered back in his seat.

The gunman stepped back, cursing louder than before. "Dirty *schwein*! You're coming with me, now!" He reached into the Rolls, groping for Spengler's ankle. Spengler lashed out with his other foot, catching the man in the arm and he staggered.

"*Nein*!" Spengler scrambled to pull the door closed, to seal himself inside once more. The gunman grabbed for the handle and they engaged in a momentary tug-of-war.

Then Gentry rushed forward with a roar, catching the other man in his arms and lifting him up, then slamming him down onto the tarmac. The automatic skittered away and Gentry pressed his own weapon to the gunman's head.

"Move and you get a new hole in that thick skull of yours," Gentry growled.

"*Ich scheib d'rauf*! So much as twitch, and my friend with the rifle will plug you good, *Amerikaner*." The German grinned savagely and twisted, looking up at Gentry. "Give me Spengler, and I'll let you live."

"Yeah? Real generous of you, Jack."

"The name's Karsten, *du schwein*." He pushed himself up slightly, his hat tilting forward. "You get one more chance. Give us the Professor, or else…"

"Yeah, I wouldn't bet on that." Gentry cocked his head, as if listening, then grinned. Looks like your pal with the rifle has problems of his own," he said and slammed his pistol across the back of the German's head, sending his hat rolling away.

Then, Gentry was up and slamming the driver's side door of the Rolls. The car gave a somnolent growl as Gentry threw it into gear and spun the wheel. The car barreled away from the tarmac, heading for the road. The back window puckered as a shot smacked the glass, and Spengler instinctively ducked.

"Whoo! That was a close one," Gentry said, glancing over his shoulder at Spengler. "Hope I didn't scare you, Professor."

"I-but how-you-" Spengler gestured helplessly. "How did you survive?"

Gentry rapped his knuckles against his chest. "One of Jimmy's patented bullet-proof vests. Would have had one for you, but Jimmy figured they wouldn't want you dead."

"But the window-" Spengler gestured at the cracked window.

Gentry grunted. "Warning shot. Whoever they had on the rifle was a cracker-jack. Plus, I'm betting they knew the Rolls was armored." He looked back. "Guy was tough. Recognize him?"

"N-no. But he's one of them."

"Yeah." Gentry laughed. "That's for sure. These guys think things through, don't they?"

"They would have taken me if you hadn't stopped them," Spengler said.

"Naw." Gentry waved a hand. "Jimmy figured they'd be coming for you sooner rather than later. We planned all this out ahead of time."

"I thought you said he thought I was paranoid!" Spengler gaped at Gentry. A plan? Hope surged in his breast. Maybe this had been the right decision after all. Maybe Jim Anthony really could save him.

"Just because you're paranoid don't mean they ain't out to get you, Professor," Gentry said. "Jimmy can explain it better than I can."

"Let's hope so," Spengler said slowly. "I do not like being used as bait, Mr. Gentry."

"Call me Tom." Gentry gripped the steering wheel so tight it creaked. "And if you were bait, well, Jimmy should be springing the trap right about now."

"What?" Spengler blinked.

"Don't tell me you figured we went to all this trouble just to draw these bozos out?" Gentry said, smiling widely. He slapped the steering wheel. "Damn but it's good to be back in the saddle again!"

3.

Ten minutes earlier.

At the first crack of the rifle, Jim Anthony surged to his feet, tossing aside the camouflaged tarpaulin. It had been painted to resemble the roof of the aerodrome he had positioned himself on earlier in the morning, rendering him, for all intents and purposes, invisible. An old hunter's trick his grandfather had taught him; one of many lessons the wizened old shaman named Mephito had imparted to his grandson.

Clad in linen trousers and a baggy gray sweater, he ignored the chill of the metal beneath his bare feet with what in another man might have been confused with an almost superhuman stoicism. In truth, Jim enjoyed the feel of the city beneath his feet. Instinctively, he checked the belt at his waist, the deceptively sharp-edged buckle, and finally the shoulder holster which held a slim automatic.

He took an instant to calculate the angles, his keen eyes flickering over the scene. The night before he'd made a study of the airfield and the potential sniper's nests. That Spengler's pursuers had someone on the plane as well was a given. He tested the wind, sniffed the air, and then gave a tiger's grin.

His prey scented, Jim moved swiftly, bounding down the slope of the roof and leaping towards the next in the row. Landing with a clatter of corrugated metal, he pushed himself up and towards the apex of the next roof, moving with a pantherish agility.

Anthony was tall and broad and his skin was burnt bronze by a lifetime spent out of doors. His face was all sharp angles between the thatch of curly hair on top and the strong jaw opposite. Once, the hair had been the color of melted brass. Now it was shot through with premature streaks of silver, scars of a lifetime spent as the world's foremost murderist.

As a hunter of criminals and killers Jim had achieved international repute, and, as the controller of one of America's foremost fortunes, he even had the pleasure of doing said hunting for free. Law enforcement agencies the world over had requested his help at one time or another and Anthony was only too glad to help.

Those times were past him now, for the most part. As the Thirties slid towards the Forties, so his presence was seen less as a public service and more as an intrusion by the Powers-That-Be. Bloody-minded vigilantes like the Black Bat garnered headlines and cast a pall over the whole business.

Jim smiled as he slid down the slope and sprang for the next. He'd met the Bat once. A good man, driven by a need that Anthony understood well enough. Not for vengeance, but for justice.

Jim reached out, grabbing an aerial, and swung himself around, diving for the square roof of an outbuilding. It was empty of everything save a few gas cans. Those, and the few spent spatters of an unusual variety of chewing tobacco he'd found on the roof.

The tobacco was of a variety used almost exclusively by certain tribes of the Anishinaabe peoples of Canada. That alone would have been enough to perk Jim's interest. That he'd found similar spatters at every other location he'd marked as a potential ambush point only cemented his suspicions.

At first, he hadn't quite believed Helmut Spengler's story. The man was a friend, but also prone to becoming obsessed with minutiae. Spengler suffered from a very specific form of tunnel vision, one that he'd refused all help with.

Spengler's telegram, requesting Jim's help, had merely been yet another example of that disorder. Or so Jim had thought at the time.

But the tobacco, and the worrying rumbles Jim's few remaining contacts among the European underworld had passed to him, had convinced him that there might be something to Spengler's fears of being followed. Europe was a powder keg waiting to go off, with belligerent participants on either side, and there were rumors that someone-something-was in the wind.

And now it was here, apparently.

Spengler hadn't said why he was being followed, and Jim hadn't pressed him at the time. It was obviously important, though.

Jim landed on all fours, surprising the sniper who'd only moments ago fired a third shot at the retreating Rolls-Royce. The man spun, raising his rifle. Jim blinked as he took in the fringed buckskin the man wore, and then whistled softly as the man unfolded to his full height.

"What the hell are you supposed to be?" the giant grunted, holding his rifle like a club.

"I might ask you the same question. Buckskin went out of style a few decades ago," Jim said, rising into a crouch.

The giant grinned, displaying tobacco-stained teeth. "Me an' style ain't exactly on speaking terms, fella." Then, with barely a flicker of effort, he swung the rifle out in a vicious arc. Jim bounced backwards as the stock of the weapon cut the air where his head had been.

"Stand still," the giant said.

"Wouldn't bet on it," Jim said. The rifle looped towards him again, and he caught it on crossed forearms. The wood was reinforced, but it cracked nonetheless. Jim's arms went numb from the force of the blow, but he ignored it and caught the stock in a vise-like grip and wrenched it from his opponent's hands.

Jim spun the weapon and tossed it aside. "There now; feel like a chat?"

"Alaska Jim ain't one for small talk, fella," the giant said, whipping out a heavy-bladed hunting knife. Jim jumped back as the blade dug for his belly. One bronze hand snapped out, catching Alaska Jim's wrist, and a second caught the giant's throat.

"Alaska Jim, hunh? I've seen that name somewhere," Anthony said, shoving the other man back. "Why are you trying to kill Spengler?"

"Ain't," the giant rasped. A wide hand fastened on the side of Jim's head, the fingers tightening with iron-certainty. Pain flared behind Anthony's eyes and he drove his knee up. Alaska Jim bent with a high-pitched whistle, and Anthony spun, hurling him across the roof.

"No? Looks like you gave it a damn good try to me," Jim said, waiting for the giant to rise.

"Maybe you weren't looking close enough." Alaska Jim got to his feet slowly, waving the knife back and forth. "Still, ain't no matter."

"No?"

"Not for you," the giant snarled. He came in low, a long arm sweeping up to drive the knife into Anthony's belly. The other hand grabbed for his head. Anthony glided into the other man's reach, slapping aside his arms and thrusting stiffened fingers into a handy nerve cluster. Alaska Jim coughed and staggered. The knife dropped from his suddenly paralyzed fingers and he sank to one knee.

Jim snatched up the blade and pressed it to the giant's throat. "I think you're wrong. I think it does matter to me. Why are you here? What do you want from Spengler?"

"Go to-ah!-to Hell!" Alaska Jim gasped. He clawed at Anthony's arm with his only working hand. "I ain't saying nothing!"

"No?" Anthony wrapped an arm around the giant's throat and sank the knife into the rooftop, leaving it quivering. Then, with nimble fingers he reached up to the shoulder holster he wore. Opposite the automatic was a reinforced set of long pouches. One held an extra clip for the pistol. The other was divided into a series of easy to access sections, each of which contained a number of tiny gel spheres. Jim popped open one section and removed a sphere, rolling it between his fingers to activate the dissolution process. Then he angled his arm, forcing Alaska Jim's mouth open and popped the sphere between his lips. Forcing the struggling giant to swallow the sphere, Jim said, "Relax big fellow. It's just an amobarbital derivative I designed. You'll feel like telling me everything in a few minutes-"

"Minutes you don't have!"

Anthony rolled out of the way as a truncheon crashed down, nearly taking his head off. Alaska Jim toppled, dazed, but Anthony was on his feet a moment later. While he'd been distracted, several men dressed in dark clothing and wearing masks had climbed up onto the top of the building. They all carried truncheons, except for the one who'd spoken. He, unfortunately, had a Thompson cradled in his arms. He swung it towards Jim with deadly intent.

"In the name of Thule...DIE!"

The Thompson chattered and Jim sprang up, running for the edge of the building. Bullets chewed the rooftop a half-step behind him and, desperate, he flung himself off of the rooftop.

The ground rushed up to meet him. The building was only a story or so high. Jim twisted and turned and when he hit the tarmac, he rolled roughly to a stop. Unhurt save for a few cuts and bruises, he climbed to his feet, reaching for his automatic.

The sound of rubber on pavement alerted him at the last second to the car hurtling towards him and he threw himself aside. The car slewed to a stop and more men got out, dressed much like the ones on the roof, in ragged masks and laborer's clothes. One took aim with a Mauser, and Jim ducked, looking for cover as bullets struck the tarmac around him.

Diving behind a makeshift barricade of engine parts and empty gasoline barrels, Jim hunkered down, waiting. When the shots stopped coming, he peered around the edge of a bent propeller. The car was gone. And so were the men on the rooftop, most likely. Jim released an unsteady breath and let the adrenaline leave his system.

"Well. That didn't work out as well as I'd hoped," he said out loud. He looked up and sighed.

At least no one had died.

4.

"I'm going to kill him," the woman said. "Slowly. With fire and sharp things."

"Aw Lady D," Gentry began, half-rising from his seat. The woman spun, pinning him in place with a finger.

"Nope. No, Tom. And don't call me that."

"Delores," Gentry said, making a placating gesture. "Have you met Professor Helmut Spengler?" He motioned to Spengler, who sat nervously on the couch, clutching a cup of tea in both hands. "Professor, this is Delores Colquitt-Anthony-"

"*Ja*, I know who she is. *Guten morgen*," Spengler said softly, eyeing the woman. Delores Colquitt-Anthony was tall and slim, with hair the color of sun gold and pale blue eyes. She was dressed comfortably, in an unpretentious dress, a fur stole over her shoulders and a cloche hat perched on her head. Arms crossed, she stood in front of the sliding doors to the balcony of Jim Anthony's penthouse apartment at the Waldorf-Anthony.

Or, rather, his former apartment. He'd moved out once they'd gotten married, though he kept this apartment and the two below it available for guests and friends. Delores hadn't made an issue of it, but it was something of a relief nonetheless.

"*Guten morgen, Herr* Spengler. Professor, rather," Delores said, pinching the bridge of her nose. "Forgive me. I'm being rude. Did you have a pleasant trip?"

Spengler looked sharply at Gentry, who shrugged. Delores caught the look, and her eyes narrowed to slits. "What? What happened? Tom?"

"There was an-ah-incident," Gentry said.

"An incident?"

"A scuffle?" Gentry tried.

Delores frowned. "Unh-hunh." She turned as Dawkins, Jim's long-suffering, and long-serving butler, stepped out of the penthouse's kitchen, carrying a tray of deli meats, cheeses and crackers.

"A snack, perchance?" he said, his Cockney accent contrasting ever so slightly with his impeccable attire. Thin, spare and hawk-faced, Dawkins had served both Jim Anthony and his father before him, yet never seemed to age. For as long as Delores could remember, he had been silver-haired and burnt brown by a youth spent fighting for the Empire in far-flung climes. "To whet your appetites before lunch."

"We're having lunch? Here?" Delores said, looking around. The Penthouse looked terribly empty these days, since she and Jim had been married. There were empty spaces where pictures had once hung from the walls and empty nooks and crannies that Jim's obsessively collected objects d'art had once occupied. His laboratory was still fully functional, but it had been sealed behind its blast-proof door for a year at least. The other two floors were similarly stripped bare of all save the essentials. There was some furniture, a few odds and ends, but nothing to indicate that anyone lived here.

"Jimmy said you wouldn't mind," Gentry said, biting into a slice of cheese.

"Did he?"

"I did," Jim said, stepping out of the private elevator that led up from the equally private parking garage that extended beneath the illustrious hotel. "Marriage is about taking liberties, isn't it?"

"So intelligent, and yet so stupid," Delores said, smiling slightly. She stepped into his arms and delivered a quick peck to his cheek. Tasting blood, she jerked back, examining his scraped features. "What happened to you?"

"I had a disagreement with some fellows," Jim said lightly, "Nothing too serious."

"Lying to make me feel better?"

"Quite possibly," Jim said, stepping past her and snagging a slice of meat and a sliver of cheese off of the tray. Chewing slowly, Jim looked around the apartment. He glanced at Dawkins, who appeared at his elbow, a cup of tea in his hands.

"Tea, sir?"

"Thank you, Dawkins. Are the party favors still in residence?"

"As far as I can ascertain, sir," Dawkins said.

"Expecting trouble?" Gentry said.

"Unfortunately," Jim said, looking at Spengler, then at Gentry. "Did you have any trouble?"

"The vest did most of the work," Gentry said. He rubbed the side of his head. "Got my bells rung some though. A Kraut named Karsten."

"Karsten," Jim said, sounding out the name. "I had some trouble of my own. Our friendly neighborhood sniper went by the *nom de guerre* of 'Alaska Jim'."

Gentry choked on a cracker. Coughing, he looked at Jim. "Alaska Jim? Geez-louise!"

"That name sound familiar to you?"

"Should to you to. We nearly had a run-in with him a few years back, that thing with Yukon Sally and the Deer Woman?"

"Yukon Sally?" Delores said, one eyebrow arched.

Jim pretended not to hear her. "Hunh. I thought he sounded familiar."

"The Mounties brought him in to help find Sally's plane, after it crashed," Gentry said, pounding on his chest to clear out the last vestiges of cracker. "Guy is supposed to be one of the last honest-to-gosh mountain men."

"He was certainly tough enough," Jim said, rubbing his jaw. "The question is, what would he want with Helmut?" Jim looked at Spengler. "Well, Helmut?"

"Names. All I have is names," Spengler said harshly. "I don't know who. All I know is why."

"Well that clears it up," Gentry said.

"Tom," Jim said, without looking around. Gentry fell silent. "Go on, Helmut."

Spengler opened his mouth, then closed it, unable to speak. Jim waited for a moment, then said, "You have a lot of explaining to do, my friend."

"You first," Delores said, seating herself in the chair opposite Spengler. "I insist. Start with Yukon Sally."

Jim looked at her, a slightly pained look on his face. "Delores, I-"

"You told me we were coming into town so that you could have lunch with an old friend," she said.

"And here he is," Jim said, motioning towards Spengler.

"Right. And Tom brought him here because?"

"He'll be staying here for a few days." Jim looked at Dawkins. "As will we. Make up the bedrooms, please, Dawkins."

"Yes sir," Dawkins said, pouring more tea into Spengler's cup.

"Why are we staying here?" Delores raised a hand. "Please don't tell me you thought it would be fun. Give me some credit."

Jim hesitated. Then, "He's in danger."

"Of course he is," Delores said, sighing. She leaned back in her seat, stretching her legs. "And now, by extension, so are we, right?"

Jim opened his mouth, then merely nodded. Delores smiled after a moment. "Right then. Now that we're all on the same page, let's get on with it."

"Thank you," Jim said, returning her smile. "Helmut?"

Spengler was silent for a moment, looking back and forth between Jim and Delores. Then, slowly, softly, his face crumbled and he began to sob. Hunching forward, he buried his face in his hands. Jim stood frozen, momentarily taken aback.

Delores, however, reacted immediately. She rose and sat beside Spengler, patting his back and murmuring smooth comforting things into his ear. Jim frowned as Gentry looked at the tableau, bewildered.

"What crawled out his gut?"

"Of course. I'm an idiot," Jim muttered. He glanced at his friend. "His wife. Helmut's wife."

"What happened to her?" Gentry asked, a trifle too loudly.

Spengler, face flushed, looked up. "I killed her. God help me, I killed her!"

Jim gravely waved Gentry away and sat down in Delores' vacated seat. Pressing his fingers together in front of his face, he said, "I was given to understand that she died in an accident, Helmut."

"*Ja, ja*," Spengler said, nodding jerkily. "My fault. All my fault." He scraped at his face with his fingers. "My *verdamt* experiments." He spat the word. He looked up at Jim, his face twisted with grief. "I killed her, in a moment of inattention. Just one moment." He held up a shaking finger. "One!" He grimaced. "I know it exactly. I know when. I know how. It is why I began to work on…what they want. What I created, and they now wish to possess!"

"Slow down," Jim soothed.

Spengler shook his head. "No time! There is no time, Jimmy." He shuddered. "*Der Wurmloch…*"

"The-?" Jim sat up straight. "No. Impossible. Helmut, tell me you didn't?"

"Oh yes. I did it, Jimmy. I made it work." Spengler's smile was a crooked, pitiful thing. "But they took it from me before I could use it. Before I could-she-I didn't-" His mouth slammed shut and he shook his head wildly.

"Helmut! It's imperative that you tell me whether it's operational!" Jim snarled, lunging forward. Startled, Delores shot from her seat like a scalded cat. Jim grabbed Spengler's shoulders and shook him gently. "Helmut!"

"Jim! Jimmy, what are so worried about?" Gentry said, looking concerned.

"*Der wurmloch*," Delores murmured. She snapped her fingers. "Wormhole! Ha! Who says you can't get an education at boarding school?" Then, puzzled, she said, "But what does that mean? Jim?"

Jim sank to his haunches in front of Spengler, who was rocking back and forth slightly, murmuring to himself in German. Not looking away from his friend, Jim said, "It means trouble. I thought it was theoretical at best. Nothing more than an intellectual exercise. But if he's succeeded…"

"Succeeded at what? What was he working on?" Delores said.

Jim looked at her, his face grim. "Time travel."

"No time! There is no time, Jimmy." He shuddered. *"Der Wurmloch…"*

5.

The Waldorf-Anthony rose gleaming into the sky. Built in 1897 and then gradually enlarged until it had reached its current height of eighty-six floors, the Waldorf-Anthony was one of the greatest examples of modern structural engineering and the most expensive hotel on the East Coast. Or, it had been, in years past. Now it was merely one of the most expensive.

The woman wrapped in black looked up at the gilded edifice, her dark eyes narrowing behind the diaphanous veil that hid her face. At first glance, this place was merely yet another enclave of the rich and idle. But to the eyes of those trained to see, it was, in truth, a fortress.

Heavier structural supports than were fashionable, and windows that were slightly too thick. The man on the door was alert, far beyond the call of duty. Beneath his wrap-around coat, she could see the bulge of an automatic pistol. How many doormen in New York City went armed?

In a subtle gesture, she squeezed one of the bangles that dangled from her ear. "You were correct," she murmured.

"Of course I was," a voice replied, echoing tinnily from the miniature transceiver hidden in her bangle. "How long?"

"Ten minutes," the woman said, reaching over to idly stroke the golden snake coiled around her arm. "I'll need to use the elevator."

"Do you require aid? Karsten is-"

"Karsten is a fool. He failed at the airfield. I will not be so careless." She cocked her head, peering up. "Make sure that the others are in position."

"Be careful, Shani," the voice said.

The woman didn't reply. She stalked gracefully towards the door of the Waldorf-Anthony, considering how to best approach things. As always, her first inclination was to simply go the direct route. Efficiency was a proper Aryan trait, and one that her Master valued highly.

Thoughts of him suffused her with a warm glow, and she smiled. He was a worthy man, a man far beyond all others. It was his genius that had brought life to the fool Spengler's experiments. And it was that same genius that now set them on the path to changing the very destiny of the world.

Close by, but far above, on the roof of a building near the Waldorf-Anthony, a man clad in black and gray fatigues and an alpine military hat checked the combat harness he wore for the third time in as many minutes, his thoughts similar to those of Shani. He too thought of destiny, and the world.

What price, that destiny, however? It was an unusually complicated thought for the man, and he brushed it aside. Regardless of his own feelings, he had thrown in his lot with his Master, and he would not waver now, not when they were so close to victory.

He hefted the heavy grapple-line launcher that sat beside him. Capable of puncturing concrete, the grapple itself would easily cross the distance between the two buildings. His eyes narrowed as he tested the wind. He had practiced this maneuver many times, but never at so great a height in a city.

Still, he had every confidence that he would succeed. The transceiver earbud he wore in his left ear squawked and he winced.

"Rolf?" a voice said. The same voice that had spoken to the woman only minutes earlier.

"*Ja*," Rolf said, sighting down the barrel of the grapple.

"Ten minutes."

Rolf grunted, "Too slow."

"I would hardly call her slow. She is being cautious, as must you. The others failed. We must not."

"The others walked into a trap. We are not," Rolf said.

"And how do you know that?" the voice said, a hint of heat to the words. "Are you so wise then, oh mighty Sturmvogel?"

"I am a Knight of Thule," Rolf said, as if that explained everything. The voice made a disgusted sound, but beyond that, did not reply. Rolf smiled, satisfied. "Ten minutes," he said. "And you are, of course, in position?"

"The *Zaunkonig* is cruising just above you, in the cloud bank. Radio me when you are making your exit, and I will be there, never fear."

"I do not fear," Sturmvogel said. "I cause others to do so. For Thule!"

"Yes, yes," the voice said, tersely, before signing off. Feet scraped on the roof, a moment later.

Sturmvogel didn't turn. "You are late."

Behind him, a number of men, six in all, dressed in black settled themselves down to wait. They cradled weapons, and wore masks. Sturmvogel smiled and settled down to wait. He pulled a pair of binoculars out of a pouch on his harness and focused on the penthouse of the Waldorf-Anthony, where his targets waited, all unknowing and intent on other matters.

Down below, Shani sauntered past the doorman, locking eyes with him as he moved to stop her. He hesitated, then stepped back, his gaze blank.

Among the gifts bestowed upon the woman known as Ashanti Garuda was a mastery of such mental disciplines as hypnosis. Simply by locking eyes with a subject, she could exert the force of her unconquerable will against them, and cloud the minds of most men.

It was these gifts that made her so useful to her Master. She had used them at his behest again and again over the last few years, ensuring his position and influence in a hostile world. And now, she would use them to see to it that that world became something…finer.

She strode through the lobby of the hotel, ignoring the staff and the other guests. Her eyes sought and found the elevator and she tapped the button. After a few moments, the doors hissed open.

The porter looked at her expectantly. "Going up?" he said.

"All the way," she said, letting the doors close behind her. The porter made idle small-talk as they ascended, seemingly unconcerned with her lack of response. As the floor numbers lit up one by one, the elevator slowed, and finally stopped at the eighty-third floor.

She looked at the porter, who began to open the doors. "I want to go to the top."

"Where do you think you are, lady?" the porter said, doffing his cap. "Eighty-third floor. Enjoy your stay."

"Hmm." Shani nodded and then spun, driving a foot into the man's side with bone-crushing force. He bounced off the wall of the car and staggered. Shani closed the doors and twisted, sweeping her other foot across his jaw. The porter fell heavily, his jaw broken in several places. She looked down at him and sank to her haunches in front of the control panel.

Swiftly, she ran her fingers across the panel, and then down. She gave a soft chuckle as she found the camouflaged lock. A quick rifle through the porter's pockets revealed the key that fit that lock and she opened the secret panel. Another set of controls were within.

"Which floor?" she murmured.

"Eighty-six. The penthouse. Sturmvogel is watching them now," the voice said quietly. "He and our local friends will provide you with a perfect distraction."

"If this isn't a trap," she said, stabbing the button for the penthouse. The lights in the elevator flickered and changed hue as the car switched tracks. It was yet another example of the nearly superhuman ingenuity their quarry possessed. Luckily, they had a living god on their side. She smiled and stroked the tikala mark on her forehead.

"He is certain it isn't," the voice said. "Even so, be wary. We have no way of knowing what alarms or warning devices this Anthony has installed."

"Hmm. Yes. It would be a shame to do so," Shani said, grinning wickedly.

"Do not lose sight of why you are there, woman."

"Do not use that tone with me, *man*." Shani stretched, rotating her limbs in brief, dancer-like movements. "I sit at the hand of the Emperor of the World."

"As do I. As do we all," the voice said sharply.

"For Thule," Shani said. The voice fell silent. Shani nodded in satisfaction.

The elevator bell chimed as the doors slid open, revealing a lushly carpeted hall beyond. Shani left the elevator without a backward glance at the unconscious porter and started down the hall.

"Pardon me, Miss. I do not believe that you should be here," someone said. Shani spun, reacting with an instinct honed by a life of nigh-constant training. Her hand flashed out.

Dawkins leapt back with an agility that anyone who didn't know him would have found surprising. He straightened his tie and the sleeves of his black coat as he examined the woman facing him.

"I'm thinking that you're not paying a social call, hmmm?" he said, his accent becoming rougher.

Shani's eyes narrowed to glittering slits. "English," she spat.

"By the grace of God," Dawkins said.

"Die." Shani flung her arm out, and the golden serpent coiled there shot forward, striking out with vicious intent!

At the same time, a building away, Sturmvogel shot to his feet. "Time to go!" he roared, firing the grapple. Simultaneously, the men behind him clambered to their feet. Two of them unlimbered grapple-guns similar to Sturmvogel's and fired them. Three piston-powered grappling spikes shot across the gap between buildings, embedding themselves in the brickwork of the Waldorf-Anthony's upper spire.

"Go, go, GO!" Sturmvogel said, setting the grapple-gun down and activating the air-pressure powered mooring clamps. The guns locked themselves in place on the roof with a splintering of concrete. Then, one by one, the men snapped hooks onto the lines and slid off the roof and towards the Waldorf-Anthony!

6.

"I'm all for jokes, but time-travel?" Gentry said, looking askance at Jim. "C'mon Jimmy."

"I'm serious," Jim said, looking down at the man on his couch. "And if he's succeeded…"

"Then it's a very bad thing," Delores said. "Especially considering that someone's after him."

"Yes. It means that someone else knows what he's created, and likely knows the implications besides." Jim stood and crossed his arms.

"Implications," Spengler murmured, looking up. His grin was painful to look at. "Implications? *Ja*, so many of those." He wrung his hands together helplessly. "I didn't consider them all. Still haven't, actually." He chuckled. "I couldn't, you see. I couldn't allow myself to be distracted."

"Distracted?" Gentry said.

"His wife," Delores said, softly. She touched Jim's arm and he looked down at her. He covered her hand with his.

"Yes. You wanted to bring her back, didn't you, Helmut?" he said. "To save her." He put his hand out, clutching Spengler's shoulder. "There's no sin in that."

Spengler hunched for a moment longer, then grabbed Jim's hand in his. "Thank you Jimmy," he said hoarsely. "But regardless of my intentions, I have sinned. And terribly." He took a breath, and sat back, seemingly more in control of himself. "I needed funding. Badly. I needed space to work, and money for materials and, at times, protection for my staff." He closed his eyes and smiled bitterly. "Some of them were Jews, you see."

Jim frowned. "Who did you get the funding from, Helmut?"

Spengler hesitated, his jaw working as if he were chewing over his words. Then, "They call themselves the Thule Society." He looked at Jim. "It is-"

"I know what it is," Jim said sharply. He waved a hand. "An occult society, like a hundred others that sprang up in the wake of the Great War. I was a member of one or two myself."

"Jimmy!" Delores said, sounding shocked.

Jim looked at her, smiling crookedly. "A man needs hobbies," he said, by way of explanation. He looked back at Spengler. "But the Thule Society is more than just a collection of dilettantes and the curious."

"They are dangerous. And even now, they yet have power in the Reich." Spengler ran his hands through his hair. "They sent a man to talk to me. A man named Minx. He knew of my research, which in itself was impossible. No one save a few like you, Jimmy, knew what my theories entailed."

"They were watching you, even then," Jim said.

Spengler nodded jerkily. "I was so grateful though. I was on the cusp of it. I knew I was! I just needed money…" He trailed off for a moment. "And they gave it to me. Gold, even." He reached into his pocket and pulled out a strange, flat coin.

Jim took it and examined it. It was heavier than it looked, which spoke to its purity. Stamped on both sides with an aquiline profile that Jim didn't recognize, surrounded by writing in a language he couldn't decipher at first glance. A thrill of atavistic disquiet rippled through him as he made the coin dance awkwardly across his knuckles.

"When did you start to worry?" he said.

Spengler shook his head and looked away. "Not soon enough. Not until close to the end. Some days Minx would show up, others it would be someone else. A woman, sometimes. Not German. Dusky and cruel," he said. "Always, they watched and oversaw my progress. I thought nothing of it until the end." He looked at Jim. "When I performed the first successful transfer of matter through time."

"I still say that this is baloney," Gentry barked, looking uncomfortable. "It's hokum! Science fiction!"

"Quiet, Tom." Jim's face looked as if it had been carved from stone. "Go on, Helmut."

"He was a prisoner. A convict, they said. I didn't notice until later how malnourished he was," Spengler said slowly. He stared at his hands. "I activated *der wurmloch* and one of them shoved him through." His eyes were wet. "There was a sound like lightning trapped in a bottle, or a hundred thousand fiery hornets rattling inside a steel hive, and then he was gone."

"Gone?" Jim said.

"We weren't sure where. Or how. Anything, really." Spengler sniffed. "He was just gone. And oh, they were excited." His hands clenched into fists. "They wanted to know everything. Everything!"

"And?" Jim prodded.

"I spent days, trying to trace him. To find where he had gone," Spengler said. "I nearly burned out every Tesla coil in Vienna, but I did it. And when I brought him back, the bastards shot him!" He pounded his fists into his knees. "They shot him, for nothing. For seeing whatever it was he saw. They shot him like a dog."

"You don't know what he saw?" Jim said.

"*Nein*," Spengler said tersely. "He was bustled away by Minx and that *schweinhund* who accosted Mr. Gentry and I at the airfield. Karsten." He massaged his temples. "They questioned him for hours, then, Karsten shot him. Right there in my lab." He fell silent for a moment. "He just shot him."

"I knew he was a creep when I laid eyes on him," Gentry said, pounding his fist into his palm. "Guy that fights that dirty has got to be a man of low moral character." Jim and Delores looked askance at him, and Gentry blushed. "I'm just saying!"

Shaking his head, Jim turned back to Spengler. "Helmut, what aren't you telling me?"

"Coordinates," Spengler said, after a moment.

"What about them?"

"It was part of the deal. I was given a set of chronological coordinates for the initial test. I thought nothing of it at first, but when they shoved that poor devil through..." He paused. "I wondered where he was going. And where they had gotten those coordinates."

"You couldn't tell?" Delores said.

"It's not like I had a map of time, *Frau* Anthony." Spengler gave a little laugh. "Dates, times, it doesn't work like that. Not like *Herr* Wells' fictive time machine."

"Not so fictional," Jim said, absently. "I've seen it. What's left of it, at any rate. Could you recall those coordinates, Helmut?"

"*Ja*, possibly." Spengler gestured to his bags. "I have my notes." His eyes lit up. "And one other thing."

"What?"

Spengler tapped his head. "Me." His smile became a vicious thing. Triumphant. "Without me, those devils will never be able to activate that machine. It's the only reason they haven't yet killed me."

Even as Spengler said those words, the hairs on the back of Jim's neck prickled in warning and his arm shot out, encircling Delores' waist. He jerked her in front of him and lunged for Spengler even as a spatter of gunfire shattered the sliding glass doors of the balcony!

Glass went everywhere even as Jim took his bride and his friend over the back of the couch. "Tom! Find cover!" Jim roared.

"Hell with that!" Tom said, pulling his pistol even as a long, dark shape hit the lip of the balcony and launched itself inside. A Mauser spoke sharply, and Tom cursed as it kissed the sleeve of his coat. The automatic in his hand replied loudly and at length.

The dark shape dove left, the Mauser spitting. Even as Tom tracked it, a half-dozen other shapes suddenly occupied the balcony, their hands filled with death!

Tom gave a yelp and hurled himself into the kitchen, just as a bevy of bullets plucked at the carpet where he'd been standing.

Jim, after a quick glance to make sure that Delores and Spengler were unhurt, rose to his feet, sweeping the couch into the air with him. Then, with a war cry worthy of his mother's people, he hurled the sturdy chunk of furniture towards the balcony.

One man, not quite quick enough to get out of the way, screamed as he was swatted backwards over the edge by the hurtling couch.

Then, long arms swept up under Jim's own and a mighty pressure fell onto the back of his neck. "You are strong, *Amerikaner*, but Sturmvogel is stronger!"

Jim didn't bother replying. He jerked forward, dislocating both of his arms in one sinuous movement, and then shoved himself back. His skull connected with something soft and he heard a satisfying crack as cartilage crumpled. His captor stumbled back with a moan, and Jim spun, planting a foot in his belly.

Sturmvogel flew backwards into a pillar and slumped, covered in bits of broken plaster. With a groan, Jim contorted himself just so and snapped his arms back into place with painful alacrity.

Ignoring the pain radiating through his shoulders and back, he vaulted over the island counter that enclosed the minuscule kitchen and dropped to the floor. Tom was there, his back pressed to the opposite counter, as was Delores and Spengler. Delores produced a small pistol from within her coat.

"Where did you get that?" Jim said, surprised.

"I asked Dawkins to procure one for me."

"Why?"

"Do you recall the circumstances of our first date?" Delores said primly. "Chinatown?"

"Ah," Jim said. "Never mind." He glanced at Spengler. "Helmut, I have a feeling there's more to your story than either you or I know." Then, raising a fist, he punched through one of the floor tiles that covered the small square of the kitchen. Stuffing his hand into the hole, Jim hooked the switch hidden there, then jerked his head towards one of the cupboards. "I've opened the crawlspace. It'll get you to safety."

"*Vas?*" Spengler looked at him in incomprehension.

"Crawlspace," Delores snapped, flinging open the cupboard. Then she sat back and launched a kick, dislodging the false backing within. "You. In," she said, looking at Spengler, then at Jim, "You? Try not to die."

"I live to serve, my dear," Jim said, reaching up under the counter and giving the wood a sharp knock. A hidden slot opened up and a .45 dropped into his waiting palm. "Get to safety."

"No." Delores gathered her feet under her. "Someone needs to find Dawkins and let him know that your little clubhouse has been compromised."

"Tom can-"

"Tom is sticking by you, Jimmy. Bodyguard, remember?" Gentry said, hiking a thumb at himself.

"When did you become my bodyguard?"

"When you stopped needing a chauffeur," Gentry said. He hefted his pistol. "On three?"

Jim sighed and shook his head. "One."

"Two," Delores said, slamming the cupboard shut even as Spengler pulled his leg through.

"Three," Tom said, rising to his feet, his Colt already singing. Jim and Delores followed suit, and the penthouse echoed with the sound of thunder.

7.

"Huff," Dawkins grunted as he sheltered his head behind his forearms. The woman continued with her devastating flurry of kicks and punches. He had divested himself of his coat, using it to ensnare the squirming form of the golden serpent moments earlier.

"Why won't you fall?" Shani hissed, in startling imitation of her pet. Angry, she overextended slightly, and Dawkins' fist shot out, catching her just below her ribcage. She grunted and slid back, falling into a crooked stance.

"Very good, madam," Dawkins said, slightly out of breath. "You are quite the pugilist."

Shani shrieked and spun, the sole of her foot whipping towards Dawkins' jaw. He caught her foot and rolled his shoulders, causing her to spin onto her face. She dropped lightly onto all fours and swept his legs out from under him.

Dawkins rolled up onto his knees as she drove stiffened fingers towards the top of his skull. He caught her hand and bent the fingers back, eliciting a whistle of pain. Her knee extended and cut in, catching him on the head. He dropped and rolled across the floor, dazed.

Shani hopped backwards, trying to shake some feeling back into her wrist.

The bud in her ear gave a squawk. "Having difficulties?"

"Nothing I cannot handle. Time?"

"Running out. Sturmvogel has engaged our opponents, but he is hard-pressed."

"Pfaugh. Can he not handle even one half-caste snoop?"

"Apparently not," the voice said, sounding amused. "Karsten and Jim are en route."

"I need no aid!" Shani snarled, darting towards Dawkins as he rose to his feet. The old man twisted, avoiding her cobra-quick open palm strike, and dropped an elbow onto her shoulder. Her arm spasmed and she ducked his next blow.

"Who were you talking to, I wonder," Dawkins said, his eyes narrowed shrewdly.

"No one you'll ever see," Shani said, baring her teeth. She shook life back into her arm and made a sinuous movement. "No more playing. You die now."

"We shall see."

Elsewhere in the penthouse, Sturmvogel crouched behind a hastily opened door and cursed the idiotic operatives he had been assigned. Of his five remaining men, one was wounded and busily moaning on the balcony, and another was likely dead, his brains scattered across the opposite wall.

"We should have used rifles, as Jim suggested," he growled, slapping a new clip into his Mauser. Blood dripped sluggishly from his flattened nose and pain radiated through his face.

The bead in his ear gave a whine. "We couldn't be sure those windows weren't made of the same bullet-resistant material as we encountered before. Besides, there's less chance of accidentally killing our quarry this way."

"You're worried about him?" Sturmvogel said, incredulously. He peered around the edge of the door and fired his pistol.

"Shani is on her way-"

"Shani can rot," Sturmvogel said. "I don't have time to wait." He rose to his feet and kicked the door aside. Head down, arms pumping, he charged towards the kitchen. A bullet plucked at his sleeve as he leapt up onto the counter and dove towards the bronze-skinned giant, his hands outstretched like the talons of an eagle.

Jim dropped his automatic and caught Sturmvogel's wrists, whipping the big man around and slamming him into the cupboards behind him.

"Tom! Handle the others," Jim said, kicking his pistol towards Gentry. Then he pounced on Sturmvogel, grabbing his combat belt and hauling him to his feet. The black-garbed soldier drove piston-like fists into Jim's chest and belly, but Jim held on, spinning his opponent around and running him headfirst into the icebox.

Stepping back, his breath coming in sharp gasps, he looked at his wife. "Tom and I have it from here. Go find Dawkins and get us some reinforcements!" Delores nodded sharply and ran for the door, automatic in hand.

"She won't get far," Sturmvogel rasped, pushing himself to his feet.

"Far enough," Jim said, jerking a drawer out of the kitchen counter and shattering it on Sturmvogel's head in one smooth movement. The storm-trooper staggered, and Jim was on him before he could recover.

"You made a mistake, attacking me here," Jim said, grabbing the front of Sturmvogel's shirt and jerking him around. He punched him twice, in rapid fashion and threw him bodily out of the kitchen.

Jim stalked after him, ignoring the bullets that flew through the apartment like angry hornets. "Before, I was merely intrigued. Now," he said, grabbing Sturmvogel's arm and yanking him up. Sturmvogel punched him in the side, but Jim didn't flinch. He pulled Sturmvogel forward and head-butted him. "Now I'm angry," Jim said, as Sturmvogel pitched backwards.

Outside of the apartment, Delores hurried down the hall, pistol held in both hands. Jim and her father both had given her a thorough education in the ways of the gun, but her skin still crawled at the touch of the pebbled butt against her palms.

Jim's earlier question bothered her more than she'd let on. Mainly, because she wasn't as entirely certain of the answer as she'd tried to appear.

When had she begun to carry a weapon? When had it begun to seem like a good idea?

"Stupid," she whispered, shaking her head slightly. Stupid to be thinking of that now. It was a selfish thought, and one she chided herself for even entertaining. The thought lingered, however.

Jim's life always seemed so exciting, when you were on the outside looking in. A millionaire playboy, tussling with colorful criminals and thwarting sinister schemes straight out of the pulps.

But then, you saw the other side of the coin. The late nights and threatening phone calls. The old scars coiling across the skin under his shirt, and the new ones waiting to be added. The way his body was beaten and battered, a bit at a time, like a rock being worn smooth by the tide.

The fear.

That was the worst of it. The fear that one day he wouldn't be strong enough, or fast enough, or even smart enough and that would be it. A knock at the door and a lifetime of loneliness, stretching away, forever. Her hands tightened on the pistol as she came to a bend in the hall.

Dawkins flew past her, connecting with the wall.

He slumped, with a groan, his face a puffy, bloody mess and his breathing labored. She flew to him, then turned even as the woman charged towards her, silken robes streaming around her like the wings of some great bird of prey.

Delores squeezed off three shots, grouping them as close together as possible. The woman stumbled to a halt and stepped back. She looked at Delores, her eyes becoming blazing, predatory slits.

Then, she extended a bruised hand and dropped the three flattened slugs to the floor.

Back in the apartment, Sturmvogel wheezed and pushed himself up onto all fours. He had never endured such punishment, not once in his brutal career.

It was his own fault, of course, and he damn well knew it. Jan and Jim had tried to warn him. To explain to him what he was facing. Even his master had cautioned respect for the man currently driving a kick into his belly.

Jim Anthony was an apex predator. A man born to hunt men, even more than himself or any of his companions, save possibly for Shani.

He had had his chance at victory in this encounter, and he had squandered it.

Sturmvogel caught a second kick and rose to one knee, shoving Jim back. The soldier came to his feet with a roar. A bullet struck the floor in front of him, and he danced back.

"Last man standing," Gentry said, aiming two automatics at Sturmvogel. "Unless you want that to change, I'd settle down."

"*Nein*," Sturmvogel said. "No surrender."

"Consider it a tactical cessation of hostilities," Jim said, crouching nearby. Hands dangling between his bent knees, Jim watched Sturmvogel with the patience of a tiger on the hunt, his hands flexing and curling. "The others?" he said to Gentry, without looking at him.

"Deader than Jesse James," Gentry said. "Glad to see you finally took those damn mercy bullets out of your guns, Jimmy."

"Needs must when the Devil drives," Jim said, rising to his feet. "Who are you? Your uniform is German."

Sturmvogel felt a moment of panic. He could not allow himself to be identified. Not now. "Who I am is none of your concern. Give me the Professor," he said, tensing.

"You're in no position to negotiate."

"You have no idea of the strength of my position," Sturmvogel said. A smile crossed his scarred face. "Where is your woman?"

Jim's eyes narrowed, then widened. "Delores?" He turned towards the still open door, momentarily forgetting himself.

Sturmvogel took the opportunity and spun on his heel, sprinting for the balcony. Gentry's automatics barked in unison, and Sturmvogel staggered as darts of pain cut through his arm and leg. Nonetheless, he managed to reach the lip of the balcony thrust himself over.

Jim reached the edge of the balcony even as Sturmvogel plummeted over. Moments later he was scrambling back, arms raised to protect his eyes as a great silvery shape rose up, the spinning fans in its stubby wings casting waves of warm air over him.

Sturmvogel clung to the top of the flying machine as it rose up and turned away from the Waldorf-Anthony. Jim watched it go, feeling a tingle of awe for whatever intelligence had conceived of such a craft. Then, it was gone, and Tom was calling for him. Jim turned.

"Jimmy! Get in here!" Gentry said. "It's Dawkins!"

Jim re-entered the apartment, rushing to help Gentry get the bloody, battered form of his manservant to a bullet-torn seat. Dawkins nearly toppled as they stepped back, and Jim caught him.

"Dawkins? My God, what happened?"

Dawkins caught Jim's wrists. "I'm sorry Mr. Anthony. I tried to stop her..."

"Stop who? Dawkins?" Jim looked at Gentry. "Where's Delores?"

"They took her," Dawkins said, his voice hoarse with pain and emotion. "Mr. Anthony, they took her!"

8.

Jim rolled the three flattened slugs around in his palm, his eyes closed. The muscles in his jaw hopped in time to some red rhythm. "Anything?" he said.

"You tell me," Gentry said, rising from beside the last body and dropping a collection of items onto Jim's workspace. The lab had been opened for the first time in years, and the drop cloths stripped from the work-bench and examination tables. Jim stood in the center of the lab, not looking at anything in particular.

Spengler, retrieved from his hiding spot, sat at the work-bench and shifted through the pile Gentry had deposited. "They were Society-members," Spengler said, holding up a small golden lapel pin in the shape of a strange, spinning mandala. "Even here…"

"No surprises there," Jim grated. He turned. "Dawkins?"

"Resting comfortably. He's a tough old Limey," Gentry said. "I wouldn't want to run into whoever did that to him."

"You won't have to." Jim's hand clenched around the slugs, further distorting them. "That pleasure will be all mine." He glanced at Spengler. "What else?"

"Money. Cab fare, perhaps," Spengler said, letting a number of coins drop from his fingers. "And these," he continued, lifting up a small crystal, barely even a speck of a diamond. "Though as to what they are…"

"How many?" Jim said.

"Five. I assume the fellow you sent over the edge had one as well," Spengler said, tossing it to Jim.

Jim caught it and held it between two fingers, examining it from every possible angle. When he twisted it into the path of a shaft of sunlight, it suddenly grew warm. Eyebrow arched, he brought it close to his face.

"What are you?" he murmured, to himself.

"The future, Mr. Anthony," a voice said, echoing tinnily from the now gently vibrating crystal.

Jim nearly dropped the crystal. He shared looks with both Spengler and Gentry, then said, "And whose future would that be?"

"Mine. Ours. The future of the world as you know it." The voice was mellifluous and vibrant. It was a man's voice, but something more as well. Something older. Jim's hackles bristled at the sound of it.

He eyed the crystal, trying to fathom its secrets in the seconds before he answered. He had seen similar devices before-harmonic resonators-which captured vocal vibration and transferred it to similarly shaped receivers, though never one this size. "Who are you?"

"The answer should be obvious," the voice said, seemingly amused. "You have the bodies of my men. You have met my associates. I can only attribute your lack of deduction to your heightened emotional state. Follow the facts, Mr. Anthony."

Jim's eyes narrowed. "My emotional state is none of your concern."

"In fact, it is of great concern to me. I need to know that you will act rationally. That you will not simply lash out like the wounded animal my associates believe you to be."

Jim swallowed a retort. "Where is my wife?"

"Then you *have* figured out who I am."

"Your identity is irrelevant," Jim snapped. "Where's Delores?"

"Huhm. Safe. For now."

Jim rocked back on his heels slightly, relief flooding through him. "What do you want?"

"Right to it, then? How disappointing. I was informed that you were quite the conversationalist."

"What do you want?"

"Spengler."

Jim looked at Spengler, who had gone pale. "No. What else?"

"Nothing. Spengler, for your lovely wife."

"You have his device. Why do you need him?" Jim said. He snapped his fingers at Gentry and pointed towards the balcony. Gentry blinked in confusion, but only for a moment. Then he moved to one of the cabinets at the back of the lab and snatched out a bulky duffel bag. Inside the bag was a long range listening device that Jim had used on occasion, though not often. Originally designed to trace the high-frequency signals used by the Vampire King of Harlem, the device hadn't seen the light of day since Jim had used it to locate the upper-atmospheric hideout of Reinhardt Cloud.

"Natural curiosity, Mr. Anthony? Or something else?"

"Does it matter?" Jim said. "You want to tell me."

"Do I?"

"Of course you do. Your kind can't resist it." Jim watched Gentry sink to his hams on the balcony and open the bag. He withdrew a bulky bowl shaped section, then what looked like a bisected carbine. Swiftly, he began to combine them.

"My kind?" the voice said, definitely amused now.

Jim's grin was a feral thing. "Amateurs."

There was a moment of silence. Then, a deep chuckle. "Is that how you see me?"

"I don't see you at all. You're merely a voice on the other end of a simple harmonic resonator. But I hear you just fine." Jim popped the crystal into the air and caught it. "You're taunting me. Trying to toy with me. That says 'amateur' to me."

"And a professional would-what? Kill your woman?"

"A professional wouldn't have let Spengler get on that plane," Jim said. "He certainly wouldn't have let him escape the airfield. And if all else failed, he wouldn't have let him reach this penthouse, then leave behind a number of markers as to his identity."

A pause. "A harsh critique."

"But fair, I think." Gentry raised a hand, catching Jim's attention. He had assembled the device and now had it mounted on the edge of the balcony wall. Jim made a gesture, and Gentry grinned, pulling the trigger. "Your whole operation to date displays an over-reliance on timing and a wholly undeserved confidence in your own abilities."

"Now who's taunting who, Mr. Anthony?"

"Point. That craft was quite impressive, by the by."

"I cannot take credit for it, regrettably. One of my associates is quite the inventive genius." There was another pause. "I did suggest a few modifications, mind."

"I'm guessing that it's a short range craft," Jim said. "By the smell, an electrical engine, rather than diesel."

"Very impressive," the voice said. "Why are you trying to distract me, Mr. Anthony? Perhaps you are trying to trace this device's signal?"

"And if I am?" Jim said.

"I can assure you that it is quite impossible. The technology which created them is far beyond anything you might have cobbled together in that tiny aerie of yours."

"So far, I have to say that I'm not impressed." Jim signaled to Gentry, who shook his head. Jim blinked, momentarily surprised.

"Funny, you look quite impressed to me."

Jim froze. "Hnh. Maybe I spoke too soon." He glanced around surreptitiously, then looked at the crystal. Could it possibly be transmitting images as well as sound?

"Perhaps you did. Now, as to Professor Spengler-"

"I've already said no."

"We will not harm him, Mr. Anthony. Indeed, we cannot. We need him." The voice was smooth. Persuasive.

"Who's we? The Thule Society?"

"Once, perhaps. We prefer another *nom de guerre*, in truth."

"Feel like sharing it? I like to know who I'm doing business with," Jim said.

"Do you really expect me to tell you that, Mr. Anthony?"

"No. I suppose not."

"Good. You have displayed some certain modicum of intelligence so far, and I'd hate for you to disappoint me at the eleventh hour." The voice sighed. "Spengler. Bring him to that ingenious little landing platform you installed on the roof of your penthouse. My inventor-associate will pick him up, and deposit your woman. Then we shall wash our hands of one another."

"And if I don't?"

"Then everyone you have known or cared about will die, including your woman."

Jim looked at Spengler. The latter opened his mouth to say something but then slumped, as if resigned. Jim frowned and held up the crystal. "Fine. Give me three hours."

"Two."

Jim bared his teeth. "Fine. Two."

"It was a singular pleasure, Mr. Anthony," the voice said. The crystal flickered, then went dull. Jim shook it slightly and then tossed it to Gentry, who was staring at him in shock.

"Jimmy, you can't be serious!"

"I'm not even going to dignify that with a response," Jim said, looking at Spengler. "Have you ever been to the Catskills, Helmut?"

"N-no?" Spengler said.

"They're lovely this time of year. Tom, take one of the cars from downstairs. The most nondescript one you can find." Jim turned to his friend. "Get Helmut to the Teepee."

"So you're not-" Gentry grinned.

"No."

"And what of myself?" Dawkins said, leaning weakly against the doorframe. Jim stepped quickly to his side.

"How much did you hear, old friend?" Jim said.

"Enough. I will help you rescue Mrs. Colquitt-Anthony," Dawkins said, his eyes glittering despite the scabbed and bruised flesh surrounding them. "I will-"

"Inform the police what's going on," Jim said firmly. "I need someone I can trust to get hold of Lieutenant Healy."

"Hey!" Gentry said.

"Someone who Healy won't arrest on sight," Jim continued, smiling slightly.

"And you, Jim? What will you be doing?" Spengler said softly.

"Me?" Jim said. "I'm going to find out where they're holding Delores before the two hours are up, and then I'm going to make them regret they ever set foot in my territory."

9.

Delores' eyes fluttered briefly and then sprang wide. She could smell the tang of water and wood rot. She coughed, and looked down at the heavy ropes keeping her upright. Cold metal pressed against her back, and she craned her neck, trying to see what she was attached to.

"It's a buoy," someone said, in lightly accented English. "If you were curious, I mean."

Delores looked around. The speaker was a tall man, well-dressed, with slicked back hair and wide eyes. He sniffed a carnation on his lapel and trotted towards her, one hand in his pocket. "Mayen. Jan Mayen."

"What?"

"My name. I thought you might like to know it," Mayen said, leaning towards her. He smiled slightly and cocked his head. "So. What's a nice *fraulein* like you doing in a place like this?"

"You kidnapped me," Delores said. She took in her surroundings at a glance. It was a warehouse, likely near the Hudson, or perhaps the harbor, judging by the water visible through the gaping holes in the floor. The structure had been gutted at one time or another by a fire, and there were vast swathes of area where the wood had been burned black and brittle looking.

Mayen grinned. "So we did." He stepped back and turned around. "Rest assured it was for the very best of reasons."

"Yeah?" Delores said, trying to shift herself. She was tied tight to the buoy, but there was just enough slack for her to rub her arms raw. Which meant, at least according to Jim, there was likely enough space for her to slip free. They had taken her coat, but if she could just reach her garter-

"Looking for this?" Mayen said, holding up a thin flat length of metal. He bent it and then ran a thumb up its length. "Ingenious in its simplicity. A straight razor for babies. Or women."

"Sounds like you have a problem with the fairer sex, Mr. Mayen," Delores said, trying to hide her dismay. "Too many *frauleins* turn you down for a date?"

"Hardly," Mayen said, tossing the tool into the water. "And, frankly, such insults are beneath you, Mrs. Anthony."

"I would think kidnapping would be beneath you, Mr. Mayen. Considering your work for the Austrian government and all," Delores said.

Mayen raised an eyebrow. "You know me, then?"

"My husband is one of the world's greatest amateur detectives, Mr. Mayen. I know quite a bit about the members of his particular fraternity." Delores frowned. "I saw you once, I think, at a party in Paris."

"Really?"

"Yes. I thought you were an ass then, and my opinion hasn't changed."

Mayen frowned. "Pity. Still, if you would permit the touch of a mongrel-"

"A logical fallacy, my friend. As well as a scientific one," a deep voice said. Mayen flinched back, eyes widening slightly. Delores tried to twist in her chair, to see who the voice belonged to, but she couldn't manage it. She heard the tread of heavy boots across the wooden floor, which stopped just out of her range of vision. "Mrs. Colquitt-Anthony, a pleasure to see you, despite the regrettable circumstances."

"Whom do I have the pleasure of addressing?" Delores said.

"My identity is of little importance at this juncture, especially to you. No offense meant."

"No offense taken, though I could argue the point with you," Delores said, flexing her hands slowly.

"That you don't fills me with hope that you grasp the true measure of your position." More footsteps. "Your husband is a fascinating man. A blending of two hardy sub-species to create a supernormal hybrid. I wonder if he will prove fertile?"

"We haven't discussed that yet," Delores said stiffly.

There was a humming chuckle. "Forgive me. I did not mean to be so blunt, but genetics is something of a hobby of mine."

"How nice for you."

"Insolent witch," a woman said. Delores felt hands grip the back of her chair and she was suddenly spun around to face Ashanti Garuda. "Speak respectfully or not at all!"

Delores reacted instinctively, lunging forward using all the slack the ropes allowed to bring her skull into contact with Shani's. The Indian woman stumbled back, eyes widening in shock as Delores toppled over. She started forward with a hiss.

"Stop," the voice said. Shani halted, as if frozen. Then she stepped back, frowning.

"As you wish. I will make sure our transport is ready." She strode off in a swirl of her *sari*. Delores chuckled despite the pain in her head.

"She's feisty," she said as her chair was pulled upright.

"She's lethal," Mayen said brusquely. He knelt, checking her bindings.

"And disrespectful," he added sourly.

"She respects me," the unseen voice rumbled, seemingly amused. "And that is all I ask of you, is it not, Jan?"

"Yes," Mayen said softly. He stood and looked down at Delores. "I expect your husband is on his way. I need to prepare for his arrival."

"You do that," Delores said, watching the detective walk away. She flinched as a strong hand dropped onto her shoulder.

"Even now, Jan and the others have little conception of what lengths your husband will go to in order to reclaim you."

"And you do," Delores said.

"Of course; I have planned for it, as a matter of fact."

"I've heard that before."

"I'm sure you have." The weight of the hand vanished. "We have a bit of time. I feel that I should make some attempt to warn you, and through you, your husband."

"Warn us about what?" Delores said. She heard the creak of wood, as if someone were taking a seat.

"The perils of miscegenation," the voice said.

Delores gave a bark of laughter. "Bull puckey!"

"I thought you might react that way. Still, my…people have some experience with it. The blending of blood-lines is not a thing to trust to nature, Mrs. Colquitt-Anthony. Especially blood-lines like yours and your husband's."

"Jim. His name is Jim." Delores closed her eyes. "And you know nothing about us."

"I know everything about you. You, for instance, spent the most formative years of your childhood in various boarding schools, including the Kingscote School for Girls, St. Trinian's, the Minchin's Seminary and, briefly, a dance academy in Freiburg of dubious reputation. You were tutored in various martial arts, including that of the shootist by your father's bodyguards. A fact that you, by the by, hid from your husband."

Delores flinched slightly, and her eyes narrowed. "Fine, so you know what any half-wit G-Man could dig up. Bully for you."

Her captor chuckled. "You're naturally aggressive. You hide it well behind a sheen of manners and respectability, but you frequented a number of illicit establishments during the so-called Noble Experiment, and came close to arrest no less than three times due to volatile confrontations. You were briefly engaged to the gangster Salvatore Maroni, also known as 'the Panther', before his timely death at the hands of the FBI."

"I had a thing for Italian poetry," Delores said, trying to wriggle around so she could face her accuser. "A girl is allowed a bit of fun."

"There's fun, and then there's fun, Mrs. Colquitt-Anthony. You are, in your own way, as vicious and unprincipled as Shani."

"I'll take that as a compliment, considering the situation."

"I thought you might," the voice said. "Your husband, on the other hand, has spent years attempting to cage his own innate savagery behind a wall of willpower and intelligence. I'd admire him for that alone, even if he hadn't become involved in the Great Work."

"The whosits?"

"Forgive me. The-ah-what is the phrase-'status quo', I believe you call it." Another humming chuckle. "The maintenance of an orderly society by excising those elements which disrupt it, though I'd wager he doesn't see it that way."

"No bet," Delores said.

"Your husband's mission, however, is doomed to failure. The status quo will be altered, returned to a prior state of grace, and such fierce men as he will be the ones scheduled for excision." Wood creaked again, followed by the sounds of steps. "I have a list, you see. And your husband is close to the top."

"Why?"

"What he represents," the voice said. "Feral genetic spread is a threat to order. It creates burrs in the blade. It throws the human pattern into disarray." The hands fell on her shoulders again, and she couldn't help but marvel at the strength in them. "Did you know that the ancient Aryan words for 'hero' and 'monster' are completely interchangeable? A bit of chemical drift one way or another, and you have trouble. And trouble seeks trouble." The fingers tightened on her shoulders like talons and she gasped. "And trouble squared breeds trouble. A bit of docility in the mix might prevent future heart-ache, Mrs. Colquitt-Anthony. Remember that."

"Get your hands off of me," she said, the words slipping between her clenched teeth. A moment later, the weight vanished, and she heard the sound of receding steps.

Two minutes later, a knife thudded into the boards between her feet. She looked up and saw a dark form crouched on one of the many tarp-covered boxes that littered the area.

The man called Alaska Jim dropped down and approached her, his face purple with bruises. "Just in case," he murmured. "I got no doubt that you can get to it, when the need comes." He patted her on the leg with one of his big hands and moved past her.

"Wait," Delores said. "Why are you doing this?"

The big man stopped. "Ain't right that a woman should come to harm," he said. Then he was gone, padding silently away.

Delores bristled slightly, but reined her natural inclinations back. She looked down at the knife and with a flick of her heels, discarded her shoes. Then she wrapped her bare feet as best she could around the flat of the blade and began to wiggle it free.

She wrapped her bare feet around the flat of the blade.

14.

Jim lowered the binoculars and grunted in satisfaction. The strange, electrical vessel was rising into the air even as he watched. He pulled the communication crystal out of his coat pocket and bounced it on his palm. "Far beyond me, hunh?" he murmured.

It had taken him forty-five minutes to discover the frequency which the crystal resonated at, and a further twenty to reactivate it and reverse the harmonics, allowing him to get a glimpse of the sending crystal's location.

A further twenty minutes had been required to narrow down the potential locations and eliminate the variables involved. Now, with thirty minutes to spare, he was crouching in the weeds near an old bootlegger's port on the Hudson, watching as the people who'd kidnapped his wife left to collect their ransom, a ransom that would not, needless to say, be waiting for them. Jim smiled wolfishly and jumped to his feet. Hands in the pockets of his overcoat, the collar pulled up, he trotted towards the warehouse, doing his best to look inebriated.

The building had been the scene of a fire at some point, likely during a Federal raid. According to county records, there were still plenty of shipping containers and other debris left inside. The ownership rights were tied up in litigation and search and seizure red tape. Not quite big enough for a small army to hide in.

Still, there would be guards, likely armed. He calculated no more than a dozen, probably less. In his pocket, his fingers tapped the squat shape of a snub-nose revolver. He had an automatic as well, holstered beneath his arm. And his gimmick belt, as Tom referred to it.

Thought of Tom made him chuckle. Right now, Gentry was driving Spengler out of the city and to the Catskills, where the scientist could hole up in the Teepee-Jim's home away from home in the mountains.

As soon as Jim had extricated Delores from her current predicament, they could join them. Their mysterious opponent might know a good bit about Jim, but the location of the Teepee was one of the best-hidden secrets in Jim's repertoire. And even if they did find it, it was as heavily defended as Jim could make it. Dawkins had trained the security personnel himself.

Jim moved closer to the building, humming snatches of a bawdy cabaret tune as he tried to scope out the best way to get inside.

"Hey! What are you doing here?" a voice barked. Two shabbily dressed men rounded the corner of the warehouse, carrying shotguns.

"Iamswharrywhat?" Jim slurred, wobbling around and making a show of almost losing his balance. The closest man jabbed out with the barrel of his weapon, prodding Jim in the ribs.

"Who are you?" the poker said. Jim replied with a spurt of nonsense syllables and the poker glanced at his companion. "What do you think?"

"Just a rummy," the other one said. "Give him a swat and let's toss him in the river."

"Easier to shoot him," the first one said. As the words left his mouth, Jim's hand snapped out, fastening on the barrel of the shotgun and wrenching it aside. His other hand, still in his coat, pulled the trigger on his revolver.

"Couldn't have said it better myself," Jim said, as the second guard folded up. The first man gaped in shock, then crumpled as Jim slammed the shotgun across the side of his head.

Tossing the broken weapon aside, he stepped over the bodies and ran towards the door. He hit the street-door of the warehouse with his shoulder and broke it off its hinges. As he fell, riding the door to the ground, he fired his revolver again, sending a third man spinning with a scream.

For a moment, he wished that he'd had the time to finish working on that noise suppressor he'd been fiddling with. Still, if his unknown enemy was who Jim suspected he was, then the guards had already been alerted to a potential rescue attempt.

Jim was up and moving for the closest bit of cover a moment later, jerking his automatic free of its holster as he went. Back pressed to a box, he counted to ten, waiting. He heard the boards creak and the sound of running feet. Four men, according to the varying treads.

He looked up, seeing that there were two other heavy boxes on top of the one he was sheltering behind. Grabbing a handful of tarp, he hauled himself up and scrambled to the top. Below, several shapes moved through the tangle of boxes and fire debris. Jim growled low in his throat and began to rock back and forth, causing the crates to wobble. With a whining shift of wood, they toppled and Jim leapt for the next stack, heedless of the screams from below. He skidded slightly upon landing, a motion that undoubtedly saved his life as a gunman on one of the parallel catwalks opened up with a Thompson. The crate was chewed to flinders around him as he leapt for safety.

Jim landed and rolled, his youthful apprenticeship to a professional tumbler once more coming in handy. Crates crashed around him as he surged to his feet, pistols barking. He swung his arms out and fired again, in opposite directions. As the dust cleared, he saw that he was surrounded by bodies. On any normal day, the scene would likely have evinced a feeling of revulsion in him.

Now, however, he merely felt an ugly satisfaction. These men had dared to come after him, had dared to take that which was his. And now they would be made to pay.

Jim was aware that the psychologists of his acquaintance would find something aberrant in this, but he couldn't bring himself to care. Not now. Splinters struck his cheek, and he jerked out of his haze, swinging the automatic around instinctively. Teeth bared, he fired. Bullets carved the air like angry wasps, and he returned fire until both weapons gave ominous clicks. Holstering them, he darted to all fours and scrambled into the warren of debris.

Think. He needed to think. There were more than a dozen here, too many men for him to take on head to head. He was at a disadvantage, thanks to his impatience. Now he needed to even the odds. Crouching, he reached under his shirt for his gimmick belt. It was wide and flat and strapped around his belly like a money belt. He popped open one of the myriad pouches and retrieved two color-coded capsules-one red and one blue. Swiftly he shook them and smashed them together. Keeping his hands tightly clamped, he rose and ducked momentarily into the open before throwing the mixture straight towards the nearest of his opponents. A thick, stinging purple smoke billowed instantly into being and Jim darted into it.

The purple smoke was a concoction of his own devising, created as an antidote during the Subway Riots Affair. He'd used it to negate the effects of the poisonous black cloud the instigators had unleashed and had since found that it made for excellent improvised concealment in a pinch. As he moved through the cloud, he stripped the fibrous belt out of his trousers and gave it a hard twist. Composed of a unique South American fiber, the belt was unusually strong and springy and more than once he'd used it to support his own weight. But it had other uses than holding up his trousers or himself. One of the ends was weighted and when he gave it a yank, it stretched to its full length. Wrapping the loose end around his forearm, he plowed through the smoke, swinging the belt at his side to stir the smoke.

A guard broke into view, turning blindly, and Jim snapped his arm out, causing the weighted end to crash against the man's skull with an audible crunch. As the man fell, Jim spun, swinging the belt out in a wide arc. A man howled in pain and stumbled forward. Jim's free hand shot out, his fingers fastening on the man's windpipe. He wrenched him into the air and slung him into another dim shape.

A gun went off, nowhere near him. Jim's keen ears led him to the shooter and he sprang on him, wrapping the belt around his throat and choking him into unconsciousness. Letting the body drop, he turned. The smoke was clearing. Two men stumbled forward, waving their hands. Jim swung the belt over his head and let it fly, catching them both around the neck. Their skulls collided with a hollow thud and they fell.

"Gotcha," someone snarled. Jim froze. "I got you, you bloody *kaffir-*lover," the man said, coughing. He held a Mauser in one hand and was slightly better dressed than his companions.

"Your accent-South African?" Jim said, raising his hands. "You're a long way from Orange River, chum."

"No chum of yours," the man snapped. "Keep those hands up."

"They're up," Jim said, turning. "How many of you are left, out of curiosity?"

"It doesn't matter." The Mauser went up. "Dead men don't care about numbers."

A pistol barked. Jim flinched. The gunman toppled at his feet, the Mauser sliding away. Jim looked up as Delores stepped out from behind a crate, a pistol in one hand and a knife in the other. "Well, this is another fine mess you've gotten me into," she said.

With a wordless growl, Jim swept her into his arms and crushed her to him. Their lips met hungrily for a moment and then they broke apart. "I should have known you'd get yourself out of this," Jim said.

"We're not out of here yet," Delores said. "I-"

"Hsst!" Jim said, his head jerking up. In his pocket, the crystal began to vibrate. Swiftly retrieving it, he held it up. The crystal's hum was matched by a dozen other similar tones. No, more than a dozen. Soon, a vast piercing whine filled the air. Jim held Delores tight, and his face went pale.

"Jim? What is it?"

"He knew!" Jim snarled. "He knew!" He hurled the crystal away in a fit of realization. "Come on, we have to get-"

Unfortunately, the realization had come too late. The warehouse erupted in flame a moment later, blotting out the lives of all within!

II.

Across town and twenty minutes earlier, Tom Gentry took the black coupe out into traffic, his keen eyes searching the immediate area for anything unusual. He'd intended to take the Rolls, but Jimmy had put the nix to that. Better to be inconspicuous, he'd said. The coupe certainly was that, if nothing else. He glanced at the rearview mirror. "Comfortable, Professor?"

"*Ja*," Spengler said, sitting hunched the backseat. "Where are we going again?"

"The Catskills. Jimmy's got a nice joint up there. You'll be safe and sound."

"The mountains?" Spengler said.

"Place is a fortress. Year-round security force, the works." Tom looked over his shoulder. "As soon as Jimmy and Delores get there, we can plan our next move."

"Next move? What move can we possibly make?" Spengler said tiredly. "They are everywhere."

"They ain't here," Tom said flatly. "And I aim to keep it that way. There's no way they know what Jimmy has planned. Like as not those goons are going to be waiting at the Penthouse until long after we're out of the city. So just sit back and-*Mother Mary!*"

Spengler was thrown across the seat as Tom stamped on the brake. The coupe squealed like a frightened animal as the truck brushed across its path. The armored windshield spider-webbed as shotguns roared. Cursing, Gentry spun the wheel and crashed past the truck, sending it slewing sideways in a shower of sparks.

"Guess I spoke too soon, hunh?" Tom said. He looked at the mirror again, spotting two cars gliding after him. "We've got two on our tail, Professor. Keep your head low!"

"What can this mean?" Spengler said. "I thought they didn't know!"

"Guess Jimmy was wrong! It happens," Tom said, grudgingly. "Cops are all over the area, what with that guy who took a header off the balcony. We just need to get their attention!" He hit the gas and the coupe seemed to bounce and rattle as it forced its way into the flow of traffic. Indignant horn-honking followed in their wake, as well as the screech of tires and the sound of shattering glass. The truck barreled after them. Spengler yelped as the back windshield received the same decoration as the front.

Gentry cursed virulently as one of the trailing cars drew up alongside and swerved into the coupe, causing it to slide dangerously close to a city bus. Gentry spun the wheel, returning the favor. The coupe was built to take a lot of punishment, and it dug into the side of the parallel car like a boar goring a hunter's horse. The other car peeled off and bounced up onto the sidewalk, vomiting smoke.

Tom gave a howl worthy of Cuchulain and stamped on the pedal. The second car tapped his rear fender, and Tom traded the gas for the brake, letting the coupe's reinforced bumper hammer into the other vehicle. There was an audible grinding of metal and the second car spun out. "Got you!" Tom roared, speeding up again.

The truck continued the pursuit. It was heavier than the coupe, and Tom's tricks weren't going to be enough. "Where are the cops when you really need them?" Tom muttered, trying to lose the truck in traffic. As he jerked the coupe in and out of the flow of cars, he wondered whether Jimmy really had been wrong...had they somehow known what he was planning? Or was this just a backup plan? If it was the latter, well, it wasn't the first time Jimmy hadn't foreseen everything. If it was the former...a shiver ran the length of Tom's spine. If it was the former, then whoever they were up against was a lot smarter than the goons they'd tangled with in the old days.

So caught up was he in these thoughts that he failed to notice the third car as it came out of a side-street and caught the coupe a seemingly glancing blow on the side. As Tom fought to regain control, however, the front of the car was suddenly engulfed in flame!

Out of control, the coupe charged up onto the sidewalk and crashed through a display window, scattering glass and burning mannequins everywhere. Coughing, Tom scrambled out of the car, pulling his pistol. He jerked open Spengler's door. "Professor, get out of here!"

"But where?" Spengler said desperately.

"Into the store! Keep your head down and try and mingle! I'll find you later!" Tom gestured wildly as he peered around the end of the coupe.

"But-"

"Go, Prof!" Tom shoved the smaller man out of the display. Spengler went. Tom checked the automatic's clip and took a breath. Then he swung out around the car, weapon raised. Both the car and the truck had stopped and were blocking the street. Masked men were trotting towards the display window, weapons held loosely. "Looking for me boys?" Tom said. He fired, plucking the life out of one of them. The rest opened up, rattling the rear of the coupe. Tom took cover behind it, hoping he could hold their attention long enough for Spengler to get away.

His attackers spread out, trying to come at him from multiple sides. Tom potted another one who got too close, sending him staggering back with a crimson-stained trousers leg. Shotguns spoke and the rear tires of the coupe blew out, causing the whole vehicle to shift suddenly in the display window. Tom scrambled back instinctively. Another shotgun barked and the window frame nearest to him exploded into splinters, and he shrugged away, diving out of the window and onto the street. He landed hard and the automatic flew out of his hand.

Tom lunged for his pistol, but a hard-soled shoe came down on his hand. Grunting in pain, he looked up into the bruised face of Karsten.

"Remember me, *schweinhund*?" Karsten growled, a moment before his other foot caught Tom in the belly. "Not wearing your fancy armor now, are you?"

Tom rolled with the blow, snatching up a chunk of glass as he went. Karsten stalked towards him, pulling a pistol as he came. Tom bounced to his feet and lunged with the glass. He cut a slice out of Karsten's shirt and the pistol cracked against his head, sending him stumbling. Head ringing, Tom staggered against the coupe and narrowly avoided a pistol shot. He spun and tackled Karsten, driving him back against a phone-booth. Karsten's pistol went flying, and the two men traded punches for several minutes.

Finally Karsten shoved Gentry back, and the masked men rushed forward. Shotgun butts raised up and crashed down, felling Tom like a tree. Feet and fists rained down thereafter until Karsten finally began pulling them aside.

"Find Spengler damn you! Find him!" he barked, looking down at Gentry's battered and bloody form. He frowned for a moment, then picked up his pistol. "No less than you deserve," he said, aiming the weapon at the man.

"M-Matter of p-perspective," Gentry mumbled through mashed lips. He tried to heave himself to his feet and Karsten stepped back, eyes widening in amazement.

"You're tough, I'll give you that," Karsten said. "But not tough enough."

"Gimme a few seconds, we'll see h-how tough I am…" Gentry grunted, trying again to get up. His limbs felt like wet noodles, and the beating had sapped his strength. He fell onto his side, breathing heavily, his vision spinning.

"No. No more time," Karsten said. He drove a foot into Gentry's jaw, snapping his head back and rolling him over. Karsten then took aim with his pistol. "Time to die."

"No," a voice said. Karsten spun, seeing one of his men standing behind him. Before Karsten could snap out a reply, the man seemed to swell. He pulled off his mask and Karsten's reply died in his throat.

Finally, he managed to say, "But he-"

"No. We are not murderers," the large man said softly. He sank to one knee beside Gentry and checked his pulse. "He'll live, provided the police arrive in time." Ice-blue eyes, as cold as legendary Hyperborea, swiveled towards Karsten. "Sirens. Let us go collect our reluctant seer, shall we?"

"Yeah," Karsten said, following his master into the department store and leaving Tom Gentry bleeding in the street.

12.

Two heads broke the surface of the Hudson even as the first police cars pulled up near the burning warehouse. Arm around Delores, Jim made for shore with long, powerful strokes.

Seconds before the explosion, Jim had broken through the rotten floor and opened a hole to the river below. Snatching up Delores, he'd thrown them both into the icy waters even as the warehouse had been filled with fire for a second time in its history.

"That-gah-that's one way to go about it," Delores said as she and Jim reached shore. "Could have warned me."

"No time. You're welcome, by the way," Jim said, helping her to her feet. He looked at the warehouse and ran his hands through his hair. "He knew."

"You said that before," Delores said through chattering teeth. The Hudson had been bone-numbingly cold, and the shock of it was starting to set in. "What do you mean he knew? He who?"

Jim swung around, his face set in a tight grimace. "He knew I'd come after you, rather than make the exchange!" He pounded a fist into his palm.

"He who?" Delores said again. Jim hesitated, then pulled her close.

"I'm not sure," he said.

"You're lying."

Jim looked down into her pale face and then stroked her cheek gently. "No. I'm simply not leaping to conclusions. I can't afford to. Whoever he is, he's smarter than I am."

"That's-" Delores began. Her eyes narrowed as she peered up at him. "You're serious."

"As a bullet." Jim turned towards the sound of sirens as a police car slowed in a slew of gravel, and a lanky figure hopped out before the car stopped.

"Anthony! I should have known!" Lieutenant Turkish Healy barked. Coat flaring, his battered fedora pushed back on his narrow head, Healy looked little different from the bulldog detective that Anthony had so often worked with and clashed against. Older now, like Anthony himself, and frozen at his current rank thanks to an inability to play the system, Healy still worked cases like a regular detective.

"Was it the fire or the gunshots that clued you in?" Delores said, pushing

125

away from Jim. Healy stopped short and grinned, flicking his hat brim in an offhand and borderline insulting salute.

"Well if it ain't Mrs. Anthony. It's like old home week, what with Gentry and all."

"Tom?" Jim said sharply. "What about him?"

Healy looked at him, the smile slipping from his narrow face. "We found him about ten minutes ago. They're taking him to Mercy General now."

"Found-" Jim's voice had gone hoarse. "Is he-"

"He's alive, Anthony," Healy said, stepping close. "Dawkins got me your message. But by the time I got enough men together..." He trailed off. "Looks like he put up a fight though."

Jim said nothing. His hands curled into fists, his knuckles popping like gunshots. Healy took a step back, his eyes narrowing.

"Easy, Anthony," he said.

"Jim-" Delores began, touching his arm.

"I'm fine," Jim said with deceptive softness. "Just fine. Where's Dawkins?"

"At the hospital with Gentry. When we found him, the Limey insisted on heading over there. He looked like he'd been through the wringer himself."

"We all have," Delores said, touching Jim. He put a hand over hers.

"What the hell is going on here, Anthony? We got a body out on the street outside your place, two more out where we found Gentry, and now this?" Healy gestured to the burning warehouse. "Someone declare war and forget to invite the NYPD?"

"In a word-yes," Jim said. "Was there anyone with Tom when you found him?"

"Nobody but stiffs." Healy shrugged. "Dawkins mentioned that he was escorting someone, but-" He shook his head. "We're taking statements though. Somebody saw something. They had to. What's going on? Who are these guys?"

"Evil," Jim said. "Pure evil." He flexed his hands. "They won't stop until they get what they want."

"And what do they want?"

"Everything," Jim said softly. "The world, and every solitary soul in it." Healy stared at him in shock. But his reply was interrupted.

"Hey! Stop him!" a cop shouted. Jim whipped around and caught sight of a masked figure fleeing from the area. The figure darted between the police cars, head down, arms pumping.

Jim gave a snarl worthy of a hunting cat and bounded after the fleeing figure. His bare feet pounded across the gravel, then crashed against the hood of a police car as he jumped from vehicle to vehicle in pursuit.

The masked man didn't turn, even as Jim launched himself through the air. He crashed against the man, and they fell in a tangle of limbs. The man screamed as Jim surged to his feet, dragging his prey with him.

In that moment, a red tide seemed to sweep over Jim. Frustration boiled over into rage. He turned, hurling the hapless man straight into the side of a police car. Glass cracked and metal creaked as the masked man fell with a groan.

He didn't try to get up as Jim stalked towards him, fingers flexing slowly like talons. Jim bared his teeth in a silent growl. "Get up," he hissed.

"Nuh-no!" the masked man squeaked. He rolled over, holding up his hands. "I give! I give!"

"You give?" Jim said, staring down at him. "You give?" Jim's hands snapped out and he grabbed a handful of the man's coat and hauled him to his feet and jerked him into the air. Then, even higher, swinging the screaming man into the air as if to dash him onto the ground.

"Anthony! No!" Healy barked, hurrying forward, hands raised.

"Jimmy!" Delores said, following him. "Stop!"

For a moment, the tableau held-Jim held the screaming man above his head, his face contorted in a horrible expression. Then, with a hissing sigh, he lowered his prisoner to the ground and let him drop harmlessly into the dirt. Jim turned away as Healy dragged the man to his feet and whipped off his mask.

"Hell. He's a kid!" Healy said. Delores touched Jim's arm and he turned back. The boy was fifteen at most, and scrawny-a bowery boy.

"I-I ain't saying nothing!" the kid said, shivering in Healy's grip. He tried to slide away from Jim's gaze, but Healy held him tight.

"You don't have to say anything," Jim said after a moment. Reaching out, he stripped the boy's jacket from him and turned out the pockets. He pulled out a handful of pamphlets. Jim gestured with the pamphlets. "I've seen these around...they're for the German-American Bund and the American Thule Society."

"Fascists?" Healy said.

"Mystics," Jim said, "And Fascists." His hand clenched, crumpling the pamphlets. "He was out delivering these, most likely. His mask is homemade, and of a lesser quality than those worn by the others." Jim dropped the crumpled pamphlets. "He's nothing."

"He's a person of interest is what he is," Healy said, spinning the youth towards several waiting officers. "Cuff him." Healy turned back to Jim. "I'll get you a ride to the hospital."

Delores thanked Healy, and hooked her arm through Jim's. He had fallen silent and his face resembled a stiff mask.

"Healy said he was fine," she said.

"Healy said he'd survived," Jim corrected. He put his hand over hers. "They let him live. As a warning. Just like they took you as a warning. They're toying with us. With me." He looked at the burning warehouse. "And now they've got what they came for."

"So what are you going to do about it?" Delores said. Jim looked at her, his eyes gleaming weirdly in the light of the fire.

"Me? I'm going to hunt."

13.

Tom had been in no condition to talk.

Jim had left Delores at the hospital with Dawkins, the latter having taken on the position of bodyguard. It was amusing in a way to see the normally taciturn butler fussing over a man he, by all appearances, loathed.

"When Mr. Gentry is capable of movement, I'll see to his removal to the Teepee, sir," Dawkins said to Jim as they stood outside of Tom's room. Jim's connections had secured him the best treatment money could buy, but it was small consolation.

"Make sure Mrs. Colquitt-Anthony goes as well," Jim said, watching Delores sit with Tom. "I need to know that you're all safe-that includes you, Dawkins." Jim raised a hand to forestall protest. "I don't think we're even on their radar at the moment, but I'm not risking it. Go. Keep them safe."

Dawkins closed his mouth with a snap and nodded. Jim clapped him on the shoulder. "Good man." He took a last look at Delores and Tom, and then turned away. "Now, there's work to be done."

Jim left the hospital at a trot. A police car was waiting for him at the curb, and the driver had orders to take him to the scene of Tom's near-demise. Jim was silent for the trip, barely even glancing at either the driver or the city streets. Instead, he stared straight ahead and tried to organize his thoughts into some rough approximation of coherence.

It had been a set up from the beginning that much was obvious; a casual demonstration of power by Spengler's pursuers.

No, rather by the man who pulled their strings. Jim's jaw clenched. There were stories coming out of Europe. It had become a cauldron of hostility as decades of political, economic and social blunders built to a boil in the East as well as the West. Jim had lived through one war, he had no interest in witnessing a second. Unfortunately, his interest wasn't as highly prioritized as he might have wished.

Amidst the disturbing rumors, however, were stories of a different cloth. Europe was no different from America; it too had its share of what the Press was coming to refer to as 'mystery men', some of whom Jim had even encountered. Judex, for instance, who'd been instrumental in bringing a successful conclusion to Jim's encounter with the second woman to bear the name 'Irma Vep'. But in Germany, the rumors had a different tint. Darker. The days of the Siegfried Legion and the Twilight Men were long gone and in their place…what? Who?

Just a name…Sun-Koh. An alias, Jim was sure. The name had an alien ring to it, more like a title, almost. Regardless, it was a name that hung over a number of others. More, in fact, than he'd first realized.

Alaska Jim, for instance. As far as Jim knew, the mountain man's activities were almost entirely confined to North America. Or, they had been. Delores had mentioned Jan Mayen as well. Detectives, adventurers, all connected seemingly with the Thule Society. And through the Society, with Sun-Koh.

It was a name to conjure with, apparently. Jim restrained a snort. All he had was the name, and the voice. Jim closed his eyes and rubbed his temples with his fingertips. The human voice was an entryway into the soul of thing, even as the eyes were windows. You could tell a lot by a man's voice. You could tell how serious he was, how far he was willing to go.

Sun-Koh's voice didn't say much, however much its owner liked to talk. But actions sometimes spoke louder than words, and the actions he'd witnessed told of a man who thought three steps ahead and two to the side. Jim was certain that what he'd witnessed-what he'd undergone-was only a series of strands in a much larger web. Whichever strands he'd plucked, that was the plan his opponent had implemented.

It bespoke a mind capable of lightning-quick calculation, but also long-term preparation. This wasn't a man who made many mistakes, and recovered quickly when he did. Sun-Koh, whoever he was, had engineered Spengler's capture efficiently and with pinpoint timing. More, he had shown Spengler that there was no escape. Nowhere to run for help. He hadn't just recaptured the man. He had effectively killed his hope.

Funny thing about hope though…it was easily snuffed, but just as easily re-lit.

Jim had the officer stop by the Penthouse, and he went upstairs quickly. In his lab, behind a false wall panel, there were a series of steel deposit boxes-his backup files. Jim had learned early on to keep meticulous records. Rifling swiftly through the boxes, he plucked out several thick folders and placed them in a buffalo hide saddle bag. Then he slung the bag over his shoulder and stepped out of the lab, locking it behind him.

He took a moment to survey his once and future home. The Penthouse had been the aleph of so much of his adult life. Not simply adventures or unpleasant incidents, but also a life fully lived. He recalled the Gun Club Christmas party he'd hosted, and the sound the elevator had made when the party-goers had been forced to deposit a stew-pot of explosives into it. He thought about the women who'd made this place their home, before Delores. And some of the men.

There were bullet holes decorating the bare walls now, and blood-stains on the carpet. Other than the lab, this place was dead. He wouldn't be returning. Not any time soon at any rate. He flipped off the lights and returned to the waiting radio-car.

As the car made its way back out into traffic, Jim flipped through one of the files. It contained most of what he knew, or might need to know, about Jan Mayen. The Austrian was a flamboyant figure-a Tesla for the new century. The craft had likely been his design. Mayen was a 'society dick', something Jim had been accused of being more than once. He investigated the troubles of the wealthy or the fashionable; people for whom the common man's law was more hindrance than comfort.

As a consequence, Jim knew quite a bit about Mayen's activities, including the ones the Austrian probably hoped no-one knew about, such as, for instance, his connection to the German-American Bund, via an introduction from Charles Lindbergh. Mayen had participated in the Lindbergh Baby kidnapping case along with a dozen other 'super-detectives' from around the world. Jim had stayed out of that particular mess, for a variety of reasons, not the least of which was that Lindbergh the elder had once pulled a gun on him and not in a funny party-trick sort of way.

Mayen had contacts within the upper ranks of the GAB, several of whom were also members in good standing of the Thule Society. Jim wondered if those same men had provided Mayen-and Sun-Koh-with his dogsbodies. Tracing those men would likely lead into dark corners. Nonetheless, Healy had already begun an investigation.

The car pulled to a stop and Jim hopped out, the bag over his shoulder. A series of chalk outlines sprawled across the pavement in front of the department store where Tom had made his last stand. Uniformed officers lounged nearby, displaying little interest in Jim, despite his bandaged hands and charred sweater. Healy had called ahead, obviously.

Jim crouched and traced his fingers across the spot where Tom had fallen. He took a breath and turned, imagining what must have happened. Then he bounded to his feet and hopped through the display window.

The car had seen better days. Jim moved past it and into the store. He looked into the store, thinking. Where would they have taken Spengler after they recovered him? Where would they go?

Resting against the car, Jim flipped open Mayen's file again. "Ha," he grunted. Mayen had three private airfields: one in New Jersey, one near London, and a third near Vienna. Jim tapped the paper, his smile becoming feral. Vienna. He looked at the address for the New Jersey base, and headed back to the radio car.

He tossed the bag into the car and said, "Get Lieutenant Healy on the horn. I know where we need to be." The driver blinked, but then grabbed the radio mike as Jim slid inside.

A half hour later, Healy handed Jim his binoculars back and grunted, "I suppose you want me to say thank you?"

"Best to hold the thanks until afterward, Lieutenant." Jim peered through the binoculars at the airfield. Men were scrambling around the hangar, setting up a number of gasoline drums.

"What are they doing?" Healy asked.

"Cleaning house," Jim said, setting the binoculars down. "They're going to blow it up. All of it."

Healy grunted. "Seems a waste."

"Mayen can afford it." Jim turned. "Still, we need to stop them. There'll be evidence down there."

"So you say," Healy said, checking his service weapon. A squad of armed cops awaited his orders, hefting shotguns. Jim himself carried a modified Thompson, the ammunition drum replaced with a heavy box filled with mercy-rounds.

"So I say," Jim replied. He knocked his knuckles against the segmented plates of the bullet-proof vest he wore for emphasis. Healy and his men wore similar vests, thanks to Jim's foresight and generosity.

"That kid you caught spilled his guts," Healy said. "Gave up his pals. Made them out to be a regular little cult."

"They're worse than that," Jim said. "They're an *organized* cult. Which makes them dangerous. Are we ready?"

"Always," Healy said, holstering his weapon. He looked at his men and swung his hat over his head. "Mount up, you mooks!"

Jim climbed onto the running board of Healy's car even as the lieutenant slammed the passenger-side door. Healy reached up and smacked the roof of the car. "Move out!" Healy barked.

One by one, the line of police cars trundled towards the private airfield, sirens wailing. Lackadaisical gunfire greeted them as the Thule Society members raced to defend the place they had been intending to blow up only moments earlier.

Jim leapt off of the running board as Healy's car slewed sideways. The Thompson bucked in his hands and several masked men staggered. The mercy-bullets packed a wallop, but were otherwise harmless. As the ammunition box rattled empty, Jim gripped the weapon by the barrel and swung it out like a club, catching a running man in the belly and flipping him end over end.

Jim tossed the weapon aside and looked around. The battle had been a short one, if not particularly vicious. Without their foreign leaders, the members of the Society didn't have much heart.

While Healy and his men saw to the rest of the group, Jim jerked the groaning man to his feet and ripped the mask off of his head. "How long?" Jim said.

"Wh-what?"

"How long since they left?" Jim said, shaking his prisoner slightly.

"G-Glory to Thule!" the man yelped and twisted, a blade sliding into one hand. Jim grabbed his wrist and gave it a vicious twist. Bone snapped and popped and the knife fell to the tarmac as the man howled in agony.

"Thule, then," Jim said softly, yanking the man's terrified features closer. "Let's talk about Thule."

14.

Six hours later, Jim was sipping a Martini in first-class on a transatlantic flight and reading Bulwer-Lytton's *The Coming Race*. He made notes in the margins, a bad habit Delores had tried in vain to break him of. Beneath the book he had several files open, and he made more notes on those.

With a sigh, he closed the book. He'd found it in Mayen's hangar, along with a lot of other paraphernalia relating to the Thule Society. He wanted to discount it as rubbish out of hand, but-well.

There had been books and pamphlets aplenty in the hangar, most of them apparently consigned to a fate as fuel for the fire the Society members had intended to set. More interesting than books, however, had been the maps and photographs left behind.

As Healy had questioned the Society-members, Jim had studied the maps, tracing Mayen's flight plan. As he'd suspected, the electric vessel was heading for Vienna. But there were other maps as well, these of areas of the Antarctic.

Puzzled, he'd tried to get information from the Society members, but what little they knew was corrupted by what Jim figured was deliberate misinformation. Sun-Koh, if that was indeed who he was facing, was evidently a believer in strict compartmentalization.

Jim reached down for a second book-Ossendowsky's *Beasts, Men and Gods*-and flipped through to the passage concerning the visit of the 'King of the World' to the Narabanchi Monastery in Tibet in 1890. He wondered if Sun-Koh fancied himself as a king. What little he knew about the man seemed to point in that direction. And not the romantic idea of a king either, but the real thing…ruthless, cold and cunning. But a king of what?

"Agartha," Jim murmured after a moment, re-reading the passage. A legendary city said to reside at the Earth's core. Also a possible name for Atlantis. Or perhaps it was the other way around. He closed the Ossendowsky book with a snap and opened Emerson's *The Smoky God*. That one he closed in disgust a few minutes later. It was obvious fiction.

Jim drained his drink and leaned back, digging the heels of his hands into his eyes. Sighing, he went back to Bulwer-Lytton.

The Thule Society, or the *Thule-Gesellschaft*, had originally been a study group for Germanic antiquity. Slowly but surely it had become something else. Something less concerned with history and more with the future. Or a future, at least, one based on a handful of half-baked prophecies and mythic writings.

Four years earlier however, the German government had abruptly cracked down on groups like the Society, and, interestingly, on individuals like the mysterious Sun-Koh. Jim pulled out several newspaper clippings from his files and scanned them. A large number of arrests had seemingly been paid to the German branch of the Society as well as to the careers of any number of 'mystery-men'.

"So what scared them?" Jim said. The stewardess looked at him in puzzlement as she refilled his glass. Jim smiled at her and turned back to his book.

The crack-down coincided with Spengler's sudden surge in funding, if the latter had been telling the truth. Jim saw no reason to doubt his friend, and assumed that Sun-Koh had simply gone underground. Austria wasn't part of the Reich, not yet. If Sun-Koh was on the outs with the government in Berlin, then Austria was a good sideways step. Not far enough away to disrupt any plans, but far enough to be out of the Gestapo's reach.

Frowning, Jim pondered the disparate facets of information before him. Facts tried to resolve themselves into coherent shape, but Jim's own innate rationality resisted the transformation.

It simply couldn't be. But the evidence-

"Hang the evidence," he muttered, draining his glass for a second time. "It can't be." He looked at the books again and a crawling sensation curled around his spine.

Spengler swore that he had succeeded. But he hadn't recognized the coordinates he'd been given. So, just where (when?) had he opened the *wurmloch* to?

Jim leaned forward in his seat, balancing his chin on his knuckles. Eyes closed, he took a breath, pushing his suspicions aside.

In truth, none of this mattered. Only Spengler mattered. Retrieving him. Rescuing him. Jim's eyes fluttered open and he bent, scooping up his materials. Carefully he returned them to his satchel and replaced them in his attentions with what he knew of Jan Mayen's operations in Vienna.

Mayen, unlike several of Sun-Koh's other associates, hadn't suffered much in the way of government attention. Thus, he was still the 'face' of what remained of the Thule Society in Europe. Which meant that if he wanted to find Sun-Koh, the best way to go about it was to find Mayen.

And once he found Mayen-Jim's hands unconsciously clenched. For everything they'd done-for Delores, for Dawkins, for Tom-he'd hurt them.

A sudden spurt of adrenalin pounded in his head and he fought to control himself.

He tried to concentrate on what was likely waiting for him in Vienna. Jim still had business interests in Austria, including a European office of the *Daily Star*. However, the government was becoming increasingly hostile to foreign businessmen. Indeed, Jim's contacts thought it was only a matter of time until Austria formally joined the German Reich. Things were tense, even in Vienna. Maybe especially in Vienna.

So, needless to say, he was likely going to find this particular row hard to hoe. Tapping his lip, he went back to the files, replacing Mayen's with what his German contacts had been able to dig up on the others. Karsten was Rolf Karsten, also known as 'Shrek'. Better known as the 'Terror of the Berlin Underworld', if you were going to be formal about it. A hard man regardless, with a history of violence.

"Far from home, Mr. Karsten." Jim's lip curled as he memorized Karsten's sharp features. He tossed the photo aside and looked at the next file-Rudolf Rauhaar, AKA Rolf Kraft, AKA Sturmvogel. The Storm Bird. This one he knew. Idly, Jim touched the healing bruises on his cheek. If Karsten was the hunting hound, Rauhaar was the attack dog. In and out of the army, he was a professional soldier. A killer with a lethal instinct.

Mayen, Karsten and Rauhaar. An inventor, a thug and a soldier. Good men to have on your payroll, especially if you were involved in something shady. Jim flipped a page. Alaska Jim, on the other hand, was an anomaly. Really, the only thing that tied him to the group was the Thule Society connection.

The same for the woman that had taken Delores and the 'Minx' individual that Spengler had mentioned. Neither of whom Jim had been able to get any concrete information on. The woman was a ghost, and the only Minx he'd been able to find had been Ludwig Minx, a professional stage magician who regularly toured the Baltic.

Jim looked hard at the blurry photograph of the magician and wished that he'd been able to get in contact with his friend St. Cyprian, in London or Harley Warren, for that matter. Both men knew a good deal more than he did about the occult. Still, it was likely nothing he couldn't handle.

He leaned back and closed his eyes. The obvious weak link was Mayen. He was high-profile and arrogant. If Jim pulled hard enough, Mayen would react, and likely without thinking, if their previous encounters were anything to go by. As the first dim threads of a plan began to form in his mind, Jim dropped off into a much needed slumber.

It was dawn when he awoke, and the wheels of the plane scraped against the tarmac. Jim re-packed his satchel and stood, joining the other passengers as they disembarked. The airfield was near the city of Schwechat, which Jim only knew the name of because he occasionally enjoyed a good Schwechater beer.

Breaking away from the pack, Jim sidled towards a hangar where he'd left instructions that a car should be waiting. The car was there, but it wasn't alone.

"*Herr* Anthony?" the tall man said, unfolding from his leaning position against the 1936 Mercedes-Benz. He was dressed casually, but wore his clothes with the ill-grace of one who preferred a uniform. A long scar decorated his left cheek and his eyes were bright.

"You have me at a disadvantage," Jim said, setting his luggage down.

"Doubtful," the man said, grinning. "Skorzeny. Otto Skorzeny, at your service." He twitched, as if fighting the urge to salute.

Jim gestured to the other man's cheek. "*Schmiss?*"

"*Ja.*" Skorzeny tapped his face. "You fence?"

"Once or twice. Skorzeny…you fought Carhart at the inter-university match between Vienna and Yale?"

Skorzeny bobbed his head. "Yes. Good fight." He patted the hood of the car. "Good car too."

"A car fancier, *Herr* Skorzeny?" Jim hefted his baggage and headed for the car boot. "Or are you part of the hospitality bureau?"

"You could say that, yes," Skorzeny said. "I am here to-ah-guide you, you might say."

Jim closed the boot and looked at Skorzeny. "I've been to Vienna before. I don't think I'll require the services of a guide."

"A liaison, then."

"Won't need one of those, either." Jim headed for the driver's side door. The soft click of a revolver being cocked caused him to freeze.

"I'll settle for captor, then," Skorzeny said, pulling a pistol out of his coat pocket. "You don't really have a choice, I'm afraid."

Jim grunted and turned. "Lot of that going around. Who sent you?"

"Why are you here?" Skorzeny countered, gesturing to the car. "Get in."

Jim got in and Skorzeny joined him. "Where are we going?"

"You have a hotel room arranged at the Kroenen-Anthony Hotel, I understand? Near the University?" Skorzeny said. "We go there, I think."

"You know quite a bit."

Skorzeny nodded. "You have entered a game already in progress, *Herr* Anthony." He glanced at Jim. "I hope you've got a good hand."

15.

The Kroenen-Anthony was one of Jim's interests in Vienna, though he rarely visited it. The hotel was a masterpiece of Hapsburg architecture, and had only recently been retrofitted with modern conveniences. Jim had paid for those, which was why his name was now on the letterhead.

Skorzeny didn't seem impressed by either the architecture or the letterhead. Then, Jim hadn't expected him to be. Jim had secured the services of the suite on the top floor which gave him a view of the city that was, to hear the porter tell it, unrivaled in Vienna. Jim ignored the view in favor of Skorzeny and his pistol, now back in his coat.

"So. Now what?" Jim said, as the porter left. Skorzeny glanced at him and then shrugged.

"Now, we wait."

"For?"

"Tomorrow. Then you get on the first flight to the United States."

Jim frowned. "I wasn't aware I was leaving so soon."

"There are many things you aren't aware of," Skorzeny said, pulling a chair away from the desk in the corner. He spun it so that the back faced Jim, and then sat, his chin resting on one forearm.

Jim tossed files out of his satchel onto the bed. "Illuminate me then."

"How do you Americans say it? You are-ah-out of your jurisdiction," Skorzeny said. He gestured with the pistol. "This is not New York. Things are different here."

"It's not Germany either," Jim said quietly. Skorzeny's eyes narrowed. Jim smiled. "Ha. I thought so. So, who do you work for *Herr* Skorzeny? Not the Austrian government."

"*Deutsche Nationalsozialistische Arbeiterpartei*," Skorzeny said, showing his teeth. "Heil Hitler," he added.

"Hail to the Chief," Jim said. "Why are the National Socialists interested in me?"

"Not you," Skorzeny said. "Him."

Jim sat down. "Sun-Koh."

Skorzeny flinched. Not by much, but Jim caught it. "Why?"

"I don't know." Skorzeny grimaced. "I am a soldier."

"So is Rudolf Rauhaar," Jim said, picking up a file and tossing it at Skorzeny's feet. "Do you know him?"

"I am not here to answer your questions." Skorzeny pulled a pocket watch out of his coat and flipped it open. "I am here to see that you get on a plane."

"It's going to get awful boring between now and then." Jim stooped and picked up the file. Skorzeny made to stand. Jim straightened swiftly and swiped the edge of the file across Skorzeny's eyes, temporarily blinding him. Skorzeny yowled and staggered. Jim grabbed his wrist and twisted, forcing the other man to drop his weapon even as he drove a punch into Skorzeny's kidney.

Skorzeny twisted, wheezing. Jim stepped back as a fist brushed past his face. His knee shot up, catching Skorzeny in the chin. The big man fell to the floor, breathing heavily. Jim picked up the revolver and checked the cylinder. Snapping it back into place, he looked down at his former captor.

"Now then, let's have a chat, shall we?" Jim said, as Skorzeny pushed himself up onto all fours. "Why don't your superiors want me here?"

Skorzeny glared at him, nostrils flaring. Jim quirked an eyebrow and lazily aimed the pistol. "You said you know about me, *Herr* Skorzeny. So you must know that I'm not the type to threaten." His thumb caressed the hammer.

Skorzeny sat up and rubbed his jaw. "You endanger our operations with your presence."

"Operations?"

"The termination of certain rogue elements," Skorzeny said smoothly. "Burrs on the blade of National Socialism."

"Sun-Koh and his people," Jim said. Skorzeny said nothing. Jim chuckled. "Rogue elements, hunh? How about that. But since Austria is still technically its own country, it's up to you loyal National Socialists to do Berlin's dirty work for it, right?"

Skorzeny's hands clenched into fists and he muttered, "I am happy to serve the Reich."

"Good for you. Sun-Koh obviously doesn't agree," Jim said. "And why is that, I wonder?" He gestured with the pistol. "What sort of operation are you mounting? What were you afraid I'd interfere in?"

Skorzeny didn't reply. He sat down and folded his arms, mouth clamped shut. Jim waited for a moment, then sighed. "Look, as much as it pains me to admit it, we both want the same thing. So why not tell me what I want to know?"

"*Nein*," Skorzeny said, his eyes mere slits.

"Earlier you called it a game. What kind of game?" Jim pressed. He cocked his head. "And how long has it been going on?" Facts thudded into place. "Something I've been wondering…how exactly did Helmut Spengler escape from Sun-Koh's people in the first place?"

"I have no idea," Skorzeny said, teeth flashing.

"You're lying. What sort of hidden depths do you possess, *Herr* Skorzeny?" Jim said. "It might even have been you who got him out and to Aspern, right?"

Skorzeny twitched. Jim nodded. "Why help Spengler get away? Why not simply take them then?"

Skorzeny pursed his lips. "Would you spring the trap before the wolf was in it?"

"You were trying to draw out Sun-Koh!" Jim said. He snapped his fingers. "And now…" He paused. "Now you know where he is."

Skorzeny frowned. "We believe so, yes."

"But you're not sure." Jim stepped back. "Get up."

"What do you intend to do with me?"

"I simply want you to look at something." Jim gestured and Skorzeny moved to the bed. "The folder marked 'Mayen'." Skorzeny opened it and flipped through the pages. Abruptly he turned. Jim nodded. "Is that the address?"

"Yes-"

The explosion rocked Vienna like the hammer of God. Jim staggered and Skorzeny lunged, grabbing for the pistol. They grappled for a moment, the younger man breathing hoarsely. Jim twisted and threw Skorzeny over his hip, throwing him into the wall. As the Austrian spun, Jim smoothly cocked and fired the revolver, plucking Skorzeny's leg out from under him.

The man fell heavily, cursing. Jim ignored him and hurried to the window. An enormous plume of smoke rose over the city. "What the devil?" he murmured.

Skorzeny groaned. Jim turned and retrieved a towel from the bathroom. He tossed it at Skorzeny as he moved to the door. "Staunch the blood. You'll be fine," Jim said. People were running through the hall. Jim grabbed the closest. "What's going on?"

"Something blew up!" the man yelped in German, wrenching his arm free. "The Communists are attacking!"

Jim let him go and stuffed the pistol into his coat. It wasn't the Communists, that much he was sure of. A grim premonition surged through him.

"Damn it!" Jim broke into a run.

The streets were jammed with traffic, and sirens split the air. Jim darted into the street and grabbed onto the back of a passing fire engine, hitching a ride.

He dropped to the street as the engine took a corner and sprang into an alleyway. Smoke filled the streets, issuing from an impressive three-story inferno. Water cannons stabbed plumes of high-pressure water into the greedy flames while across the street, uniformed police moved up and down a row of shroud-draped forms.

Jim put two and two together. He leaned back against the wall of the alleyway and cursed virulently. It was Mayen's place that had gone up, even as he'd suspected. Jim closed his eyes and forced his fingers to uncurl. The Nazis must have moved quickly when they'd learned he was coming to Vienna. And they'd gotten blown up for their troubles.

Pushing himself away from the wall, Jim watched as the fires were forced back and finally doused. Hands in the pockets of his coat, he watched as a series of ambulances carried away the bodies and the police set up a cordon. Through it all, Jim's eyes flickered back and forth across the crowd that had gathered to watch.

No faces stood out. No prickles of his sub-conscious. The crowd eventually dispersed, breaking off into ones and twos. The police followed suit, leaving only two behind to watch the scene.

From the snatches of conversation he'd overheard, Jim knew that the investigation would begin in earnest in the morning. He also knew that Skorzeny's superiors had likely already made arrangements with the city authorities. And they would already suspect that their trap had gone off in their faces.

It was child's play slipping past the policemen. Jim waited until the street-lights were sputtering to life, and in the break between nightfall and artificial light, he made his move. He slithered out of the alleyway and loped into the still smoldering ruins, his keen senses stretching to their limits.

The tang of smoke tingled in his nose as his nostrils flared. Tying his shoes to his belt, he crouched, bare-footed, amidst the drifts of burned wood and debris. He traced the patterns of the burn with an experienced eye, noting where it had seemed to burn the hottest. Padding towards the gutted stairs, he wondered whether the explosion had had a similar genesis to the one that had nearly claimed his and Delores' lives in New York.

From above, something clattered. Seared chunks of tile tumbled down, their descent loud in the silence. Instantly alert, Jim froze. Then, slowly, he looked up. The moon was visible through the remains of the roof. As Jim watched, something cut across it.

Instantly Jim was moving, scrambling up the stairs and leaping for the beams of the roof. Swinging around the circumference of the one that looked the most stable, he charged up its length, moving quickly lest his weight cause it to collapse. With a simian bound, Jim thrust himself out into the night and landed in a crouch on the peak of the roof.

He sniffed, his head swiveling from side to side, his muscles tense and straining in anticipation. A familiar tingle of scent alerted him a half-second before the blow landed, and Jim launched himself across the roof. The descending fists crashed against the roof, snapping heat-weakened tiles. A dark shape rose, arms spreading. Eyes like azure stones blazed and Jim froze, momentarily taken aback. Then his attacker was moving, lunging, more swiftly than Jim could conceive.

Fingers like steel hooks dug into his shoulder and throat and Jim gave a roar. He swept his forearms up, slapping aside the grasping hands, and brought his palms together on the sides of his opponent's skull. Or he would have, had the man not slithered bonelessly aside. A sharp blow caught Jim beneath the rib cage and he found himself sliding back, down the incline of the roof. Tiles scattered around him as he hunched and dug desperate fingers into the surface of the roof to stop himself.

Smarting, Jim looked up. His attacker hadn't moved. He was a tall man, bigger even than Jim, but perfectly proportioned. He was dressed in dull khaki clothing, now smudged with soot. Long-fingered hands flexed and veins like steel cables rippled.

"Mr. Anthony. How unfortunate to see you here," he said, in a soft, rumbling purr.

Jim straightened and raised his fists. "It depends on your point of view. Sun-Koh, I presume?"

"Mr. Anthony. How unfortunate to see you here."

16.

Sun-Koh threw back his tawny-maned head and laughed quietly. Jim's bones throbbed as the sound reached him, and he shivered instinctively. Now blazing, the blue eyes fastened on him. "I knew you'd figure it out, Mr. Anthony. Delightful." Sun-Koh clapped his hands together, just once. "Magnificent."

"Stop it. I'll blush," Jim said, tensing. A moment later, he sprang towards the other man, his fists a blur. Sun-Koh stepped aside, avoiding the first blow. He caught the second on an open palm, but grunted in surprise as Jim's knee dug into his hip. Sun-Koh staggered and tossed out a lazy backhand. Jim swung back, bending under the blow, caught himself on his hands and let his feet kick upwards, catching Sun-Koh on the chin. The big man jerked back and Jim pressed the advantage, lunging eel-quick towards him. He bounced from his hands to his feet and spun, stabbing his elbows into Sun-Koh's midsection.

Twin hammer-blows crashed down on his back a second later and Jim dropped to the roof, breathing heavily. "Muy-Thai," Sun-Koh murmured, stepping back with several light steps, "A dash of Capoeira, perhaps?"

Jim said nothing as he pushed himself upright. He took a quick step then pushed himself into the air, one leg hooking around, his heel on a collision-course with Sun-Koh's face. Hands caught his foot and ankle and twisted, sending a lightning bolt of pain shooting up Jim's leg as he was slammed into the roof. He twisted frenziedly, trying to scissor Sun-Koh. A piston-like punch caught him between the legs and Jim flopped away, his brain full of stinging hornets of pain.

"Very good," Sun-Koh said genially, circling Jim as he gasped. "Impressive, even. For a barbarian, I mean."

Jim looked up at him through tear-blurred eyes. "I'm not the barbarian here," he coughed.

"I beg to differ my friend," Sun-Koh said, dropping to his haunches. "From where I stand, your whole world is a barbarous one. Full of sound and fury, signifying nothing, to quote one of your better poets."

Jim spat and gathered his legs under him. "Where is Helmut?"

"Safe. Busy as the proverbial bee, in fact." Sun-Koh rose and clasped his hands behind his back. He looked down at Jim. "I'm impressed that you came this far after him."

"He's my friend," Jim said, simply.

"Quaint," Sun-Koh said, looking at him. "Loyalty is a valuable commodity. Speaking of such, I assume Mayen was the weak link, yes?" He shook his head. "I have told him he is far too free with his secrets, but, ah well." Sun-Koh shrugged. "The destruction of his Vienna residence will serve as fitting punishment, I think."

Jim rocked back, resting on his heels. "You blew up his New Jersey place as well." He examined Sun-Koh, trying to spot a flaw in the man's defense. "Losing two houses in two days has got to smart. If I were Mayen, I might be reconsidering my loyalties."

"Heh." Sun-Koh smiled. "Mayen is-and will be-well compensated for his sacrifices." His eyes went vague. "They all will be." He shook himself and focused on Jim. "You could be, as well."

"What?" Jim blinked, taken aback.

"It shows rather more determination than Mayen assured me that you possessed to follow me here, knowing what you obviously know." Sun-Koh sniffed and dislodged a tile with the toe of his boot. "I am superior to you in every way, yet you refuse to give in. Even now, you're feeling me out, trying to spot the chink in the dragon's armor."

"I wasn't raised a quitter," Jim said.

"No. You weren't, were you?" Sun-Koh said, "Unusual circumstances, unusual parents. It makes a potent compound."

"Want to study me?" Jim said, harshly.

Sun-Koh nodded. "Oh yes. I'm fascinated by beings such as you. It's why I had my servants sit this little confrontation out."

"I wondered about that," Jim said, flexing his hands.

"I wanted to see just what you were, and whether my suspicions were correct. I have not been disappointed." Sun-Koh's smile grew. "If only-ah." He waved a hand.

"If only?"

"Join me, as I said. A man like you would be invaluable."

"Never heard myself described in quite that way," Jim said. He rubbed his bruised midsection. "What are you offering me?"

"A truce," Sun-Koh said, "No. Better. Serve me." He held out a hand. "Pledge yourself to me, and in the world to come, you and yours will be among the highest of the high. You will have a place among my paladins."

"The world to come," Jim said, playing for time.

Sun-Koh turned, spreading his arms. "All of this, Mr. Anthony. It's all wrong. It is a mistake, a miscalculation. We called it the Great Mistake." He glanced at Jim. "It is ancient history for you, but right around the corner for me."

"*Der Wurmloch*," Jim said softly, his eyes widening.

Sun-Koh nodded sharply. "Yes!" He reached out, as if to grab Jim's shoulders. "I can correct the Great Mistake. I can return this debased world to its former glory!" He raised his hands and his eyes flashed. "And you can share in that glory!"

"And all I have to do is-what?" Jim looked at Sun-Koh's hand.

"Just take my hand," Sun-Koh said. "Serve me, Mr. Anthony. Jim. And the vast sea of history will part before us and the future will be born again. It will be born better."

Jim was still for a moment. There was persuasiveness to Sun-Koh's words, a sub-vocal trill that caressed the nerve endings and made you want to do as he said. A less aware man might have called it charisma. Jim, however, knew it for what it was. It was a trick, a lie, like the sinuous motion of a cobra. He shook himself and then he gave a bark of laughter. A crooked smile curled across his features and he stood. "Irishmen and Comanche make bad servants, mister. It's just not in our blood, you might say."

"Not even a flicker of doubt?" Sun-Koh said, blinking.

"Not about this." Jim spread his arms. "I'm done talking."

Sun-Koh sighed. "Then, I suppose I am as well." As the last word left his lips, he was moving, his body contorting into some unfamiliar martial style. Jim caught a flurry of blows on his forearms and shins, blocking the swift, stabbing movements with effort. He flipped backwards, avoiding a slicing leg sweep and landed on the peak of the roof. Without pausing he used the momentum to power a wild tackle. His arms wrapped around Sun-Koh and they both fell backward, down and on through the weakened roof!

Struggling, the two men struck a support beam, then fell and hit another, before dropping to the floor twenty feet below. Jim lay flat, his every muscle and joint screaming imprecations at him as he tried to get to his feet. But it was no use. He could only roll weakly side to side. Sun-Koh lay not far away. As Jim watched, horrified, the other man rolled onto his back and pushed himself up with barely a whisper of sound. Then he walked towards Jim, his boots sending up puffs of ash as he moved.

"I so wanted-" Sun-Koh stopped short. "No. It couldn't have been any other way, could it? Neanderthal and Cro-Magnon could no more share the same world than you and I. Still, it was a good effort," Sun-Koh said, looking down at Jim. "But not good enough." He raised a boot and then blackness claimed Jim.

17.

Jim snapped awake and jerked forward. Chains rattled as they brought him up short. He was facing forward, mounted on what might have been either an old torture device or simply an archaic examination table. The table had been tilted to give him a view of the rest of the room, which was cluttered with crates, boxes and barrels.

"So, you're awake then?"

Jim craned his neck. Alaska Jim sat perched on a nearby crate, playing with a big-bladed Bowie knife. As Jim watched he let it drop into the wood, then uprooted it and repeated the process. "Ol' Sun-Koh said you gave him quite the tussle. I can believe it," the mountain-man continued. "Must be the injun in you, cause no Irishman ever fought that hard for nothing that wasn't distilled."

Jim tested his bonds. "Why am I alive?"

"No clue. Maybe he's going soft this close to the end," Alaska Jim said. He spat. "I'd have split your gizzard, myself."

"Of course you would have, must be the white man in you." Jim twisted around. "Where am I?"

"Not forty feet from where you were," Alaska Jim said, hopping down off of his perch. He used the knife to point upwards. "Jan built this here fancy underground bunker a few years ago, just after he met Himself."

"Sun-Koh you mean." Jim didn't wait for the other man to nod. "Brilliant. Simultaneously eliminate your pursuers and hide your true whereabouts. I underestimated him."

"Yeah," Alaska Jim said, drawing close to Jim. He tapped the flat of his knife against Jim's cheek. "I owe you a bit and some change from earlier."

"Why did you give my wife that knife?" Jim said swiftly. The other man blinked and hesitated. Jim pressed on. "And why did you miss your shot? Before, I mean?"

"Wasn't ordered to kill Spengler," Alaska Jim said.

"But you could have killed the man who came to pick him up," Jim said. "Instead, your friend Karsten had to do it. Or to try and do it."

The mountain-man swallowed. "I ain't a killer. I'll gut a man in a fair fight, but I ain't no back shooter." He frowned. "Sun-Koh knows that."

"Does he?" Jim said. Then, "Why are you here?"

"He's here for the same reason I am," a harsh voice said. Otto Karsten lit a cigarette, momentarily illuminating the shadowed corner he'd been occupying. "Got to make sure that *Herr* Sun-Koh's new pet does not get out and ruin the carpets, *nicht war*?"

"You're Karsten," Jim said, slowly. "The one who put my friend in the hospital."

"If by friend you mean the big mick, then yes." Karsten stepped forward and blew a plume of smoke into Jim's face. "Only fair, seeing as he tried his best to do the same to me." His eyes narrowed. "I could have shot him."

"That earns you a head-start," Jim said.

Karsten made a face and looked at Alaska Jim. "What was that about you giving his wife a weapon?"

"Nothing you need to worry about," the big man rumbled, shooting a glare at Jim.

Jim said nothing. While the two men talked, he had been testing the limits of his bonds. The chains were new, but the wooden frame of the rack wasn't. It was downright elderly, in fact, and soft in the way of old wood in a damp environment. The soles of Jim's feet were braced against either side of the frame, and as he pulled his arms down, he pushed his legs back. Even as Alaska Jim turned his attentions back, the wood gave a wet crack and Jim was hurtling forward, his arms crossing in front of him in a motion that sent his chains flying out like bullwhips.

Both men went down in a tangle. Jim fell forward and caught himself on his hands. With a surge of muscle, he turned his momentary handstand into a jump and landed several feet away from his captors, spinning to face them even as Alaska Jim got to his feet with a bellow.

Jim swung his chains, catching the darting blade of the Bowie knife in the links and wrenched it out of the mountain-man's grip. With a snap of his bonds, he sent it sailing into a nearby crate and then swung the links up into his opponent's belly. The big man gave a grunt and dropped. Karsten was up by then, pistol in hand. It spoke, but Jim was already in motion.

He crossed the distance between them in moments and then drove on past the detective before whirling and looping his chains over the man's neck. Karsten gave a strangled squawk as Jim drove a knee into his back and then swung him around to meet Alaska Jim's fist. The mountain man's hard knuckles bounced off his companion's three o'clock shadow and Karsten jerked to the side. Jim slung him around, absorbing a second blow and shoved him forward.

Alaska Jim danced back as Karsten slumped. Jim gave him no time to recover. He charged in and wrapped his chains around one of the big man's fists, then jerked him to the side. Off-balance, Alaska Jim staggered. Jim stamped on his in-step and twisted, heaving his shoulders. With a sickening pop, Alaska Jim's shoulder was dislocated and the big man gave a howl. Jim spun him in a tight circle and released him. As Alaska Jim hit the floor, his wounded shoulder connecting first, Jim kicked his kneecap, popping it and rendering the big man unable to stand.

Then, calmly, Jim swung the chains against the side of the man's head, silencing his cries. Breathing heavily, Jim turned. Karsten was on his hands and knees, his eyes glazed over. Jim straddled him and looped the chains around his neck. Pulling tightly, he said, "Keys."

Karsten clawed weakly at the chain and gargled something. Jim pulled harder. "Keys. Now. Or I forget your head-start."

Karsten fumbled at his coat pocket. Jim released him and the detective fell gasping. Jim pulled a heavy key out of the indicated pocket and unlocked his bonds, letting them drop to the floor. Karsten tried to push himself up, but Jim's foot caught him between the shoulder blades and shoved him back down. "Not so fast."

Jim scooped up Karsten's pistol and swept it across the back of the man's head. Then he wrapped the chain around his wrists and ankles, tying him securely, and relocked them. Tossing the key across the room, he stuffed the pistol into his waistband and snatched up Alaska Jim's knife. He contemplated the wicked blade for a moment. Then, with a grunt of decision, he went to the door.

Opening it, he peered into the corridor beyond. Electric lights lit the passage, but there were no guards in sight. And why should there be? Here, in their very lair? Sun-Koh undoubtedly assumed that his 'paladins' could handle whatever was thrown at them.

Jim closed the door and leaned against it, thinking. His eyes drifted over the crates, and he blinked. A crude idea was forming. Moving quickly, he began to search the crates. There was no telling how much time he had, if any, but he needed a distraction, and a good one.

Skorzeny's group had failed, but if Jim was any judge of character, they were likely a tenacious lot. If Hitler wanted Sun-Koh dead, then Austria's Nazis were likely still on the hunt, which meant they would be looking for some sign of their prey's location.

So why not give it to them? Jim pried apart crates with the help of the knife, hunting for something that could help him do that. He found it a moment later and whistled through his teeth. He'd found a whole straw-packed box full of communication crystals, as well as the tuning device.

Grinning savagely, Jim began to arrange the crystals around the room. Then, he dragged both Alaska Jim and Karsten out into the corridor and set the tuning device to humming. His previous study of the crystals had given him a basic theory of how they worked. Fine-tuning them let you use them to communicate. And simply pouring frequencies into them caused them to explode; but what if the mass frequencies were dispersed through multiple crystals, all resonating with one another in an enclosed environment? Especially if the crystals had been positioned according to a quick and dirty geometric equation that pinpointed how to best use the shape of the room to further amplify the resonation?

Frankly, Jim had no idea. But he was going to find out.

Closing the door, Jim squinted as the high-pitched whine of the crystals caught his ears. The door was already beginning to tremble, ever so slightly. Yielding to a generous impulse, he dragged both men down the corridor a ways before abandoning them. Mercy only went so far, and he had bigger fish to fry.

Padding through the corridor, knife in hand, Jim came to an intersection. Here and there, electrical cables were visible. Jim placed a palm over one, then another, attempting to find the strongest current. Wherever the power was going, that would be where *der Wurmloch*-and by extension, Spengler-would be. Finding the current, he began to follow it. Above him, the lights flickered. Jim began to move faster.

Beneath his feet, the floor began to tremble, softly at first, then more urgently. A wave of sonic distortion crept in his wake. Somewhere far back in the corridor, a light exploded. Jim hurried on.

The elevator sat at the end of the corridor. Jim punched the button. When nothing happened, he pried open the doors and looked down. The cables rattled slightly. He didn't have much time. Stripping his shirt off, he wrapped the tough linen around his hands and placed the knife between his teeth. Then he grabbed the cables and stepped off of the edge.

Slowly, carefully, he climbed down the slippery cables hand under hand. By the time he reached the halfway point, sweat coated his lithe frame and his eyes stung as it dripped down into his face. Ten feet later, he let go of the cable and dropped onto the roof of the car. He paused, waiting. The metal shuddered beneath him and he heard an alarm begin to sound. Ripping off the grate, he dropped into the car. The alarm had become a full-fledged siren now, screeching a warning. The entire bunker felt as if it were shaking to an unheard rhythm. Jim stabbed the knife through the doors and wedged them open. Sticking first an arm, then a shoulder through, he forced the doors fully open and stumbled into the corridor beyond.

The alarm was louder here, howling to wake the damned. Jim found himself on a gantry, overlooking what looked to be some form of underground dock. To his left were stairs, and hurrying up those stairs, a wide-eyed Jan Mayen.

Jim lunged before Mayen had a chance to fully register his presence. Grabbing the smaller man around the throat, Jim shoved him back against the wall and pressed the keen edge of the knife to his throat.

"Hello Jan. Where's Spengler?" Jim growled.

"Anthony!" Mayen sputtered. "What-how-"

"Stop asking stupid questions, and answer mine. Spengler. Where?"

"You-" Mayen began. His eyes widened. "The structural alarm! What did you do?"

"Who knows? That crystal technology of yours is far beyond my primitive understanding, right?" Jim said.

"The crystals?" Mayen gaped. "You didn't-"

From far above came a dull krump. Then another. A third. The lights flickered and spasmed. Beneath their feet, the gantry rattled. "The acoustics in here are wonderful," Jim said, grinning. "Spengler! Now!"

"You don't understand! We have to get out of here!" Mayen said. "You'll bring this whole place down!"

"Then we'd better find my friend quickly, hmmm?" Jim turned Mayen around and stuffed the knife through his belt, replacing it with the pistol. Cocking the automatic, he prodded Mayen back down the stairs. "Let's go, Jan."

#

The dock was a flurry of activity. Automated loading dollies riding on cushions of static electricity hissed across the concrete towards a smooth-shaped vessel resting in the water. Each dolly carried several crates. Jim jabbed Mayen in the kidney with the pistol. "Planning a trip?" Jim said softly.

"Antarctica," Mayen said sourly. "Europe is no longer safe."

"How about that," Jim said. "You made some strides on those electric brains of yours I see." Jim jerked his chin towards a dolly.

"I am a genius," Mayen said. "Case in point, the sub-vocal radio transmitter I have in my right molar." Mayen turned slightly. "Goodbye, Anthony."

"Hands up!" someone bellowed. Jim spun, shoving Mayen down, and crouching. Bullets carved chips out of the concrete. Jim returned fire. A black-clad shape crouched down on a hissing dolly, hunkering behind a crate.

"No! Mayen snarled, getting to his feet. "You idiot! You'll damage the-"

Jim snapped off a kick, booting Mayen backwards."Thank you," Jim said, firing at the crate. It spilled open and the dolly canted with a whine, throwing both crate and rider to the ground. Sturmvogel rolled smoothly to his feet and raised his pistol. Jim put two into the center of his mass, cursing as he heard the bullets thud into the man's bulletproof vest. The impact tossed Sturmvogel backwards nonetheless and Jim whirled as a colorful shape bounded towards him across the tops of the moving line of dollies.

The woman hissed like a snake as she approached. Jim, with only seconds to react, yanked the knife from his belt and hurled it, pinning the edge of the woman's sari to a box just long enough to yank her off-balance. She spun and tumbled, trying to pull the knife free. Jim dropped down beside her and brought his fist crashing against her jaw in a thunderous backhand. The sari tore and she spun. Jim ripped the knife free. A bullet carved a gouge in the box in front of him and he whipped around, hurling the knife. It sheared through the top-hat of the well-dressed man standing behind him.

"You must be Minx," Jim said as the man scrambled for cover. "We haven't been properly introduced yet, I don't believe."

"Nor will you be," the woman said. Jim turned, surprised. A brown foot stabbed towards his chin and he was forced to drop the pistol to grab her ankle with both hands. Without missing a beat, she looped around, her other foot crashing against his shoulder. Jim slammed into another crate, and the dolly skidded backwards. Jim tumbled and the woman was on him a moment later. Stiffened fingers tore holes in the concrete as Jim desperately tried to avoid her blows.

"Those fools failed to deal with you as you deserve," she said, straddling his hips, her thighs locked about his waist with crushing force. "I will not be so merciful!" Black spots danced at the edges of Jim's vision and he bent double, toppling the woman forward. As she reared, Jim swung his hip and locked his ankles around her throat. Her eyes bulged as Jim pulled her head and shoulders down. Her thighs tightened their grip even as Jim bent her spine to the point of breaking.

In the end, it was only Jim's greater strength that enabled him to prevail. She released him abruptly and fell backwards, slithering out of his grip. Torso aching, Jim scrambled to his feet.

"You h-have studied the Forbidden Sutras," the woman coughed.

"Not as well as you," Jim grunted, shaking sweat out of his eyes. The woman stood and sinuously twisted into a fighting stance, arms and legs poised for destruction.

"Let us see," she said, eyes glowing with eagerness.

"No."

Sun-Koh crouched atop a stationary dolly, watching them. Over one broad shoulder was a familiar shape-

"Helmut!" Jim barked.

"Shani, please see to the loading of the vessel. If my calculations are correct, we are running dangerously low on time," Sun-Koh said.

"But-" Shani began.

"Go." Sun-Koh didn't look at her. "The others will help you." His gaze seemed to burn brighter. "Do as I command!"

The woman acquiesced silently, stepping away from Jim. Sun-Koh deposited Spengler onto the ground. He looked at Jim. "She would fight to the death for me, and I do not trust you not to kill her," he said softly.

Jim said nothing, merely raising his fists. The pistol lay nearby, and his eyes flickered towards it. Sun-Koh smiled. "You will not reach it in time."

"Who can say," Jim said.

"I can," Sun-Koh said. "I do. Give up, Jim. You are beaten."

"You sound awfully confident for a man in the process of running away."

"Who said I was running?" Sun-Koh said. "Europe is simply not the place for my plan to be enacted."

"Thule," Jim said. "Is that what's in Antarctica?"

Sun-Koh blinked. "How do you-" His eyes narrowed. "Ah. The Society. Of course."

"It was simple really," Jim said, shifting his weight. "Even if you do what I think you're planning to do, you'll need a staging post. And that's Antarctica. Or Thule, as it was once known. Ultima Thule, the last outpost of fabled Atlantis."

"Not so fabled," Sun-Koh murmured, "And not the last."

Spengler groaned, attracting the attention of both men. "Helmut? Are you okay?" Jim said.

"I-I-*Ja*," Spengler said, sitting up. Sun-Koh reached down and grabbed his collar.

"He remains unharmed so long as I wish it," he said.

"What do you want?" Jim said, taking note of the fuel barrels penned near the water. He shifted his feet, drawing an inch closer to the pistol.

"I want my kingdom back," Sun-Koh said. "The Empire of Mighty Atlantis, once more spanning this barbaric globe." He said it calmly, the way another man might express a desire for a good cup of coffee. As if it was nothing more than his natural right.

"Atlantis," Spengler said. "Is that what-where-you needed me to calibrate the machine for?" He grabbed at Sun-Koh's hand. "What have I done?"

"Simply made it possible for me to reverse the Great Mistake, Professor Spengler," Sun-Koh said, dragging the man to his feet. "And years ahead of schedule, in fact. Why rebuild, when I can reverse?" His eyes burned. "Why re-create what was lost, when I can ensure that it was not lost in the first place?"

"*N-Nein!* This is monstrous! You are mad!" Spengler shouted, struggling. His eyes met Jim's for an instant, and Jim nodded before flinging himself at the pistol. Sun-Koh roared as Jim slid across the floor and grabbed the pistol. He sprang to his feet and fired, but not at Sun-Koh. Rather, Jim fired instead towards the fuel barrels. Sun-Koh's eyes widened as an explosion rocked the dock. From above, the roof gave a groan as whatever process Jim had started above was hastened by the destruction he'd wrought below. More alarms were shrilling now. Jim turned even as Sun-Koh's fist caught him in the chest.

Jim flew backwards, smashing through a crate. Machinery spilled around him as Jim struggled to rise. His hand grabbed something as it rolled under his palm and he shoved it into his pocket without thinking about it. Sun-Koh loomed over him, his shape lit by the eerie glow of the crackling flames. Something crashed into the water behind them as Sun-Koh grabbed Jim by the hair and hauled him up. The giant casually slapped him, and Jim skidded across the ground, head ringing.

"Do you know what you have done?" Sun-Koh said, striding towards Jim, his blue eyes as cold as shelf ice.

"Made your little getaway a tad more difficult," Jim said, rising. Another blow, too fast for his eye to follow, sent him staggering. Something inside him grated painfully. Jim clutched his chest and caught the next blow, shoving it aside. A boot caught him high on the midsection and he fell. Strands of oil crept across the dock and the surface of the water, ridden by eager flames. Jim coughed as smoke tugged at his lungs. A hand caught his throat and he was jerked up into the air.

"Why? Why do you struggle so hard?" Sun-Koh demanded, shaking him. "I only want to make things better!"

Jim's answer was a kick to the chest. He shoved himself out of the other man's grip and landed hard, rolling away from the flames as they licked at him. A boot came down, inches from his head. Sun-Koh made a sound like a berserk panther. Jim caught his foot and tried to pull him down, but a blow to his jaw knocked him sprawling. Sun-Koh came for him again, but a dark shape lunged out of the flames, grabbing his arm.

"Jim-" Spengler began his eyes wide. Snarling in frustration, Sun-Koh whirled, smashing a fist across the little scientist's jaw. Spengler's head snapped to the side with an audible crack, and he fell, limp and unmoving. Sun-Koh stared down at him in shock, his eyes clear.

"I-no, I didn't mean to-"

Jim didn't hear the rest of it. He howled and launched himself at his opponent, crashing into him. Sun-Koh gasped as Jim's fingers dug into the meat of his throat and they staggered back and forth, grappling. After a moment, they broke apart as a curl of flame danced between them and separated them for a moment.

"I didn't mean to kill him," Sun-Koh said, rubbing his bruised throat. "It doesn't have to be like this, Anthony. No one else has to die here! And be sure, one of us will die if this continues."

Jim bared his teeth. "One more or less person dead here doesn't mean a thing," he snapped, raising a hand to shield his face from the flames. "You snuffed his life without hesitation! Is that how your new world will go? Will you blot us out like insects?"

"No!" Sun-Koh said. "I'm not the enemy here! I will bring order to the world! Peace!"

"Slavery," Jim countered. "I know what you're planning. I'll stop you, even if I have to die to do it!"

"We're on the same side!" Sun-Koh said, holding out a hand. "We both want a better world, damn it! Our methods aren't mutually exclusive! We could make this world a paradise! I-NO!"

At Sun-Koh's cry, Jim turned, narrowly avoiding the bullet that caressed the side of his skull; the bullet sped on, cutting through the flames and slapping into Sun-Koh with a sound like a tenderizing hammer slapping a chunk of beef. The golden giant staggered back into the flames, clutching his chest. His eyes were wide with shock. Jim looked around. Sturmvogel, wailing in horror at what he had done, shoved past Jim and went to Sun-Koh's aid as the latter slowly collapsed off of the edge of the dock and into the fiery water. Without hesitation, the black-clad warrior dove into the water after his master.

Jim looked around. The ceiling was bowing inwards from some massive pressure, and the fire was rushing to meet it. He looked down at Spengler, dead. Then, face set, Jim too dove into the water, angling his body away from the flames.

19.

It took Jim six weeks to make it back to New York.

He'd surfaced downriver, carried by the current. By the time he'd made it to shore, police sirens were already wailing in the direction of Mayen's bunker. Jim discovered later that he'd destroyed half a city block as well, and ruptured water lines and gas mains for three. Of the bunker, he heard nothing.

Jim caught sight of someone who might have been Skorzeny once or twice, lurking on street corners and following him at an acceptable distance. Officially, nothing had happened. Even Jim's sources in the Austrian government, of whom there were pitiful few these days, couldn't find anything. Unofficially, someone had slipped a number of photographs under his hotel room door, showing the burnt out remains of the underground dock, as well as the as-yet unidentified body of a man found there.

The vessel, whatever it had been, was gone.

Tempted as he was, Jim didn't stick around to identify the body. Helmut would have understood, he hoped, but he could feel the net closing on him. Not tightly, but surely. Someone wanted answers for what had occurred, but Jim wasn't feeling generous.

He spent the next two weeks criss-crossing Eastern Europe, looking up old friends and making a few new enemies. By the time he reached Budapest, he was ready to go home. A quick stop off in London gave him time to learn that Mayen's London residence had mysteriously been consumed in a blaze a few hours before he'd arrived.

In the time he'd spent recuperating and moving, Sun-Koh's trail had dried up. The destruction of Mayen's last public residence effectively erased all of Jim's leads in one fell swoop. And, frankly, Jim wasn't too broken up about it. He'd suffered numerous first-degree burns, bruises and two broken ribs as well as a host of other ailments. He was in no shape to hunt anyone, especially someone as dangerous as Sun-Koh.

And in truth, Jim kept remembering Sun-Koh's certainty that continued combat between them would result in someone's death. Jim had found that acceptable at the time, in the heat of things, but in the cold light of day, it was a different story. Whatever else he was, Jim Anthony was a survivor. Suicide wasn't high on his list of preferred activities.

So, after six altogether fruitless weeks, Jim Anthony came home. Tom was out of the hospital by then, and spitting mad that Jim had left him behind. Delores and Dawkins had prepared the Pueblo for war, and the latter seemed slightly let down that there was no enemy action expected. Delores, on the other hand, seemed relieved.

"You think he's still alive?" Delores said, later, as they both stood on the balcony of their room at the Pueblo, overlooking the Catskills. The sun was setting, and the mountains were bathed in a beautiful light. Jim hugged her close.

"No idea. I suspect, however, that it'll take more than a bullet to put him down." Jim hesitated. "Regardless, he's done."

"You think?"

"I know," Jim said, reaching into his pocket and depositing a small device on the rim of the balustrade.

Delores peered down at it. "What is that?"

"Not a clue. But it's necessary, I know that much." Jim bounced the object on his palm. "Or it was." He looked out at the mountains. "There was an explosion a few days ago, in Antarctica. A survey team from some university in Massachusetts saw the flare and felt it. It registered with the prototype seismic sensors they were trying out." Jim placed the device back in his pocket. "Possibly, that's the end of it."

Delores snorted. "You don't sound hopeful."

Jim smiled crookedly. "I'm not. Whatever he was trying to do, it was a short-cut to a greater goal. If he survived, then like as not he'll keep going. Keep trying."

"And what will you do?" Delores said carefully.

Jim looked at her. After a moment, he said, "There's a war brewing in Europe. A bad one. Innocent people are caught in the middle. I may have to do something about that."

Delores nodded. "Of course. Granted, you'll have to change your business cards from 'Super-Detective' to 'Super-Man' if you do that." She nudged him with her elbow.

Jim nudged her back. "I think we'll leave that to that fellow in Kansas, hmmm?" He sighed. "Besides, I think I'll be keeping a low profile from now on."

"You? Low-profile?" Delores mimed shock. "Heavens! How will you cope?"

"Quite well, I think." Jim smiled again. "It's about time I retire anyway, don't you think?"

"I may faint."

"I'm simply taking your advice, you know." Jim knocked his knuckles on the balustrade. "I'm getting older, and I'm getting tired of outrunning explosions and having Dawkins practice his battlefield surgery skills on me." He wrapped an arm around her shoulder. "And, it'll be good to spend some time together, uninterrupted." He pressed his face to her hair. "I'm looking forward to a nice quiet time of it, I think."

Delores gave a snort. The snort rapidly became a giggle. Then she was laughing loudly. Jim looked at her in consternation. "What? What did I say?"

Delores looked at him. "I'm pregnant," she said, between sniggers, snorts and guffaws.

Jim blinked. "What?"

Part 3:
'VRIL-YA'

I.

"...so by the time I'd recuperated and was able to get around, Sun Koh had covered his trail with a clinical ruthlessness I was now used to from him. Any and all leads that could have led to Sun Koh were gone. People were dead. Known houses that he and his people had used were burned to the ground." Jim sipped water from a glass before continuing. "But to be honest, I had had enough by then. I'd made up my mind to retire, to come home and stay home and be a full time husband to Delores. When I did get back home and she told me she was pregnant, that cemented my resolve."

Dillon looked over at Vera. "Mrs. Anthony was pregnant with you?"

"No," Vera responded in a voice that made it very clear that this was a line of questioning Dillon would be better off leaving alone. He took the hint.

"So why is this Sun Koh back now? What does he want?"

Jim reached down to the iron box, lifted the lid and withdrew something out of it. He placed it on the table where everybody could see it. "He wants this."

The device Jim had placed on the table could have easily fitted in the palm of Dillon's hand. Magenta in color it was and covered with chalk-white circuitry that might have been taken for ancient runes of some sort. It sat there, the circuitry pulsing softly. And it was humming slightly in a musical tone that uncomfortably sounded too close to singing. Softly, as if trying to sooth a child to sleep. What it sang, Dillon had no idea. But it most definitely sounded to him like singing. "What is it?"

"My research into the history and technology of the Vril-Ya has led me to believe that this is an Aerash Evocation Drive. And this is what Sun Koh needs to make **Der Wurmloch** fully and 100% operational." Jim tapped it slightly. "It's powered by Vril energy."

"Vril energy?" Rubio said. He seemed almost hypnotized by the device.

"Vril energy was the primary power source used by The Vril-Ya. Supposedly they're a race of technologically advanced beings who live in a subterranean kingdom that legend says has its capitol somewhere in Antarctica. This Vril energy has extraordinary capabilities. It can wipe out entire cities if used in a destructive manner. But it can also heal and grant long life. In fact, Sun Koh and his chief aides have used Vril energy to keep their youth and vitality."

"Except for Ashanti, Poppa."

"Ah, yes...Ashanti Garuda drank of the sacred Ayurveda Elixir of Life while still in her twenties and has not aged a day since then. My belief is that no one, not even Sun Koh knows when she actually was born. She is so feared to the extent that many will not even speak her name and call her The Daughter of Kali." Jim looked hard at Dillon. "There is no way to adequately impress how dangerous Ashanti Garuda is. If you meet her, you will die. It's just that simple."

"I'm not unskilled myself. Could be there's a thing or two I could show her."

"Until now you didn't strike me as being stupid," Vera said. "Don't do anything to change my opinion."

Martha now spoke. "Mr. Anthony, I still don't understand why this Sun Koh would pick now to strike at you and get this thing." She gestured at the device.

"I can only surmise that Sun Koh is once again going to try and accomplish his ultimate goal." Jim looked around the table as he spoke, his eyes rested for a time on each face looking back at him. "He's in Antarctica. He's in Ultima Thule, the last outpost of Atlantis. And he's probably built another **Wurmloch.** He's going to use it to reverse what he calls The Great Mistake and restore the lost Empire of Atlantis. That's the only reason he would be after me now."

"He's mad, of course." Vera said.

"Say what you want but Sun Koh is a man of tremendous intellectual and physical power. He's persistent, calculating and above all, patient. He knew I'd never destroy this device or let it fall into the wrong hands. He knew I'd secure it somewhere where no one could get their hands on it. The Aerash Evocation Drive was just as safe in my hands as if it were in his."

"But why didn't you just destroy the thing?" Dillon asked. "Take a hammer to it?"

"There have been several experiments where the United States government attempted to harness Vril energy. None of them ended well. I was at two of those experiments. And both times my recommendation was to stop the experiments. Vril energy is simply too unpredictable to meddle with unless you know precisely what you're doing. Now, it could be that I could just take a hammer to this thing and smash it into a thousand pieces and nothing would happen." Jim leaned forward slightly as he continued. "Or it could be that I would unleash a wave of Vril energy that would vaporize everything for miles around. Or mutate us into hideous creatures out of nightmare. Or—"

"We get the point, Poppa," Vera sighed. She rummaged in a pouch on her belt for cigarettes and took out a pack of Mancinis and lit one. "So what do we do?"

"We make plans," Jim said. "Sun Koh is going to come for this. Next time he may not send just Ashanti. He may send both her and The Storm Bird."

Dillon frowned. "Let me guess…another invincible warrior I would have no chance against?"

"Precisely. Sturmvogel is in his own way as dangerous as Ashanti herself. He's an attack dog in human form."

"I don't understand any of this!" Dillon snapped. "Why are you telling us all this if you plan on lying down and giving up?"

"Did I say I was giving up?"

"It sure sounds like it to me! You keep going on and on about how brilliant and dangerous this Sun Koh is and how his people can't be beaten by us—"

"Not exactly," Vera said. She blew out smoke and pointed her cigarette at Dillon. "Poppa said that *you* can't beat them."

"And I suppose you can!"

Vera smiled sweetly and said nothing.

Jim smacked the flat of his hand on the table for attention. "This is what I'm saying; of course we're not giving up. Sun Koh can't be allowed to get his hands on this device. But he'll never stop coming after us until he gets it. Which means we have to take the fight to him."

"Why don't you just give it to him?" Martha asked. "Mr. Anthony, he'll kill us all for this, correct?"

"If he has to, yes."

"Then give it to him!"

"You can't be serious," Rubio said.

"You can't expect me to believe that he can use this thing to turn back time or raise Atlantis or whatever lunacy infects his diseased brain! Just give him the damned thing!"

"Martha, how long have you known me?" Jim asked. "All your life, correct? In all that time have I ever lied to you?"

"No."

"Then why would I lie now? Trust me when I say that Sun Koh can do what he says if he gets his hands on this."

"And I don't want to die! Haven't you seen enough of your people killed already? Do you want to get yourself killed as well?"

"Of course not. But if Sun Koh accomplishes his goal all of us will be dead. The only way to stop him is to take the fight to him." Jim rubbed his left cheek absently. "Vera, can you get a line on his people? The way to find Sun Koh is to find his paladins. Most likely he's got them in the field doing his work while he stays in the background, planning and plotting."

Vera stood up. "You give me the descriptions of his people and I'll get the machinery working. If they're out there, I'll find them."

Martha pushed her chair away and left the building, Rubio following closely behind her, mumbling in her ear. Dillon also stood up and came closer, never taking his eyes off of the Aerash Evocation Drive. He couldn't be sure and he didn't want to say anything out loud but he could have sworn the thing had subtly and slightly changed its shape since Jim had placed it on the table.

"You do know she's in love with you, don't you, Poppa?" Vera said, blew out more smoke. "Has been for some time now."

"I'm old enough to be her father," Jim replied.

"Grandfather, actually. But I'll allow you your vanity this one time as we've got more important things to think about. But you should sit down and talk with her." Vera wagged her head at Dillon. "Come on with me, Boy Wonder. Let me teach you something."

"Just a minute, Vera." Dillon moved closer to Jim. "Look, if I'm going to work with you on this thing then you've got to trust me as much as I'm trusting you. No, I don't have anywhere near your experience but I've been in a few tight spots since leaving Shamballah. More than you can imagine. And I've come out of them with a whole skin. I've had people trying to kill me ever since I was a kid. I've survived against them and I can survive against this Sun Koh and anything or anybody he throws at me."

Jim Anthony looked up at Dillon, looked deep into his eyes and surprise tingled his spine.

Dillon's eyes were no longer the sparkling copper they usually were. They had darkened to a moody, molten gold that radiated pure, primal rage.

Jim stood up slowly and extended his hand. "Yes. I do believe that you can."

Dillon took Jim Anthony's hand and they shook firmly.

"Thank you, Mr. Anthony."
"Call me Jim."

Dillon didn't turn around as Vera Gemini came up behind him. She sat down cross-legged next to him on the warm flat rock overlooking the complex of buildings that was The Pueblo. "What are you doing sitting up here wasting time?" Vera asked.

Dillon shrugged. "Not much else for me to do, is there? Your father pulled a laptop out of somewhere and he's busy working on that. You were off doing whatever it is you do. Martha doesn't want to talk to me and Rubio is seeing to his people." He held up the book Jim had given him. "And I'm not wasting time. I figured I'd take your father's advice and do my homework." Dillon cocked his head as he said, "Which brings up a question I've been dying to ask ever since I met you. Exactly who *are* you and who or what are *Les Vampires*?"

"They began as an *Apache* gang in Paris. You know about French *Apache*?"

Dillon nodded.

"The history of *Les Vampires* begins back in the early 20th Century. Thanks to the brilliance and daring of the first Great Vampire and his paramour, the first Irma Vep, *Les Vampires* grew from being a petty street gang into the most feared criminal organization in France. My mother was the second Irma Vep and my entire upbringing from the moment I was born was designed with her single obsessive goal that I would take over from her one day. My mother seduced Poppa as physically and intellectually he was the most perfect man she knew. Genetically she wanted her child to be as close to perfect as possible. And she didn't want me to just be the paramour of The Great Vampire as she and her mother had been. She intended for me take over as The Great Vampire and run the the vast worldwide criminal organization that *Les Vampires* had grown into over many years. It now operated on a global level and the next Great Vampire had to be as exceptionally skilled as possible to see to it that the organization continued into the 21st Century and beyond. World class experts in thievery and martial arts were my teachers. Tutors in science and the arts were my constant companions. When I was older, other experts were brought in to teach me...other disciplines."

"So you're the leader of a gang of thieves? Is that it?"

"I rejected the teachings of my mother. I searched for my father and found him. With his help I broke away from her and went to work for a private detective named Nestor Burma. He taught me a lot about the world and the art of private detecting. But I always had it in the back of my mind that if properly used, *Les Vampires* could do a lot of good in the world, maybe make up for some of the misery and suffering they had caused. With Poppa's help I wrested control of *Les Vampires*, became The Great Vampire and now *Les Vampires* serve me."

Dillon sighed and said again; "So you're the leader of a gang of thieves? Is that it?"

Vera gave him a look that plainly communicated she was losing patience with him. "*Les Vampires* is an international organization that developed a vast network that crossed borders around the world. It moved weapons, guns, drugs, girls, anything that made an illegal dollar. With my father's assistance I was able over time to change that without my own people noticing."

"Noticing what?"

"Say I was moving a shipment of drugs like heroin or cocaine. I would hide it in a shipment of legal drugs that was vitally needed in that area. Every shipment moved I would increase the volume of legal drugs and reduce the number of illegal drugs so that eventually, the shipment was completely legal. I did the same thing with guns. The human trafficking I had to take more drastic measures with."

Dillon did not ask what those measures were. "So you're telling me that now *Les Vampires* is a completely legal operation?"

"No. It's never going to be that. Our roots are too deeply entrenched in crime to ever be completely legal. We still indulge in blackmail, theft, grand larceny, crimes of that nature. But I make sure that we only rob from the people who need robbing."

"And then you give to the poor?"

"Absolutely not. We keep it. We've got expenses you know."

"Then what's the point? You're still criminals."

Vera looked for her cigarettes, found them and lit one up. "You ever hear of Woody Guthrie, Dillon?"

"No. I don't think so."

"There's something he said once that I think sums up what people like me and to an extent, my father do. He said that he loved a good man outside the law just as much as he hated a bad man inside the law. I think that if you do this work long enough, you'll come to understand exactly what that means."

"He said that he loved a good man outside the law just as much as he hated a bad man inside the law."

Dillon sat there, waggling the book slightly as he thought over what Vera had said. "Maybe I should reserve judgment on what it is that you do until I know more about what it is that you do."

Vera winked. "Maybe you should."

"So do you have any brothers or sisters? Since Jim didn't tell me about you I hardly think he would tell me about any other children."

Vera's face hardened as she looked away. "I have a half-brother and half-sister. They don't acknowledge my existence and I return the favor."

"Does Jim?"

"Magee is the CEO of his company and runs it for him. They have what I call an amicable arraignment. Jim, Jr. is another matter."

Dillon said, "and that matter is—"

Her smartphone beeped for attention. "You'll have to ask Poppa about that. I've said too much as it is." She unclipped it from her belt and looked at the screen. "Data coming through. Looks like my people have found at least two of Sun Koh's agents."

"That quickly?" Dillon asked, plainly impressed. "It's only been a couple of hours since Jim gave you the descriptions."

"We don't play games in this business, Boy Wonder. Getting the correct intelligence as soon as possible can mean the difference between life and death. Mainly your own." She tapped several buttons. "There. I sent it to Poppa's laptop. He'll let us know what we're going to do after he evaluates it."

"What do you think that'll be?"

Vera looked out over the expanse of desert, smoking quietly. "Whatever it is, it's not going to be nice. Make no mistake…we're going to get bloody before this is over. Very bloody."

Z.

"These are the agents of Sun Koh currently in Buenos Aires," Jim said. He turned his laptop around so that Dillon, Vera, Martha and Rubio could see as he continued the briefing. The screen displayed side-by-side images of two men. The one on the left showed a man with a scarred face that might have been chiseled out of granite. A military alpine hat sat atop his head.

"The one on the left is Rudolf Rauhaar alias Rolf Kraft and mostly known as Sturmvogel. The man's as close to the perfect soldier as there is. He's equally at home in the desert as the jungle. Put into his hands a weapon he's never seen before and in ten minutes he'll have mastered it. Where Shani is Sun Koh's scalpel, Sturmvogel is his broadsword."

Jim pointed at the man on the right. This one had a thin face with cruelty in the eyes. A stingy brimmed hat sat cocked insolently on one side on his head. "This is Rolf Karsten. In his day he was the most feared private detective in Berlin. His nickname back then was 'The Terror.' There wasn't anything he wouldn't do to solve a case. Good with his fists, knife or gun. And he's got a natural talent for analyzing physical and psychological behavior he then turns into an advantage. He's a man you don't want getting into your head, trust me."

"What about Sun Koh himself?" Rubio asked. "Do you have a picture of him?"

"I can't find any," Jim replied. "And believe me, I tried. But I can draw a sketch of him. He's not a man you forget, trust me on that. But you won't have to worry about that. You're not going with us."

"You can't go without me, Jim!" Martha shouted, leaping to her feet. She caught herself and said quickly, "I mean, you can't go without us!"

"Dillon and Vera will be coming along with me along with Vera's Vampires. You will stay here and see after our people. You know where the planes are kept at the hidden airfield. Take them away from here. Sun Koh has his resources just as I do. He'll send his people here. I judge we have maybe another day, two at the most of safety and then we must be away. Dillon, Vera and I head south."

"If these people are as dangerous as you keep insisting they are, then you have no business going near them!" Martha insisted. "Mr. Anthony, how long has it been since you've been in a fight? A real fight? Fifteen years, twenty?"

"In fact, I was just in a couple of real fights, as you put it. Remember? A gang of armed men tried to kill me at my penthouse and at The Teepee. I didn't do so bad against them." Here he gave Dillon a sidewise glance and winked. "And it's not like I haven't been keeping my combat skills sharp. I do more than my share of practice."

"It isn't the same and you know it! You need to turn this over to others who are more capable of handling this matter!"

"Someone younger, you mean."

"Of course I do! You intend to go on with this foolish course of action backed up by an untrained boy—"

"Hey!" Dillon yelped.

"—and a glorified second story thief!"

Vera lit up a cigarette and said nothing.

"Rubio and I are young and well trained! You trained us yourself! Surely we would—"

"You've heard my wishes on this matter, Martha. I don't intend to repeat myself. Vera and Dillon will come with me. You and Rubio will look after our people and see to their safety."

Martha stood there, visibly trembling, biting her lower lip to hold back the angry hot words she wanted to give voice to. She abruptly turned, knocking her chair over and it hit the floor with a bang as loud as a gunshot. She left the building, slamming open the door and leaving it open as she exited.

Jim sighed. "Rubio—"

Rubio lifted his hands, palms outward as he pleaded; "Please, Mr. Anthony...I tried to talk to her before and she nearly bit my head off. Please don't ask me to go through that again."

Jim looked at Vera. "Would you—"

"Nope."

Jim sighed again. "I'll have to talk to her, then."

"Which is what you should have done in the first place." Vera stood up. "I'll go get the plane ready."

"There's something I want you to do for me first," Jim said. He gestured at Dillon. "Take our young friend to the shooting range and school him on firearms. I had to give him a crash course back at The Teepee and he did very well but he needs proper instruction. I'd do it myself but I have people to contact and let them know that Sun Koh is back in action.."

"I don't need it," Dillon quickly put in. "I hate those smelly, noisy things."

"Then you stay here," Jim said flatly. "Our enemy is going to have guns. Plenty of them and they have no problems using them. You go on a mission with me you go prepared or you don't go. It's up to you."

Dillon saw the look on Jim's face and nodded sharply. "Very well."

"Come on, then" Vera jerked her head at the door. "Let's go shoot something."

"You know your martial arts so you know how to take a front stance. You grasp the gun like *so*. Loosen up. Loosen up! Hold it tightly but don't strangle the gun. It's your friend. Here, move like this. Get your body weight behind the gun to control the recoil. Keep the sight straight in line. When you squeeze the trigger you want to be smooth and even. The point is not to pull the muzzle off target so that you lose time bringing it back to re-aim at your target. Okay, let him have it."

Dillon squeezed the trigger of the Jericho 941 and sent fifteen 9mm bullets toward the distant Thug With A Handgun Target commonly used by law enforcement agencies. When the clip was empty, Vera and Dillon walked down to check it. She examined it with approval. "Ten hits at one hundred yards. Three of them definite kill shots. Very good."

Dillon hefted the gun, looking down at it with obvious distaste. "I've run across men who have valued these things more than they value their own families. Why? It takes no skill or talent to use them."

"For some it does." Vera removed the old target and put up a new one as she spoke. "And guns are a tool, nothing more. They're just as useful in their own way as the swords and knives and other bladed weapons you've become proficient with."

"But those weapons take true skill and discipline to use."

They began their walk back to the firing line while Vera continued. "Same thing with a gun. You learn how to use it properly and it can be a powerful tool to intimidate, injure or disable. You don't have to kill with it every time you draw it. But it certainly helps if the other person thinks that's what you intend."

"I don't think I'll ever think that way," Dillon insisted.

They stopped at the firing line. "Okay, let's do fifteen out of fifteen. Go!"

Dillon's hands came up with the Jericho and the air filled with the booming of the weapon's fire.

They walked down to the target and Vera sucked her teeth in annoyance.

"Seven hits! And only two of them a kill! What happened?"

Dillon waggled the gun in his hand. "It just doesn't feel right, is all! You just can't expect me to suddenly take to a weapon that is so unfamiliar and foreign! I—"

"Hey, hey...take it easy! This is supposed to be fun, you know. Here, turn around." Vera reached up and sunk her thumbs into the base of Dillon's neck. "You're wound up tighter than an eight day clock." Her slim fingers that looked so deceptively frail worked Dillon's tightened shoulder and neck muscles with a strength than soon eased them and relaxed them.

"Hey...that's...really good..." Dillon murmured.

"Remember when I told you that my mother had many experts in many disciplines train me? Many of those disciplines didn't have anything to do with violence." Vera's voice softened as her fingers continued working. Tensed muscles softened and a gentle warmth spread through his torso. At the same time Vera worked his muscles. "The various methods of massage and acupressure...especially those designed to provoke certain... responses..." and now Vera Gemini's voice had become playful. Her hands slid down Dillon's muscular back, still massaging, still relaxing.

The gun slipped from Dillon's hand, thudded to the ground. His eyes were half closed as he let that wondrous warmth continue to spread through his body. "Vera...I don't think..."

"Stop thinking."

"But...your father..."

Vera's hands continued to move along his body and his breathing deepened.

"What about him?"

Dillon turned around and looked deep into her eyes which were now large seductive pools of promise.

"Oh, the hell with it," he said in a voice suddenly thick with passion and wrapped Vera in his arms, kissing her with a savage grace that she easily matched.

Jim walked to the firing range, impressed by what he was hearing and when he came up behind Dillon he became even more impressed. Dillon had Jerichos in both hands, firing at two targets with an accuracy that bordered on genius. If the targets had been men, they'd have both been dead in seconds.

Vera stood off to one side, smiling broadly, smoking.

"I'm very pleased, Vera. I give you a novice and you hand me back a marksman."

Dillon stopped firing, walked over to them and handed the weapons to Vera, smiling at her in a way he had never seen Dillon smile.

"You really want to see something?" Vera asked. She reloaded one weapon and reached into a pouch on her belt. She withdrew a ten dollar roll of quarters and unwrapped it. She spilled the shiny coins into her hand as Dillon reloaded one of the weapons. "You ready?" she asked him.

He nodded, stepped back, shaking his arms to loosen up.

"Two dollars and twenty-five cents," Vera said as she tossed the handful of quarters high up into the air. Dillon's arm went up and the Jericho boomed, silver sparks striking from the quarters that were hit by the bullets. The coins fell to the ground. Jim walked over to where they had fallen, bent down and picked up the ones hit by the bullets, bent from the impact. He brought them back to where Vera and Dillon stood, the coins in his wide, dark palm.

"Well?" Dillon asked.

"Two dollars and twenty-five cents exactly," he confirmed. He looked at Vera. "I'm astounded. What's the secret?"

"No secret," Vera answered. "Poor boy just needed to relax is all."

Jim, Vera and Dillon returned to The Pueblo to find the place in an uproar. Rubio had returned just before they did. He lay on a couch in Jim's quarters, his face battered and bruised. Several of Jim's people tended to other, minor wounds on his arms and legs. Upon seeing Jim enter, he insisted on getting to his feet. Dillon moved forward to help him stand.

"Mr. Anthony, I tried to stop her! I swear I did! I didn't know she was going to do it!"

"Do what? Tell me."

"Martha's gone crazy! She said she had to save you from yourself, that you were going to get yourself killed, that you weren't thinking straight—"

"You're not making much sense yourself," Vera snapped. "Calm down and tell Poppa what happened."

Rubio visibly got himself under control then spoke in a more controlled, quieter voice. "Martha took the Gulfstream. I tried to stop her. We fought and you see how that turned out. She said that you weren't thinking straight and that she had to stop you from getting yourself killed." And here Rubio looked at Vera. "She said you would understand."

Jim walked over to where the iron box sat on the ground in a corner and opened it. "The Evocation Drive is gone," he reported. "Martha?"

Rubio nodded miserably. "She said she was going to fly down to Buenos Aires and give it to those men. She said if she did that they would leave you alone."

"Misguided little fool!" Jim growled.

"I knew she had it bad for you but I didn't think it was quite that bad," Vera said. "We going after her, Poppa?"

"Of course we are. Rubio, can you fly the others out of here? I don't want anybody left here that will be harmed—" Jim stopped as Rubio started shaking his head in a negative. "Why? What—" "Martha disabled the other two planes so we couldn't use them. The only thing that will fly is Miss Vera's cargo."

Despite his anger, Jim had to admire her planning. "Clever. Martha knows I won't leave our people here so we'll eat up valuable time taking them to safety and giving her even more of a head start."

"Why didn't she disable Vera's plane as well?" Dillon asked.

"My Vampires are on my plane. Little Miss Martha knew better than to even set foot on my plane without permission. Besides, her purpose wasn't to strand us here with no way out, just slow us up."

"Agreed. Let's get moving. We've got to get these people to safety and then we're going south. I only pray we can head off Martha before she reaches Sturmvogel and Karsten."

3.

Dillon had never been to Buenos Aires before and during the drive from the private airport to the hotel Vera had secured lodging for them he got a good look at it. He was glad they had arrived early in the day so he could take in the European flavor and style of architecture. Even the hyper modern, futuristic skyscrapers appeared to have been constructed with an eye toward the past.

Shortly after they had landed, Vera had assembled her Vampires and issued instructions via whistles. The Vampires left the plane, scattering in seconds across the tarmac, scuttling up the sides of the hangar, storage facilities and support buildings, disappearing like smoke.

"Where are they going?" Dillon asked.

"Scouting," was all Vera would say. Aboard the plane was a midnight black Buick Enclave that Jim had packed with duffle bags of weaponry and equipment. Vera took the wheel and they drove off. The plane's ramp closed by remote control.

"Where are we staying?" Jim asked.

"A small hotel near the Puerto Madero. We won't attract any attention there unless we want it. Once my Vampires have picked up the scent and nailed down a location for Sturmvogel and Karsten we can plan our attack strategy."

Jim nodded in satisfaction as he enjoyed the ride. "Been a long time since I was down here."

"It's a beautiful city," Dillon agreed. "I wish I had time to see more of it."

"Hopefully we'll survive this and you can take a proper tour of South America one day," Jim said. "But surviving is the trick. I just hope we can find Martha before Sturmvogel and Karsten get their hands on her."

"Given time, my Vampires can find anybody, Poppa."

Jim turned to look back out the window. "Yes," he murmured. "Time. That's always the problem, isn't it?"

Hearing the knock on his door, Dillon rolled smoothly out of bed. He hadn't been sleeping but in a light meditative trance. It refreshed him totally in mind and body but he had entered into it for far more than that. Ever since meeting Jim Anthony and his mercurial daughter he'd been letting his emotions go this way and that. It wasn't something he was comfortable with. And what would happen between him and Vera now? What would she expect from him? Since leaving Shamballah he'd been very careful not to get involved in emotional entanglements. Oh, he'd had dalliances here and there but that's all they were. He had no place in this world yet, hadn't even begun to make one and he had no idea if Vera expected that place to be with her.

Dillon opened the door. Jim Anthony stood there, grim-faced. "Get dressed. Vera's Vampires have found our prey."

Dillon nodded. "Five minutes."

"Meet me in my room."

It didn't take Dillon long to get dressed. Jeans, sneakers and T-shirt. In three minutes he stood in front of Jim's door, knocking. Jim opened the door.

Vera sat in a chair, conferring with one of her Vampires. It was impossible to tell if it were male or female in the head-to-toe black outfit. The Vampire perched on the back of a chair like a huge vulture, so perfectly balanced that the chair did not tip over. Vera and the Vampire conversed in soft whistles. She turned to Dillon and Jim. "Sturmvogel and Karsten are holed up in a warehouse about ten miles from here. No sign of Martha. If we leave now we can take them by surprise."

"Maybe they know we're here?" Dillon asked.

Vera shook her head. "From what my Vampires tell me, they don't act like it. They're coming in and out of the warehouse far too casually to be on the alert. I think we're ahead of the opposition for once. My Vampires are watching the place."

Jim issued swift orders. "Inform them to continue to watch the place closely but take no action against Karsten or Sturmvogel but if either or both of them leave, follow them wherever they go. But if they see Martha they are to capture her at once and hold her for me."

Vera nodded, turned back and whistled to the Vampire who whistled in response and then was gone out the window so quickly that Dillon blinked in surprise.

Jim nodded. "Okay. Let's go work."

They went to the hotel's garage and Vera drove the Buick. She had explained to Dillon that the vehicle had been customized so that it was a rolling fortress. It could withstand anything up to and including a rocket launcher. Jim half turned in the front seat to talk to Dillon. "You'll hang back. Under no circumstances are you to engage either Karsten or Sturmvogel. And especially not Sturmvogel."

"I don't run from a fight."

"You won't have to. Sturmvogel never travels without at least of dozen soldiers he's trained himself. Trust me, you'll have your hands full with them. Vera and I will deal with Karsten and Sturmvogel."

Dillon nodded. "Fair enough."

Jim passed back a belt with a holstered Jericho and a combat knife. "My hope is to take one or both of them alive and force them to tell us where Sun Koh is. The quicker we bring this to a conclusion, the better."

Vera stopped the vehicle and pointed. "There's the warehouse."

The warehouse occupied an entire block. Two stories tall, it had been painted an atrocious lime-green. Jim examined the building with binoculars while Vera contacted her Vampires who were in hiding, watching the warehouse. She said to her father, "Karsten came back about ten minutes ago with Martha. No sign of Sturmvogel or anybody else."

"I don't like it," Jim said. "I wish we could wait until night but we can't. We've got to go in now."

"This doesn't feel right, Poppa."

"No, it doesn't. But we don't have much of a choice. How do we get in?"

"Service entrance on the west side of the building. My Vampires have already secured it. They say there's no booby traps, alarms or guards."

"Why don't they just put out a welcome mat saying 'come on in'?" Dillon muttered. "We just going to walk in like they obviously want us to?"

"We are," Jim said. "Vera, you find another way in. Dillon and I get captured or run into more opposition than we can handle, you're the cavalry."

Vera nodded.

Jim climbed out of the vehicle and walked toward the warehouse, followed by Dillon who buckled the belt around his waist and draped his T-shirt over it so that it wouldn't alarm passers-by.

The two men walked past small coffee shops, restaurants and modest office buildings. Not far away on their right they could see the waterfront. Jim and Dillon approached the west side of the warehouse. The loading dock was deserted. Steep stone steps led up to the service entrance and the warehouse office. Jim motioned for Dillon to hang back as he led the way. Jim opened the office door. Nothing inside but a chair. Jim's nostrils flared. A slight odor of bacon and cheese. Someone had been here not long ago, eating.

They left that office, entered another, larger one. Several wooden crates resting on pallets were stacked in a corner. Jim examined the door carefully before opening it. A long flight of metal stairs went up to the second floor. Jim's hands went into his pockets, withdrew something, Dillon couldn't tell what it was. Jim whispered without turning around; "when you see me move, close your eyes." He followed closely, wishing that something, *anything* would happen.

And when it did, he would never make that wish again.

Upon reaching the second floor landing, hidden men came out of the storeroom they had been hiding in and crept up the stairs behind Jim and Dillon. The second floor blazed into sudden illumination as strong lights were turned on. To reveal the blood-freezing sight of Martha strung up by her heels, hanging ten feet above the concrete floor. Dillon had to look away. Judging from the final expression on her face, Martha had not died well.

Karsten himself emerged with half a dozen men sliding out of the shadows to cover Jim and Dillon with their weapons. The picture Dillon had seen on the laptop did not do justice to the cruelty in Karsten's face now that he saw it for real. Karsten lazily held a silver-plated automatic in his hands, supreme in his confidence that they were in control of the situation.

"Jim Anthony. When Shani told me you were back in the game I could hardly believe it. I fully expected you to be content staying retired."

"I was," Jim said quietly. His eyes were on the slowly twisting body of Martha. "Your work?"

"Me? Nooooo…Shani reserved that honor for herself." Karsten gestured at Martha's body with the automatic. "Can you believe the silly girl actually thought she could bargain for your life? She said you were a deluded old man who didn't know what you were doing. Said that if we promised to leave you alone she'd give us the Aerash Evocation Drive." Karsten laughed softly, showing very white teeth in a very red mouth. "Ignorant child. I actually think she was in love with you, Anthony. Naturally Shani killed her and recovered our master's property. It was fun to watch, actually. I always appreciate watching Shani work." Karsten looked at Dillon with interest. "And who's this? Some new pet you've adopted?"

"A pet who's going to break your neck, Karsten," Dillon said through teeth clenched so hard the hinges of his jaw ached. "You didn't have to kill Martha. She was harmless."

"Anyone who involves themselves in the affair of our master is not harmless and suffers the consequences of doing so."

"Where is the Evocation Drive, Karsten?" Jim asked in a voice strangely calm.

"On its way to our master as it should be. We knew you'd be following the girl so we arranged for this reception. It will be my honor to dispatch you once and for all. It should have been done years ago if you—"

Jim threw the objects in his closed hands onto the floor. Dillon covered up and closed his eyes as the chemicals in the spheres mixed together to create a powerful flare that overloaded the optic nerves of everybody in the room. Karsten cursed, fired his gun as his other men did so, firing wildly at the last place they saw Jim and Dillon standing.

Neither man was still there, naturally. Both of them moved with terrible swiftness, weaving in and out of Karsten's men with surety and economy of movement, striking with precision and skill. Karsten's men weren't soldiers, simply local criminals he had hired and against men with the training Jim Anthony and Dillon had, they had no chance.

But the men pounding up the staircase *were* trained soldiers and as they entered the second floor, the flare died away.

'Died' being the operative word here because as Dillon looked, slim black forms seemed to appear out of the shadows. Thin ebony razors in the hands of *Les Vampires* made whickering noises as they sliced through the throats of the soldiers and in brief seconds, six dead soldiers joined the unconscious men Jim and Dillon had already laid low.

Dillon went over to where the rope binding Martha's feet had been tied to a handle on the wall. He untied it and slowly lowered her body into Jim's waiting arms. Dillon looked around for Karsten's body. "Where is he?"

"The slippery bastard moved as soon as I did. He talks too much but he's no fool. And he saw no reason to stick around and fight it out with us. He did his job." Jim stroked Martha's cheek tenderly and kissed her forehead. He gently closed her eyes. "But that doesn't mean he's not going to die for this. They all will."

"Then I suggest we get a move on," Vera said from the staircase. "The Garuda woman's in a car, hightailing out of here like her ass is on fire. She must have the Drive. If we hurry—"

"Say no more," Jim laid Martha down and got to his feet.

"You can't just leave her here!" Dillon insisted.

Vera whistled and two of her Vampires gently lifted Martha's body. "They'll see to her. C'mon!"

Vera led the way down the stairs, following closely by Jim, who was so focused on the hunt he did not sense the massive form that slammed a fist against the side of his head. He went tumbling over and over, stunned from the sheer force of that sledgehammer blow. He recovered and rolled smoothly to his feet, clearing his head, looking at the huge seven foot tall man advancing on him. Vera stepped in between the man and her father, her hands going to her holstered guns.

Dillon leaped on the man's back and they both hit the ground hard. Over his shoulder Dillon yelled, "Go get Ashanti! I got this!"

Vera nodded and ran over to Jim, "Come on, Poppa!"

"No! That's Sturmvogel! Dillon can't take him! He'll kill him!"

Vera shook Jim hard enough to make his teeth click together. "Then he gets killed and we mourn! But right now Ashanti is our business! Leave Dillon to his!"

Jim swallowed hard and followed his daughter.

Dillon and Sturmvogel got to their feet, Dillon stepping back to take him in. And he was a lot to take in. An even seven feet tall, dressed in black fatigues, black combat boots and a black alpine military hat he stood there like a living tombstone, his eyes radiating quiet authority and total menace.

"This is your lucky day," Sturmvogel said in a voice like two bricks being rubbed together. "I will be satisfied with having the great Jim Anthony run away from me. Go on back to wherever it is you come from, boy. I only kill men."

"So do I," Dillon replied.

Sturmvogel's eyes opened wider in surprised amusement. "You have heart. That is good. But heart is not enough."

"We gonna fight or what?"

Without another word Sturmvogel exploded into action and incredibly for such a big man seemed to levitate as he came off the ground with an agility more appropriate for an Olympic gymnast. The sheer speed and power of his attack completely took Dillon by surprise as he planted his size sixteen boot square in the middle of Dillon's chest.

Dillon flew backwards as if hit by a shotgun blast into a wall. He hit the ground heavily, fighting to draw air in his lungs, wheezing with the effort. But he sprang to his feet to meet Sturmvogel's next charge.

Again, Sturmvogel took him totally by surprise a move somebody that big shouldn't have been able to do that fast; a spinning back kick to the chest that again sent Dillon to the ground and now his entire torso was one just one big throb of pain.

Sturmvogel didn't give him time to recover, either. He ran over to where Dillon lay, his foot came up and then down, intending to stomp Dillon's head into jelly. Dillon rolled out of the way barely in time as the foot smashed downward.

Dillon flipped to his feet, coming back at Sturmvogel with a series of sidekicks, backing up the bigger man as Sturmvogel blocked the first three kicks. But the fourth one never landed as he simply seized hold of Dillon's leg and threw him across the warehouse as if he were a sack of trash. Dillon hit some stacked wooden crates, hardly able to believe he was being treated as if he were no more than a misbehaving child. Fueled now by rage, he grabbed one of the crates and chucked it at Sturmvogel, cords of muscles thick as round files standing out on his arms and shoulders.

The Storm Bird simply punched the crate. It burst apart like a water balloon, the contents inside pulverized into pieces that flew in all directions as if a hand grenade had went off inside of it. Dillon gawped. He was beginning to understand at last that Jim Anthony hadn't been exaggerating when he described how dangerous this man was. Dillon tried to get past him, to the door Jim and Vera had used to leave. Maybe if he could get outside, get some room-

Then Sturmvogel was right there in front of him, again having moved with uncanny speed. Sturmvogel's massive arm came out and around in a left hook that would have done to Dillon's head what it did to the crate if Dillon had stayed there. He ducked and once again tried to make a dash for the door and once again Sturmvogel blocked his way. The Storm Bird smiled. "It is too late for that, my friend. Far too late." The Storm Bird's smile widened into a grin. "You may actually be worth killing."

Dillon charged Sturmvogel. The giant's arm shot out in a straight punch but again, Dillon wasn't there. He threw himself under the punch, slid right through the gap between Sturmvogel's legs and by the time Sturmvogel turned around, he was out the door and running flat out.

He heard the door shatter behind him as Sturmvogel pursued, bellowing his rage. Dillon leaped off the loading platform, hit the dock and ran, turning the corner and going flat out down the street, weaving around amazed pedestrians.

Sturmvogel wasn't as gentle. He simply swatted people out of his way as he pursued and soon a trail of injured, battered men and women were left in his wake. One man he hit so hard that unfortunate actually somersaulted up twice in the air before coming back down, crashing onto the roof of a car. The windows burst into thousands of sparkling bits as the alarm blared.

Dillon came to an outdoor café and instead of going around the tables, simply monkey vaulted over them, not heeding the cries and curses of the shocked café patrons as their drinks and food was sent flying. But it couldn't be helped. If he was to have any chance to survive against Sturmvogel he was going to have to have room. In any enclosed area, Dillon would have no chance at all.

But for right now then main thing was to gain some distance so he would have time to formulate a plan of attack and then-

-Dillon rounded the corner and there Sturmvogel stood, grinning as if he'd just heard the funniest joke ever told.

Igosalek ortorli! Dillon thought; *where did he come from! He was behind-*

And then there was no more thinking as Dillon defended himself from the blizzard of punches Sturmvogel threw at him. Punches powered by arms as solid and thick as the rafters of ancient German drinking halls. But Dillon compensated as he had to punch *up* to reach his target and he was rewarded by a solid blow to Sturmvogel's right cheek that snapped the bigger man's head back.

Sturmvogel's shrugged it off and he came back in, all attack and no defense, his arms and his knees a blur. Dillon allowed the knee strikes to his already sore ribs so that he could deflect those devastating punches he knew would take his head off if he allowed them. He blocked out the screams of the citizenry as they scattered in all directions, running as fast and as far away as they could from the two huge men who apparently seemed interested only in battering each other to death.

Sturmvogel charged Dillon, picked him him up and slammed him against the brick wall of a drugstore. Dillon brought his right elbow down again and again on Sturmvogel's back, taking a savage satisfaction in hearing a sharp cracking sound with the fourth strike. *The animal CAN be hurt! He's human! Da-*

Sturmvogel roared as he backed up, seized Dillon by clothes and flesh with such force that Dillon had to scream. Sturmvogel lifted him up and slammed him back against the wall so hard that Dillon now did feel muscles in his back tear from the impact. He wrapped his legs around Sturmvogel's neck in an attempt to break that neck but Sturmvogel simply pivoted, spinning like a dancer and with nothing more than the strength of his neck and shoulder, slung Dillon away.

Dillon flew through the air into the street, bounced, rolled and came up on his feet to meet Sturmvogel's attack. It was unnerving how the man ever was on the offensive. No matter what, he was coming at Dillon, always on the attack, always the aggressor. Dillon blocked his strikes to his head and too late saw where where he had made his mistake.

Sturmvogel had directed Dillon's defense to his upper body, leaving his lower body unguarded. Sturmvogel grasped Dillon's crotch with his huge right hand and Dillon's neck with his left. Sturmvogel lifted him up completely into the air over his own head. Sturmvogel then slammed Dillon back down onto the ground with bone-cracking force.

Dillon could only lie there, his entire body nothing but one massive pain. The sheer savage speed, strength and power of The Storm Bird was like nothing he had ever encountered, even among his training with The Warmasters.

Sturmvogel's foot smashed into his mouth. Blood exploded from his mangled lips. Sturmvogel's massive foot came down again and again as Dillon barely was able to block it from crushing his head.

I'm not going to die here today. I'M NOT GOING TO DIE HERE TODAY!

The next time Sturmvogel's foot came down, Dillon shifted to one side, caught it as it came down and locked it with his own leg. Sturmvogel tried to counter but it was too late, he had let his blood lust take him and now he had to pay.

Dillon yanked, twisted and felt tendons in the leg tear as the huge body of Sturmvogel twirled in mid-air to crash to the pavement. That leg was hurt, Dillon knew. He rolled away, got to his feet and stumbled over to where Sturmvogel lay, clutching at the injured leg.

Dillon yanked The Storm Bird to his feet and pistoned one punishing blow after another into the bigger man's face until blood gushed from the lips and nose. Dillon let Sturmvogel go but he didn't let up punching him. Left. Right. Left. Right. Left. Right. Left. Right.

One punch after another. But not aimlessly. Every punch with precision and with purpose. Dillon meant to make a statement with every blow. No matter how this fight ended, win or lose, The Storm Bird would remember Dillon.

Astoundingly, Sturmvogel wavered. He reached down to clutch at his injured leg and Dillon surged in like a blood-mad tiger, his arms reaching out to claw at Sturmvogel's sides, slamming into him, taking him across the street into a small pottery shop. They went right through the outer wall and into the store itself in a storm of masonry and glass, Dillon's yowl of rage mingling with Sturmvogel's German curses.

The silence seemed longer than it actually was. People gathered outside, looking inward to the ruined shop, wondering what they should do as it seemed impossible that the two men were still alive, so furiously and ferociously they had fought.

Dillon pushed rubble aside as he sat up, coughing to get dust out of his lungs. He rolled over onto to knees, trying to get his heaving guts under control. He shakily pushed himself to his feet. The lower half of his face was bloody, bruised. And his chest felt like hamburger. He clutched at himself. His heart pounded as he had never felt it pound before. His breathing was labored and raspy.

Dillon dragged his left leg as he attempted to stumble out of the now ruined shop into the street. The leg was numb and he had no idea why.

Sturmvogel burst from under a pile of rubble. He grinned through the blood on his face. "Good...good...we get to play some more."

And he came again at Dillon.

A double handed blow smashed Dillon to the floor and more blood gushed from Dillon's mouth.

Sturmvogel kicked Dillon in the side. "And *you* thought you were good enough to stand alongside Jim Anthony?"

Sturmvogel kicked Dillon again in the side. Dillon yelled as he felt a rib crack.

"Anthony ran today, yes....but even on the day that he ran...he is still more of a worthy foe than *YOU!*" and The Storm Bird kicked Dillon so hard that Dillon actually came up off the ground and flew across the ruined shop to smash into a display case. Dillon landed hard to the floor, showered in broken glass and trinkets made in Taiwan.

Sturmvogel walked slowly over to where Dillon lay. His Aryan pride would not allow him to admit he was injured. But his entire left side felt as if every bone on that side was broken. He knew he was bleeding internally. He would pass out in another few minutes. But he would kill this boy before he himself succumbed.

Dillon saw The Storm Bird coming at him. And one thought solidified in his mind: *You're going to tell everybody in Hell I'm coming you sonof-*

Dillon's right arm came back. His left arm came up to block Sturmvogel's right arm which came down in a sledgehammer strike. Sturmvogel's right hand didn't matter because Dillon's right fist moved with the speed of a true Warmaster's thought behind it to strike Sturmvogel's chest right above the heart.

Sturmvogel gasped.

Dillon stepped back and drew back his right fist again.

Sturmvogel had too much pride to ask for mercy but his eyes spoke for him and his hands going to his chest punctuated the request.

Dillon ignored the request and his fist went in again, the very air sizzling with the speed and power of the punch that slammed into the area above Sturmvogel's heart and stopped it.

Sturmvogel fell.

Dillon stood over The Storm Bird, holding onto his own side. He felt as if he were full of wet cotton and he could not believe that the body lying at his feet was one he had defeated. Dillon grinned. This was a battle The Warmasters would have loved to see.

And then Dillon fell over and into complete unconsciousness.

4.

The Buick Enclave's supercharged engine snarled like an enraged beast as it sped in pursuit of Shani's Mercedes-Benz W220 which easily kept its distance without any effort at all. Vera cursed in French. "Her car's got just as much under the hood as ours," she said in English as she twisted the wheel, speeding around slower moving vehicles. "Probably just as armored as ours as well."

Jim reached over and took one of his daughter's Magnums from its holster. "Just get me close enough. Maybe I can take out a tire."

"We'd have a better chance running her off the road," Vera muttered but she tromped on the gas, continued weaving in and out of traffic. They were rocketing down a wide, four-lane highway that thankfully was straight, with no curves and no exits in sight that Shani could have ducked onto and maybe lost them.

"Good thing is that she can't drive and shoot back," Vera said.

As if on cue, a section of the roof flew off as explosive bolts detonated. Shani popped up with an evil grin on her face and a AR-15 in her hands. She directed a burst at the windshield of the Buick. The bulletproof glass held, the deflected shells leaving small nicks in the surface but that was all.

Jim powered down the window on his side, leaned out and fired three shots, forcing Shani to duck back down. He then took aim at the tires and fired four more shots. He knew that he hit the right rear tire with at least two of those shots but nothing happened. He ducked back inside as Shani reappeared, firing on his side. Bullets ricocheted off the passenger door in sheets of sparks but otherwise there was no damage.

"Puncture proof tires!" Jim reported. "We're going to have to ram her! We're going to have to ram her!"

Vera grinned, "Now you're talking."

The Buick responded smoothly as Vera's superior driving skills closed the gap between the two vehicles. And now they could hear sirens rapidly approaching their position.

Then, a veritable barrage of bullets lashed the Buick on Vera's side as another Mercedes roared out a side street. Two men were enthusiastically firing their weapons. These were Colt 9mm submachine guns and they must have been loaded with armor piercers as some of them got through the bulletproof glass.

The three speeding cars came up on a tunnel and they wildly swerved in and out and between other vehicles. A truck's rear tires had the misfortune to be hit by bullets from the car chasing the Buick. The driver cursed, fought the wheel to regain control of his fishtailing truck.

The truck hit the wall, bounced off and slammed into the Buick. Vera hit the brakes, twisted her wheel, fighting to keep the Buick from being thrown out of the lane into other cars. She manipulated the wheel, shifted gears and the Buick performed a one-eighty spin, freeing it from the truck. She again twisted the steering wheel. The Buick's tires smoked as she got the Buick under control and sent it in pursuit of Shani's Mercedes again.

All around them, other cars were veering wildly out of the way, smashing into each other. The screaming of brakes and the hideous sounds of metal colliding against metal filled the tunnel.

The Buick emerged from the tunnel, in the wrong lane and Vera just barely managed to avoid hitting a bus head on. The Buick's tires screeched insanely as Vera got it back in the right lane, the bus's rear view mirror clipping the Buick's.

Shani again fired and the Buick's armor held, the bullets deflecting off the hood. A police car pulled up alongside the Buick on Jim's side, sirens whooping and lights flashing. Jim looked into the car at the angry face of the driver whose mouth worked wildly. So excited was the officer that he didn't realize Jim couldn't hear his orders due to his window being rolled up.

Shani at last had a target she could take out. She sent a withering burst right through the windshield, killing the police officer instantly. The police car careened across two lanes as the driver's dying hands wrenched the wheel to the right, smashing into other cars.

Shani dropped down to reload, also ducking out of the path of the two shots Jim fired at her.

More rounds from the car pursuing them hammered on the rear and driver's side of the Buick. Jim pulled his head back inside the car. "This is intolerable," he said calmly.

"Then I suggest you do something about it," Vera just as calmly.

Jim climbed into the back seat, reached over to one of the duffle bags, zipped it open and drew out an FN FNC assault rifle. It was already loaded. He didn't want or need standard ammunition. Jim rummaged around in the duffle bag, picking up various ammunition magazines. They were color-coded depending on what they were loaded with. He discarded the blue and yellow ones, looking for-

More bullets from the chase car slammed into the Buick's left side.

Vera's window burst into thick chunks under the relentless pounding. She threw up her left arm to protect that side of her face. "Poppa!"

"Hold on!" Jim shouted back. He had the magazine he wanted. He double-checked it, loaded it into the weapon then set it to full automatic. He then rolled down the window. "Enough is enough," he muttered as he squeezed the trigger. The results were as satisfying as they were devastating. The windshield simply disintegrated and the three men inside were turned into hamburger in a matter of seconds, thanks to the blizzard of armor-piercing shells. The FN FNC assault rifle was no joke at close range and in the hands of someone who knew how to use it.

The car crazily weaved back and forth, slamming into other vehicles before flipping over on its side where it continued sliding on for another twenty feet or so, throwing up great sheets of sparks in its wake.

"Poppa, hold on!" Vera shouted.

Jim didn't ask questions, just dropped the smoking assault rifle and held on as Vera once again sent the Buick into a gut-busting, tire-abusing tight turn to avoid the pair of grenades Shani had thrown in their path. The Buick rocketed across three lanes of traffic, narrowing avoiding being hit by other cars.

The explosions upped the already considerable level of chaos and destruction they had already left. Jim estimated there had to be at least six miles of mayhem in their wake. He pointed. "Take this exit ramp. Soon as you can turn around and let's go back for Dillon."

"You're breaking off pursuit?"

Jim pointed in the sky. A number of police helicopters were converging on the scene and judging by all the sirens he was hearing, every police car in the city was heading their way. "Above all, we can't risk being detained by the police down here. I could call in some favors and get us released but that would still eat up precious time."

"But we'd have Shani!"

"And how many more innocent people would be hurt or even killed? God only knows how many we've left back there as is. You saw how easily she killed that policeman. Human life means nothing to her and if she's cornered she'll kill civilians if for no other reason than to make me feel responsible for their deaths. No, we'll let her go for now. In any case, I know where she's going. We'll get back to the plane and head for her destination."

※ ※ ※

Jim sat behind the steering wheel of the Buick, trying not jump out of the vehicle and go see for himself what was keeping Vera. It had taken them nearly three hours to get back to the warehouse due to them having to keep off of the main roads so that the damage to the Buick would not be seen by the seemingly hundreds of police cars cruising the streets.

Back at the warehouse there were even more police. Vera Gemini had climbed into the back seat. She opened a panel in the armrest. Within the armrest were a number of wigs and a professional theatrical makeup kit. After twenty minutes thanks to a wig and the kit, Vera Gemini looked nothing like herself. "You stay put, Poppa. And try not to worry."

But he was worried.

Vera returned and climbed into the passenger seat.

"What took you so long? For a while there I thought maybe you had been ambushed."

She took off the blonde wig. "My Vampires were out of sight looking after me. I was in no danger." Impulsively she leaned over to kiss Jim on the cheek. "But it is nice to know that you care."

"Where is Dillon?"

"It appears that he and Sturmvogel had a fight they'll be talking about down here for years. The two of them battered each other into unconsciousness and were still out when police arrived. They were both taken to the Hospital Italiano." Vera held up a hand to cut off Jim. "I know what you're going to say and I've taken care of it. I sent my Vampires to spirit Dillon out of the hospital. They can do it far more efficiently and quickly than we can. Our time can best be used by getting back to the plane and prepping it for takeoff so that when my Vampires return with Dillon we can lose no time getting into the air."

"And what of Sturmvogel?" Jim said as he started up the car.

Vera smiled. "Oh, trust me when I say I gave my Vampires most explicit instructions as to what to do with him."

"What do you mean, 'he was gone'?"

Jim asked the angry question as The Vampires brought Dillon aboard the Hercules cargo plane. They had placed him in a cocoon like mesh that they used to transport him out of the hospital and across town. They gently laid the cocoon on a bunk bed and opened it. Upon seeing the extremely battered condition of the young man, Jim couldn't help but gasp in amazement. His entire body was one huge purplish bruise. His face looked as if Sturmvogel had used it for a speed bag.

The 'he' Jim had referred to was Sturmvogel. Vera communicated with her Vampires, whistling softly. She turned to her father, shrugged. "He was gone when they got there. According to what they overheard, Sturmvogel just got up, broke the necks of the nurse and the two doctors examining him and simply walked out of the hospital. It all happened so fast that by the time the police were alerted he had just plain vanished."

Jim dropped to his knees next to the bunk bed to do his own examining of Dillon. "That man's not human."

"None of Sun Koh's people are, Poppa. Not anymore. They've lived too long and submerged whatever humanity they had for him and his dream." Vera reminded him. She was looking at Dillon's hospital chart which her Vampires had thoughtfully brought along. "And I'm no medical expert but if I'm reading this right, our young friend there may not be entirely human either."

Jim looked up sharply. "What do you mean?"

"Here. Look at the extent of his injuries when they brought him in."

Jim ran his eyes over the chart. Unlike Vera, he *was* a medical expert. And what he read on the chart made him tilt his head to the side in slight surprise. "Hm. This *is* interesting."

Vera eyed her father as intently as he eyed the chart. "You're not totally taken by surprise by what's on that chart, are you?"

"Not really. I had asked him for a blood sample back at The Teepee before Shani destroyed it. I had been examining him visually during sparring sessions and it seems as if he never got tired even after hours of prolonged strenuous physical activity. It made me curious and I figured that if I analyzed his blood and gave him a physical exam it might prove interesting." Jim tapped the chart. "And this is even more so. According to this, the beating Dillon took at the hands of Sturmvogel should have crippled him. But he didn't receive any of the treatment someone in that condition should be getting."

"Meaning?"

"Meaning that I'm going to take a sample of his blood and examine it. In the meantime, shouldn't you be getting us in the air?"

"Just as soon as you tell me where we're going, Poppa."

"Cape Horn."

"Cape Horn?" Vera frowned. "What's there?"

"The gateway to the bottom of the world, daughter. The gateway to the bottom of the world."

Three Days Later

The yelping and barking of twenty Alaskan Malamutes filled the cargo hold of the Hercules C-130 as Dillon moved among them, stroked their heads, smiling like a little kid as they licked his hands. He ambled down the ramp to where Jim Anthony and Vera Gemini stood next to Vera's two remaining Buick Enclaves. Her Vampires were already inside them. They had removed their black outfits and now were dressed in regular everyday clothing but they all wore large dark sunglasses. None of them looked at Dillon as he walked by, raising his hand in greeting.

Jim and Vera each held one end of a map in their hands. Jim traced a route on the map as he spoke. "Once you get to Colcail you should be able to rent a plane with the capabilities to get you back to the States. I can't thank you enough for letting us take the Hercules, Vera." Jim looked at Dillon. "Everything ready?"

"The dogs are secured. So are our sleds and supplies. We can leave anytime you want."

"What else could I do, Poppa? You got to stay on the trail while it's still hot. I only wish you'd let me go with you."

Dillon heard that. "Still don't think I can help your father?"

"Not at all. Anybody who can take the beating you did and walk around laughing about it two days later is okay with me."

And it was true. While his face was still bruised and he was still sore, Dillon looked more like he had been in a car accident rather than beaten nearly to death in a savage hand-to-hand battle.

"It's just that three stand more of a chance than two."

But Jim shook his head firmly. "Nobody knows where we are, Vera. It is vital you get back to the States. Go directly to Washington and speak to Dan Fowler. Tell him what's happened. He'll know what to do then."

"I don't understand," Dillon said. "Your Mr. Fowler is Director of The FBI, correct? He's got no jurisdiction down here. What can he do?"

"In England sometime around the mid-19th Century, British Intelligence formed a...you might call it a league of individuals with extraordinary talents, gifts and skills to protect the interests and safeguard the security of the Empire. Over the years that concept was adopted by many other countries such as France, Germany and of course, America. These individuals are only gathered together in times of global peril. This is most definitely one of those times. Trust me, Dan knows who to call and what to do." Jim looked at Vera and Dillon with utter seriousness. "The stakes are too high and we can't rule out that we may not succeed."

"I don't like what I'm hearing, Poppa."

"I don't like what I'm saying. But you must know what the stakes are and you must know that Dillon and I may very well just be buying time until you can get to Dan Fowler and he can get help and get down here." Jim handed Vera another map. "This is the route to where Dillon and I are going. Guard it with your life and give it to Dan."

"I will." Vera rolled it up and placed it inside a tube. She slung the strap around her neck so as to have her arms free to hug her father. "I know you won't be careful so I'm not going to ask you to do so. I love you, Poppa."

Jim lifted her head up by the chin so that he could look directly into her eyes as he said; "There's something I've never said to you and I have to say it now if this indeed turns out to be the last time we see each other. I want you to know that the circumstances of your birth have never mattered to me. I couldn't have asked for a better or more loving daughter. I'm so very proud of you, Vera. And you have made me happy." He kissed her tenderly on the forehead and they hugged again.

Vera finally let go and wiped her eyes dry. She turned to Dillon and grunted, "I suppose I should give you a hug as well. Come here." As they embraced, Vera whispered in his ear so that only he could hear; "Don't come back without him. I mean what I say. Do you understand me?"

Dillon drew back and looked in Vera's eyes. He gulped. "Oh. Yeah, I understand."

Vera turned away and walked over to the lead vehicle. Soon, the three vehicle convoy kicked up clouds of dust as they drove away. Jim and Dillon stood side-by-side as they watched them go.

It was some time before Jim spoke. "I'm sorry for getting you mixed up in this."

"Awfully late for that, don't you think?"

Jim laughed. "Yes. Yes, I suppose it is. Still, I felt I had to say it. We've come a long way in such a short time, haven't we?"

Dillon nodded. "And we've still got a long way to go, don't we?"

Jim clapped the younger man on the shoulder. "Indeed we do. Let us go, my young friend. The final confrontation awaits."

Dillon and Jim Anthony boarded the cargo plane and within minutes, the ramp was up and secured. The big plane started down the runway and shortly was in the air, heading south.

"Don't come back without him. Do you understand me?"

5.

It was a vast desert of ice that seemed to go on into infinity. A painfully flat plain of white under an azure sky. Both disturbing and glorious in its arcane beauty Dillon had never before seen anything like it. A few feet ahead of him, Jim Anthony led the way, his ten dog team pulling his sled as efficiently and as easily as Dillon's own team.

They had flown the Hercules as far as they could before taking to the dog sleds. Jim had even admitted he'd pushed it, flying further than it actually was safe to but he explained to Dillon that travelling on the ice was physically debilitating and he wanted them to be as fresh as possible when they reached their final destination.

Jim apparently knew the way to Ultima Thule as he did not use a GPS but yet kept them on a steady course. Jim raised his hand, calling for a halt. Dillon did so, wondering if they had come to another crevasse. Jim had told him that his two major fears was hitting brittle ice and falling through into a crevasse or being caught in a blizzard. Either one would bring their trip to a sudden and sure halt.

Dillon walked over to Jim, patting the heads of his dog team as he did so. The animals looked barely winded even though they had been pulling the sled for a good three hours so far today. Dillon lifted his goggles with the polarized lenses to guard his eyes against snow blindness. Jim had explained to him that catching snow blindness was at all costs to be avoided as it could last anywhere from two to four days.

"Anything wrong?" Dillon asked.

In answer, Jim lifted his own goggles and pointed. "There's a range of ice mountains up ahead. But I think there's a canyon we can get through."

"I don't see anything," Dillon said.

Jim continued to point and gradually Dillon saw it. Again he was amazed at the eyesight Jim Anthony possessed. Dillon's own eyesight was pretty remarkable but Jim's eyes, even at his age seemed to have telescopic or microscopic properties depending on what he was looking at.

"So what's the plan?" Dillon wanted to know.

Jim put his goggles back on, adjusted them so that that sat comfortably on his face. "Let's make it through the canyon and then camp for the night. We should reach Ultima Thule by tomorrow or the day after if the weather stays with us."

"How far do you think Shani is ahead of us?"

"No more than half a day, I should think. There's no way for her to get to Ultima Thule except by dog sled, same as us. Only a madman or an idiot would take a snowmobile out this far. If it breaks down, you're dead. And I've been looking for the tracks of a larger vehicle and haven't seen one. Shani wouldn't want to be burdened with worrying about gas or if it breaks down. She'd want to move fast, quick and hard like we're doing."

Dillon nodded and replaced his goggles as well. "You give much thought as to how we're going to stop Sun Koh once we get there?"

"Let's worry about getting to Ultima Thule first, youngster. We can figure out how to save the world later."

Dillon grinned and climbed back aboard his dog sled. Shortly, the two companions were once more speeding across the ice, their dogs charging ahead as if they themselves realized the urgency of their mission and they pulled with a will.

Gradually the range of ice mountains came into clearer view as they drew closer. The sunlight reflecting from the crystalized surface of the mountains made them appear to be ablaze with an inner light that even through the polarized lenses of his goggles made Dillon's eyes ache if he looked at it for too long. Instead, he kept focused on Jim, who lead the way and only shifted his vision every minute or so.

Once again, Jim was proven right as after thirty minutes of hard traveling, Dillon could see the entrance to the canyon. Dillon urged his dogs to speed up until he was close enough to Jim to shout a question; "How do you know the way to this place?"

Jim shouted back, "Once I retired I had a lot of time to do research on a lot of things. Purely from a scientific point of view I was interested in Ultima Thule. Back in the 1930's there were a number of scientific expeditions sent here to Antarctica to try and find it. There were a number of other ruins found here. But none of them were Ultima Thule. If we survive this you really should plan to visit Miskatonic University in Massachusetts. There are some fascinating documents there that—" Jim suddenly stopped speaking. He cocked his head, trying to hear something over the howl of the wind.

"What is it?" Dillon said. He strained his own ears to try and pick up whatever it was that had alerted Jim but he couldn't hear a thing over the wind.

And now both Jim and Dillon brought their dog teams to a mutual halt. The dogs themselves had either heard or smelled whatever it was that Jim had. The dogs growled softly, tossing their heads, digging with their forepaws at the hard-packed snow.

Jim looked directly at the entrance of the canyon for a long minute. Too long for Dillon. Finally, he could contain himself no longer. "What the hell—"

"Be silent!" Jim snarled. He continued to listen and look.

And then Dillon saw what Jim and the dogs had long ago heard.

Emerging from the canyon were half a dozen huge grey-black shapes with spotted hides. At this distance they looked like giant slugs to Dillon but they certainly didn't move as slowly as slugs. They undulated across the ice at a frightening speed, using their broad flippers to help them along. And now the dogs were yelping and barking furiously.

Dillon had never seen anything like these creatures. They had to be at least fifteen feet long and looked to be about a thousand pounds each at least. Despite their size they moved as quickly as serpents and the hooting, honking bellowing they were making filled their air with a cacophony that sounded like the shrieks that the damned in Hell made when being whipped with red-hot cat-o-nine tails.

Jim ran to his dogs and began unstrapping them from their harness. "Turn your dogs loose! Hurry!"

"Why?"

"So they can defend themselves! Move, damn you!"

Dillon did so with fingers suddenly gone numb. The dogs were going berserk, the clamor they were making easily matching that of the creatures charging at them. "What are they, Jim?"

"Leopard seals! The most dangerous thing alive in Antarctica! Get a gun and start picking them off! Hopefully we can get most of them before they kill all the dogs!" Jim yanked at the straps tying down his equipment on his sled, looking for his FN FNC assault rifle. Once his dogs were all turned loose, Dillon also began ripping his sled apart to get at his.

The dogs quickly closed the gap between themselves and the leopard seals and leaped to the attack. Two of the dogs landed on the lead leopard seal. One of them chomped down on the leopard seal's snout while the other went right for its throat.

Two more dogs went for another leopard seal but they weren't as fortunate as their fellows. The leopard seal opened its fearsome mouth, saliva sparking on its horrendously sharp teeth. The leopard seal bit down on a dog's head, biting it clean off. A geyser of blood exploded from the headless dog, startlingly bright against the pristine whiteness of pure snow and ice. The leopard seal tore into the second dog, chomping down on its hindquarters. The dog yowled pitifully.

By now Dillon and Jim had their assault rifles out. They took cover behind their sleds, leaning on them to steady their arms and aim more accurately. Jim set his weapon to single fire and took his time, shooting one leopard seal right in the head. Even though half the creature's head had been blown away, still it came on, hooting and braying another eighty feet before crashing on its side, a crazily twisty trail of blood and brains in its wake.

Dillon placed three bullets in the leopard seal he had targeted. Following Jim's example he also had his weapon set for single shot. But his leopard seal was moving too fast for him to shoot it in the head. The leopard seal's thick layer of blubber underneath its skin acted like natural body armor, blunting the impact enough of the bullets so that by the time the bullet penetrated, it was slowed so much that it couldn't get through the tough layer of muscle under the blubber.

The bedlam of the sled dogs fighting the leopard seals drowned out the lonely shrieking of the wind as the leopard seals snarled and the dogs barked. Spurts and gouts of bright red blood splashed through the air. A leopard seal reared up on its tail, four dogs hanging off of it. One dog furiously chewed at the leopard seal's throat as it scrabbled to hold onto the thrashing creature's back. Another went for the tail. Blood fountained in spurting arcs as the beast thrashed about. Two more dogs latched onto the flippers, tearing them to ribbons.

The dogs depended on their speed to get in and tear at the throats of the leopard seals with their razor sharp teeth. Like dancers they weaved in and out, slashing at the huge beasts. But the leopard seals had thick layers of fat under their skin that protected their vitals.

One leopard seal headed for Dillon and Jim, its eyes fixed right on them. Jim fired, trying again for a head shot. Amazing, this leopard seal seemed to have learned from the example of two of its brothers who lay dead, their skulls ripped into bloody pieces thanks to Jim's accurate shooting. The thing wasn't coming head on at them but bounding from side-to-side, vaulting clumsily, true, but good enough to keep from getting its head blown off.

Jim suddenly realized Dillon wasn't shooting. The young man stood frozen in place, the assault rifle held tightly in his shaking hands.

Jim realized that Dillon had stopped breathing as he saw no puff of condensation coming from his mouth or nostrils.

"Dillon!"

Dillon didn't hear Jim at all. In fact he could not hear anything except the voice of his mother. It had been years since she had died but her voice now rang in Dillon's ears as if she were standing right next to him…

…*"No! You have to go! Don't be afraid. There are people on the other side, friends of mine who will love you and care for you just as much as I do. Now go and do as I say! Go!"*

…and Dillon remembered the snow and the cold on the last day of his mother's life. It had been cold just like this and there had been snow just as white…until it had turned crimson from soaking up his mother's blood…

Jim Anthony slammed into Dillon, knocking him out of the way of the charging leopard seal. Dillon's sled shattered into toothpicks thanks to the size and weight of the blood-crazed creature. The smell of so much blood had driven it nearly insane with lust to taste blood itself, to feel the hotness of it as it spurted over its muzzle. It had been too long since the creature had tasted man meat. And it loved that taste.

It checked its charge. Sliding and scrabbling on ice now slicked with its own blood pumping from gunshot wounds, it sought to turn around to eat Jim and Dillon. Jim emptied his weapon right into the leopard seal's chest. The reptilian head bobbled and weaved like a human boxer's as the creature came in closer.

Jim kicked Dillon out of the way and swung his now empty weapon at the sea leopard's head. The beast's right eyeball burst like a tomato in a suddenly clenched fist, drenching Jim in fluid and blood. The leopard seal honked in pain that fueled its rage to an even greater level. It swung it's head, slamming into Jim, sending him flying through the air to land on the ice, sliding like a poorly hit hockey puck.

Jim's entire body quivered as if it were a badly plucked banjo string. The leopard seal swung its head back and forth, looking for Jim with its good eye. Upon spying him it let loose with a booming roar and flopped toward him, the ground shaking as it came closer. Its one good eye glittered with rage and its mouth opened up at as impossible angle as it lunged at what it considered to be lunch.

Jim scrabbled to his feet, trying to gain foothold on the slippery ice, the cleats on his boots digging in. But it was too late and the leopard seal was too fast. He'd never get out of the way in time-

The leopard seal covered the remaining distance between it and Jim

in one last froggish leap. The beast's head lunged forward, snarling and snapping. Holding the assault rifle in both hands, Jim thrust it forward to keep back those fearsome fangs. The leopard seal bit through the assault rifle as if it were a French fry and Jim was left with nothing but shards of ruined metal in his hands. He stumbled and fell on his back. The leopard seal eagerly dived in again-

-Dillon appeared from seemingly out of nowhere, foot long survival knives in both hands. He ran so quickly it appeared that he was on skates zipping across the ice. He leaped into the air in a soaring arc and came down right on the leopard seal's back.

The knife in his left hand whistled through the air and went into the leopard seal's remaining eye like a red hot poker through ice cream. The leopard seal screamed and reared up, bucking like a crazed bronco, trying to dislodge Dillon who held onto the knife. He raised up his right hand and brought the knife in that hand right down through that reptilian skull into the brain.

By now, Jim had gotten to his feet and dived out of the way as the leopard seal, gushing blood from its terrible wounds, crashed to the ice, zig-zagging cracks radiating outwards in all directions from the impact. The beast let out one last blubbering cry that sounded disturbingly like a human cry of despair and died.

Dillon slid off of the creature's back, breathing heavily. Jim ran over to help him up. "You okay, boy? Anything broken?"

Dillon shook his head. "No. I don't think so…"

Jim nodded. "Come on, we'd better help the rest of the dogs—"

He stopped. An undulating warbling filled the air. The two remaining leopard seals stopped and turned their heads in the direction of the warbling. Surrounding them were the seven remaining sled dogs. Battered and bruised, they were still more than game to continue the fight. Around them were the bodies of their fellows and the leopard seals they had killed. The ice was no longer white. It was red.

The two remaining leopard seals flopped away, pushing themselves along with that same bizarre speed that belied their bulk. They went back toward the opening of the canyon they had emerged from, leaving broad bloody trails from their wounds on the ice as they did so.

"What the hell is that?" Dillon asked.

"Those beasts were trained to attack and kill," Jim said slowly. "Leopard seals normally stay near water as that's where their food is, penguins, fish and other sea life. They're also solitary creatures. They only get together to mate and they don't hunt in packs. These creatures have been trained. And there's only one of Sun Koh's crew I can think of who would be able to train leopard seals." Jim looked off in the direction of the canyon opening, squinted slightly. "And here he comes."

Dillon looked and saw a man coming towards them. He walked with a curious long-legged lope. He didn't seem to be hurrying at all but he covered ground in an amazingly short amount of time. He approached the remaining dogs who slunk away from him as if sensing that here was the master of the leopard seals and he was not to be trifled with.

"Let me do the talking. I know him."

"He's one of Sun Koh's people?"

"He is. He's the very last of the genuine mountain men. His name's Alaska Jim Hoover."

Alaska Jim Hoover stopped about five feet from Jim and Dillon. A big man with deep-set eyes that missed nothing, his dark skin had the appearance of old leather. Fur boots were on his feet. He had on layers of fur over the fringed buckskin shirt and pants he wore. A coonskin cap with a striped tail sat squarely on his long, narrow head. Held in the crook of his arm was a weapon Dillon was unfamiliar with but Jim knew very well; a Henry repeating rifle.

Alaska Jim Hoover nodded slightly. "Anthony. Heard you were back in harness and carryin' on somethin' cranky." Alaska Jim looked at Dillon. "This'un yourn?"

"This is Dillon. He's my partner in this."

"You got a problem with me?" Dillon demanded.

Alaska Jim looked at Dillon with some amusement and what might even have been some approval. "Not if you're the one who took ol' Sturmvogel down."

Dillon blinked. "I thought he was a friend of yours?"

"Jus' because we work together don't mean we take long walks in the moonlight holdin' hands. Fact of the matter is that for the past thirty years or so, Sturmvogel has been getting jus' a lil' bit beside himself. Do him some good to have gotten his ass kicked good n'proper."

"I was wondering where and when you were going to show up, Hoover," Jim said. "Where's Minx?"

Alaska Jim shrugged. "Your guess is as good as any. Minx disappeared about fifteen years ago. But for about ten years before that he dedicated himself to drinking hisself to death."

"And Sun Koh just let him go? Just like that?"

Again that careless shrug. "Poor Minx wasn't much good even before he started his drinkin'. He just didn't care anymore. Himself knew that and even felt sorry for him, I think. That's why he just let him go."

"Where's Sturmvogel now? And Karsten?" Jim asked.

"Still back in Buenos Aires." Alaska Jim again looked at Dillon. "I don't know what kinda whoopin' you put on Sturmvogel but it took. He left outta that hospital, hooked up with Karsten at a safe house and promptly passed out. Th' word I got is that he's too busted up inside to travel."

"Where's Mayen?"

"He's with Himself and Shani in Ultima Thule. She come through here a few hours ago. She'll just be getting' there about now."

Jim said, "So now what, Hoover? Why didn't you let your pets finish us off?"

"You may not believe this, Anthony, but if I hadn't been busy with some other stuff I wouldn't have let the seals attack you."

"Busy with what?" Dillon said.

"Gettin' a couple of snowmobiles ready for you."

Jim and Dillon swapped shocked looks.

Jim looked back at Alaska Jim and said slowly. "Is there something I'm missing?"

Alaska Jim Hoover turned abruptly and said over his right shoulder. "Let's collect your dawgs first. Then you come on up to the cabin and set a spell. We need to jaw for a bit. An' then you got to move on. 'Cause you don't have a whole lotta time if'n you're fixin' to stop Sun Koh onct an' fer all."

It didn't take them long to get to Alaska Jim Hoover's log cabin. The seven remaining Malamutes followed behind Jim. Dillon followed behind Alaska Jim Hoover. He didn't give a flying kitty for what Alaska Jim said. The man had sent a horde of killer beasts after them and to Dillon, that was all that mattered. Jim Anthony didn't seem particularly worried or concerned but Dillon himself was half convinced that the man was leading them into a trap and if so, he intended to get his hands on him and break his neck.

Located at the other end of the ice canyon the log cabin looked incongruous, situated on the crest of a snowy hill. Smoke came out of the chimney. Jim Anthony chuckled. "A regular 'Little House On The Prairie' isn't it? Where on earth did you find enough wood here to build a log cabin?"

"The wood came from Ultima Thule," Alaska Jim replied. "You'll see for y'self when you get there. C'mon inside. The dawgs can come in as well. Been a long time since I've had dawgs around."

They entered the cabin which Dillon was surprised to find was well lit, immaculately clean and even had a solid wooden floor. Alaska Jim noted the look on his face and grunted. "Think that just because I live in a log cabin I must be some kinda uncivilized yokel?"

"No...no...I..."

Alaska Jim pulled off his furs and hung them on a hook made from deer antlers next to the door. He motioned to the fireplace with his Henry rifle. "Go on over and warm y'selves. Y'want grub? I'd advise you to. May be quite a while before y'eat again."

Jim nodded. "We appreciate the hospitality. Yes, we'll eat."

Alaska Jim grunted. "Be right back." He went outside without his furs but obviously he wasn't going far. And sure enough, in a few seconds Dillon and Jim heard a gunshot. A minute later Alaska Jim came back inside the log cabin. "Hope you like seal meat," he said. He held up a huge slab of raw meat.

"You killed one of your seals?"

"I don't much like the critters in the first place. But they make the perfect watchdawgs for this region." Alaska Jim walked over to the fireplace, rested his rifle on hooks above the mantelpiece then seated himself on a stool. He threw the slab of meat into a large cast iron skillet hanging from a swinging metal arm and used his Bowie knife to slice it up right there in the pan. He then gave the arm a push so that the pan was over the cheerfully blazing fire.

Dillon and Jim shucked their cold weather gear and found chairs to sit in. The dogs had made themselves very comfortable indeed in the log cabin. Some wandered around, sniffing everything. Others flopped on their bellies, never taking their eyes off the pan as the smell of cooking meat quickly filled the one huge common room of the cabin. Dillon's stomach quietly rumbled.

Alaska Jim stood up, selected some small jars from the mantelpiece and added herbs and spices to the frying meat. Dillon looked at Jim Anthony who sat in his chair as easily as if he and Alaska Jim Hoover were old friends. It was Jim Anthony who opened the dialog.

"Why here, Hoover?"

Alaska Jim knew what he meant. "I'm th' first line of defense. That's why I trained the leopard seals." He used his Bowie knife to turn the meat over. It sizzled and popped. The dogs whined. Alaska Jim smiled suddenly and with one quick twist of his knife flipped two thick pieces of meat across the room into their midst. The dogs fell to struggling over the morsels.

Alaska Jim continued. "You'd be surprised at how over the years various folks have come down here. Either to settle old scores with Himself or to try and take the secret of **Der Wurmloch** for themselves. And for a while there, Germany was sendin' hit squads down here on a reg'lar. Seems like some documents or papers or such came to light detailing some of the missions Sun Koh and us did on behalf of them Nazis back in dubya dubya two. Turns out some folks were really embarrassed by our affiliation with them Nazis even after all this time. Funny how people hold a grudge fer so long, ain't it?" Alaska Jim directed that last bit directly at Jim Anthony who simply shrugged.

"Anyway, here I be. Just holdin' down the pass, so to speak. Fact of the matter is, I prefer it this way."

"Why is that?"

Alaska Jim gave the meat one last turn. He stood up again, walked over to another shelf for metal plates, forks and spoons. He gestured over to the sink. "There's plenty of fresh water to drink. I don't reckon you or the boy will be wantin' anything stronger than that." He returned to the skillet and forked meat onto the metal pans. He gave one to Dillon, the other to Jim. He himself did not partake of the meat but did throw another couple of pieces to the dogs. He then walked over to a corner of the room where his unmade bed was and pulled a brown jug from underneath. He returned to his stool, pulled the cork and took a long swallow from the jug.

"What happened to you, Hoover?" Jim said, cutting small pieces of the meat in his plate.

"Well, I'll tell you the truth, Anthony. Plain an' simple I think we all just done lived too damned long. You too. Alla us shoulda got ourselves killed back then in the 40's, '50's. Gone out in a blaze of glory. Instead you knock around your Catskills mansion just hangin' on, pretendin' you're still doing something useful by helpin' out your ol' buddy Fowler. An' Sun Koh hides out in Ultima Thule still thinkin' he's gonna change the world. Correct The Great Mistake. Turn back time and restore The Earth to the Garden of Eden." Alaska Jim snorted and took another swig from his jug. He looked back at Jim.

"I was one of the first, did you know that? One of the first who swore allegiance to him. So I was there at th' beginnin', Anthony. You should have seen us then. We *shone*, Anthony. Sweet Jesus did we *shine*. And we had ideals. We *knew* we were destined to save the world."

"What happened? What changed you?"

"Too many setbacks, I reckon. Too many years hiding down here. Oh, every so often we would go back into the world on one mission or another. But I soon realized th' world was movin' too fast for us. Ludwig Minx realized it too. As our failures racked up and Sun Koh became more distant we realized that we had no place in the world as it was now and we would have no place in Sun Koh's world if he brought about correcting The Great Mistake." Alaska Jim took another healthy swig. "You knew him back then, Anthony. He had nobility then, didn't he?"

"Yes," Jim agreed quietly. "Yes he did."

"But so many years of seeing his dream unfulfilled…it's done something to him, Anthony."

"But why hasn't he opened **Der Wurmloch** before now?"

"He couldn't. He tried once before and damn near brought down Ultima Thule on his head. It's taken him this long to rebuild the damned thing. He was planning on moving on you but not quite so soon. I heard a couple of his overzealous pretty boys took it in their heads to jump you and got jumped."

"That they did. Thanks for the food." Jim pushed his plate away.

Alaska Jim gestured with his jug at Dillon. "Shani and Sturmvogel couldn't figure where the boy came into this. Shani thought he was a new bodyguard or sumptin.' Who is he?"

"He's my friend," Jim said simply. "So where do you stand now, Hoover?"

Alaska Jim took another swig. "You know how I come to be here? One day, must have been about thirty years ago I was standin' as close to Himself as I am to you. Sun Koh and Minx had just finished arguing. Seems like they were always arguing then. Time was when none of us would dared have question any of Sun Koh's commands. But more and more Minx was becoming rebellious. We'd just come back from a mission to Africa. Sun Koh had heard of some kind of miracle mineral that he thought he could use as an alternate power source. Didn't work out the way we thought. But by then Minx had had enough.

"Truth to tell, I had enough as well. I even thought about using ol' Abigail there—" Alaska Jim nodded at his Henry rifle. "An' puttin' a bullet right in the back of Sun Koh's head. But he turned around and looked right at me as if he knew what I was thinkin.' You know me from the old days, Anthony. You know I don't scare. But the way Sun Koh looked at me that day scared me like nothing had before or after. Once he was through arguin' with Minx he took me to the side and suggested I build an outpost here to guard the canyon pass. I think he was givin' me a way to stay alive more than anything else. Because I do believe that he did know what I was thinkin'. And I believe that if I hadn't taken his suggestion, Sun Koh would have killed me sooner or later. And I honestly think he didn't want to do that. But he was content as long as I stayed here away from him."

Alaska Jim took another swig. "It was a bad time. Things were falling apart. Sturmvogel and Shani were the worst. Ain't none of us ever pretended to be anythin' more than what we were, Anthony. But Sturmvogel and Shani began to do things that turned even my stomach. Especially Shani."

"Is she with Sun Koh in Ultima Thule?"

Alaska Jim nodded. "Shani...there's nothing human inside of her anymore, Anthony. All she wants to do is watch the world die, even if she dies with it. She worships Sun Koh as if he were a god and if he decrees th' end of th' world, it's fine with her."

"Well it's not fine with us." Dillon swallowed the last of his fried seal meat and pushed the plate away. "Are we going, Jim? We're wasting our time with this drunk."

Alaska Jim looked up at Dillon with eyes that were perfectly sober. "You last long enough in this business, boy and I think you'll be pullin' a cork or two yourself after a while. The voices of the dead speak long, boy. They don't speak loud...but oh, they speak long. Lord have mercy on my blasphemin' soul do they speak long."

Jim Anthony stood up and walked over to Alaska Jim and placed a hand on his shoulder. "Who else is with Sun Koh, Hoover?"

"Jan Mayen is there, of course. Where else would he be? He wants to be there when **Der Wurmloch** works finally, after all these years of waiting. And there are...the others."

"What others?"

"They who have waited even longer than Sun Koh. You'll see." Alaska Jim took another swig. "There's a shed out back. Two snowmobiles. You'll see the trail. It'll take you right to Ultima Thule. An' hurry. You don't wanta be out in the open. Not now."

Dillon started forward, his face angry but Jim raised a hand, shook his head in a firm negative. "Leave him."

"You sure?"

Jim looked down at Alaska Jim Hoover who was staring into the fire.

Perhaps he was looking into the past. A past where he still shone.

"Yes, I'm sure. We've got to go to work." Jim and Dillon headed for the door and the Malamutes followed them.

"Anthony!" Alaska Jim said. "C'n I ask a favor?"

"What is it?"

"C'n you leave me the dawgs? Been way too long since I had dawgs here. An' I do so hate them damn seals."

"Of course, Hoover. Take care of them for us." Jim spoke a few words of command to the dogs and they sat where they were.

"Thanks, Anthony. 'Preciate it." Alaska Jim went back to staring moodily into the fire. Dillon and Jim retrieved their cold weather gear and donned them again.

Dillon threw a last look over his shoulder at Alaska Jim. "Should we just leave him like this? Shouldn't we tie him up or something? He may warn Sun Koh."

"No. He won't. He's all used up, Dillon. Leave him be." Jim opened the door, motioning for Dillon to go on out. He closed the door firmly behind them.

Alaska Jim Hoover barely heard it. He was lost in his own memory. A memory that sometimes seemed more real to him than the world he lived in now.

One of the dogs hesitantly got to her feet and quietly walked over to Alaska Jim. She placed her head in his lap. Alaska Jim looked down into the dog's wide eyes. Slowly his hand came up to stroke the animal's head. He smiled and turned back to again gaze into the fire, stroking the dog's head.

6.

The desert of ice sparkled as if diamond dust had been sprinkled on the surface. The two snowmobiles easily sped across the wide road that had been marked with halogen light poles every thirty feet or so on both sides. Jim reckoned that the road doubled as as a runway if and when planes brought supplies in. He led the way on the road, heading toward a towering gray-black rock cliff looming ever closer before them.

Jim took his hands off the handlebars one at a time and flexed his stiff fingers. Even in the gloves, especially made to insulate against the extreme cold of Antarctica, it seeped into his bones. Or maybe because since he was older he just simply didn't have the tolerance for the cold that he once had. He briefly smiled to himself as he remembered the days when he walked around Manhattan barefoot, even in the dead of winter and he was just as comfortable as if he had been wearing expensive handmade Italian loafers. He looked over at Dillon who was slightly behind him and to his left and wondered what had made the younger man freeze up back there when they had been fighting the leopard seals. That was the first time Jim had seen him hesitate in battle. Whatever it was, it appeared to have passed. Dillon was once more focused on the job. Jim hoped so. Not that he honestly expected either of them to survive the day. Oh, he was confident that they would stop Sun Koh. But it was more than likely they would both die doing it.

But the thought did not trouble him. He had lived with the bony hand of Death on his shoulder for many years. Death had woken up with him in the morning and sung him a lullaby at night when he went to bed. Death was nothing to fear, especially when you lived with it as long as Jim had.

He did feel a pang of regret for Dillon. Still so young with so much potential to do much good in the world. And it would all most likely end here. But still, it would a good death and a noble one. And maybe that was all anybody could hope for. Certainly it would be a better death than many Jim had known over the years. Friends and foes aplenty he had seen die. Some died well. Some died badly. Some died as cowards. Some had died bravely. Some had died as fools while others sacrificed their lives for the greater good.

"Grandfather," Jim whispered, "grant that if this young man and I go to meet our deaths on this day that those deaths mean something." Jim continued to whisper Comanche prayers as they drew closer to the cliff.

The quality of the air seemed to be changing as Jim could swear it was getting warmer. Dillon must have felt it as well because he pushed back his hood and threw Jim a questioning look. Jim nodded in confirmation.

They soon found out why. The ice road ended at the mouth of a large square tunnel that had been cut into the side of the cliff. Where the ice road ended, a concrete road began and it was here that Dillon and Jim Anthony left their snowmobiles. Dillon removed his goggles, let them hang around his neck as he stepped onto the concrete path. "Feel that?" he said.

Jim nodded. "You got your gun handy?"

Dillon unzipped his jacket, drew it back to show the Jericho 941 in a shoulder holster. Jim grunted in satisfaction. He himself had a .44 Colt Anaconda. It was a larger gun than he normally would carry but Jim had no illusions about what they were facing. He himself didn't plan on letting Shani get within ten feet of either himself or Dillon. As soon as he saw her-

"Jim?"

Jim snapped out of it and looked into the worried face of Dillon. "You okay? You went away there for a minute."

Jim gripped his shoulder. "Yes, yes. I'm fine. We should get started."

"Look…about what happened back there. When I froze up…there's something that I should tell you about what happened to me when I was just a kid—"

"There will be time enough for that later on. Right now we have to keep ourselves focused on the mission. Come."

"I just want you to know it won't happen again. You have my word on that."

"I know. Come on."

They didn't need flashlights as the tunnel had sufficient lighting for them to see where they were going. Their footsteps crunched on the concrete under their feet as they continued on. They walked for about twenty minutes before coming to an intersection where three tunnels split off from the main one. Dillon grunted in disgust. "So which way do we go now?"

Jim said nothing. Merely walked over to each tunnel's entrance and hunkered down, staring at the ground and lightly brushing his fingers over it. Only after he had examined all three tunnels did he stand up and pointed firmly at the one on the far right. "We go this way."

Dillon nodded and followed. The tunnel gently sloped downwards and amazingly, it was getting warmer the further they went. In fact, after a solid hour of walking they shed their cold weather gear entirely as it was now far too hot and uncomfortable to wear.

They continued on, the tunnel widening gradually until it became a gigantic chamber. Amazingly, they now saw trees growing on either side of what had turned into a paved road. But these were trees unlike any either Dillon or Jim Anthony had ever seen before. They resembled ferns but were of a gigantic height and they weren't green but a dark golden red.

Jim suddenly put out a hand to stop Dillon. He pointed up at one of the trees. Something that resembled an albino alligator but with large claws resembling those of a raccoon, slick silver-gray skin and far larger eyes than that of any alligator Jim had ever seen regarded them from its perch on a thick branch.

"Should we shoot it?" Dillon asked in nervous wonderment. "Whatever it is."

"As long as it doesn't bother us we won't bother it. Let's keep moving." They did so unmolested. The creature apparently was content just to watch them walk by. The heat was now comfortably soft and the roof of the cavern became wider and higher. Dillon and Jim were now walking up a hill. They reached the top of that hill and both of them stopped. They stood for perhaps a minute taking in the breathtaking sight before them.

It was Jim who broke the silence; "Welcome to Ultima Thule, my friend."

He knew something of architecture and it was immediately apparent to him that the magnificent huge buildings were of a design he knew for a fact was not that to be found on any city in the outside world. Huge carven columns and amazingly graceful plinths decorated the wide boulevards and streets. Pyramidal towers stretched up to the roof of the cavern, a roof that Dillon and Jim could no longer see. Spectacular circular fountains sprayed what looked to Dillon to be liquid fire but Jim knew what it was. "Vril," he whispered.

"What?" Dillon asked.

"The energy source of Ultima Thule. It's what gives The Evocation Drive its power. Sun Koh used Vril energy to keep his assistants alive all these years. A Vril Master can use the energy to heal or destroy. I never thought I'd live to see so much all in one place at one time. Amazing."

"How do you plan on finding Sun Koh?" Dillon asked.

In response, Jim leveled an arm at a double line of ten marching men approaching them. "Somehow I don't think that's going to be a problem."

The double line soon reached them. Tall slender men, dressed in simple tunics and trousers with puttees wrapped around their lower legs. One man, who Jim presumed to be the leader carried a slender staff which looked like polished steel. He used this to gesture at Jim and Dillon that they should come with them. Jim couldn't help but examine them with detached scientific curiosity. They looked human enough but they were remarkably fit and tanned despite living underground for only God knew how long. Their faces held a sort of terrible calm serenity that Jim had never before seen on any face. Their entire bearing was one of cool mystery and transcendence.

"What do we do?" Dillon asked.

"Go with them. You wanted to find Sun Koh, right? Well, this is the fastest way to get to him."

"You seem to have a habit of putting yourself in a trap."

"Sometimes that's the best and easiest way to find out what you want to know or to get your hands on who you want to get your hands on. The whole trick is to make sure that you can walk out of the trap the same way you walked in."

Dillon and Jim fell in step with the men and they walked through the wide streets. They saw other men and women and even a few children. They did not look at the strangers but continued on with their business as if visitors from the outside world walked among them every other day.

They came to an ornate building that had the majesty of a temple. The entire building hummed as if an enormous power source were contained within. The building had no stairs. Instead, evenly sloping ramps afforded access inside. Dillon, Jim and their honor guard soon found themselves standing inside a circular chamber. In niches spaced evenly around the chamber were marvelously carved statues of ivory, gold and brass. So well-crafted were they that they could well have once been humans transformed into statues.

"You look upon the statues of the former magistrates of Ultima Thule," a powerful voice behind them said. "Men who wisely and well regulated the customs that all who live here must adhere to. It is how the Vril-Ya have managed to live in peace for millennia."

Dillon and Jim turned to see standing behind them a man who might well have been the most perfect human being either of them had ever seen. Spectacularly muscled, standing an even six foot six, his tanned golden skin seem to glow with energy from within his very body. He stood as if he were King of The World and even his blond hair swept back from his high forehead in a regal manner. He dressed simply in calf high black leather boots polished so well that Dillon could swear he could see his reflection in them. Crisply starched and pressed jodhpurs and a military shirt completed his outfit that he wore as if they were royal robes. Piercing blue eyes rested first on Jim Anthony. He spoke again in that powerfully resonant voice; "Jim Anthony. Believe it or not it is good to see you, old friend."

Jim's laugh was a bark of derision. "You have a strange way of treating your old friends! Most of of my time of late has been spent trying not to get killed by your people."

"Events got out of hand. My intention always was to recover the Evocation Drive without engaging you. I did not know where you had hidden it but I am a patient man and I was prepared to wait until you led me to it. People have been killed unnecessarily."

"Way I hear it," Dillon said, "You don't have much of a problem killing folks to get what you want."

For the first time the golden man turned to look at Dillon and amazingly he smiled. "You must be the young man who has been giving my paladins sleepless nights. You should hear what Sturmvogel says he's going to do to you the next time you two meet. In a way it's actually flattering. But where are my manners? I am Sun Koh. And you are—"

"Dillon."

"A pleasure. If you are an ally of Jim Anthony then you are a foe to be honored and respected." Sun Koh looked back at Jim. "Although I would not have it so. Once before I offered a place at my side for you to serve me willingly. I would make this offer again."

"What about me?" Dillon asked.

"If Anthony would have you, I have no objections to your continued existence."

"Thanks. I guess."

"Why so generous, Sun Koh?"

"Because it has been too long for all of us, Anthony. You yourself have no more place in the world today as it is than I do. There was a reason we lived at the time we did. We lived too far past that time. In my case because I had a mission to fulfill. In your case you simply continued living long after you lost your purpose to do so. But join with me and I bring about a new world, a new age. An age where men like us can direct mankind to its proper place in the universe."

Jim felt the corners of his mouth twice as they pulled back in that old familiar hunter's grin. "But I do have a purpose, 'old friend.' You gave it to me when you came back into my life. And you could have changed your name, lived anywhere in the world you wanted. With your wealth, your abilities, your intellect, you would have had no problem doing so. You could even have tried to make up for some of the harm you've done and find peace within your spirit. But you held onto your plans for all these long wasted years. And for what? Minx is trying to drink himself to death. Alaska Jim is burned out. Sturmvogel and Shani have become mad dogs that should have been put down years ago. Karsten is even more of a sadist than he used to be. I hate to see what's become of Jan Mayen. And you? What have you been doing here in Ultima Thule? Lording it over these people, telling them lies about how you're going to bring back the glory that was Atlantis?"

"Atlantis *will* live again!" Sun Koh stepped forward, blue eyes sparkling like diamond chips. "This time nothing has been left to chance or miscalculation. **Der Wurmloch** has been rebuilt and refined. The years may not have been kind to me, Anthony but they have been productive. And as always, patience has proven to be its own reward."

Anthony sighed. "Why do you think we're here, Sun Koh? This can't happen. It won't happen. And you know why? The Evocation Drive. I've tampered with it. You try using it and there's no telling what will happen."

"You would not do that. I know you were at Critias Base when the U.S. attempted to harness Vril energy! You saw yourself how disastrous the results can be when Vril energy is tampered with by those who know not what they are doing!"

"This cannot happen. I am prepared to take any risk necessary to convince you to give this up. If not, we will all take our chances here. But this cannot happen."

Amazingly, the anger faded from Sun Koh's face and he smiled. He had a rather engaging and pleasant smile. "What if I promised that you could have Delores back, Jim? Whole. Just as you remember her."

Jim kept the angry despair swelling inside his chest from reaching his face. "What do you think you know about my wife?"

"I'm sure that Alaska Jim told you that over the years we've returned to the world for various missions. During those times I took advantage of the opportunity to check up on you myself. I've had my people keeping tabs on you but there were certain areas of your life I respected and considered off limits. Mrs. Colquitt-Anthony is one of those areas."

"Whatever you think you know, Sun Koh…you don't."

And now Sun Koh turned to look at Dillon. "And what of you, Dillon. Do you have moments in your life you wish you go back and correct?

Tragedies that were not meant to have happened? I am sure you do. Men like us...our destiny is forged in the roaring crucible of calamity and cataclysm. You have known great loss as I have. As Jim Anthony has. What have you lost that that you wish to regain, Dillon?"

"Don't listen to him, Dillon," Jim ordered. He knew what Sun Koh was trying to do. Sun Koh had tried to do the same same to him many years ago. It was a sub-vocal trick that actually persuaded the listener to continue listening to the speaker, something that many charismatic speakers had mastered. Some were born with it, some learned it over years of training and practice. Jim had long suspected it was a natural talent Sun Koh had been born with. And Jim suspected that it was because he was trying to distract them from-

-Dillon exploded into action, his right leg pistoning backward to take Ashanti Garuda in the pit of her stomach with explosive force. It was difficult to say who was more surprised; Jim, Sun Koh or Shani herself. She hit the ground hard, tumbled over and over.

Sun Koh did not attack as either Dillon or Jim expected. Instead he took off, running deeper into the building with the speed of a racehorse. Surprisingly, the men who had escorted Dillon and Jim did not attempt to seize them or engage them in battle. They simply stood where they were, regarding them with remote, distant eyes.

"What gives with them?" Dillon said warily.

"The Vril-Ya have lived here for untold thousands of years with no violence. They don't even know what it is anymore. And I'm glad to see that Sun Koh hasn't taught them."

"Hey! Shani's gone!" Dillon pointed at the spot where she had landed.

"Because the goal isn't to beat us. As long as Sun Koh activates **Der Wurmloch** they've won. But we have to stop him from activating it."

"You really did tamper with that gehooka?"

"No! I just said that to throw doubt in Sun Koh's mind! I told you that thing was far too dangerous to fool around with! The Evocation Drive is fully operational!"

Without another word the two of them took off after Sun Koh, running through the circular chamber into a long corridor that took them to a simple concrete beam bridge with ornately carved balustrades on either side spanning a deep chasm.

And standing there in the middle of the bridge stood Ashanti Garuda. She smiled, looking so beautiful it seemed impossible that she was so deadly and dangerous. Her sari was as black as an undertaker's suit.

"Don't take any chances," Jim said firmly. "Shoot her." He went for his gun at the exact same moment Dillon did.

Shani's hands whipped up and out of them sped two throwing knives. They struck the guns in the hands of both men, knocking them out of their hands to spin away. They clattered to the ground, barrels bent into uselessness.

"Ooookay," Dillon said, shaking his stinging hand. "Plan B?"

Jim ignored the pain in his own hand, never taking his eyes off of Shani. "How good are you? Really?"

"I survived a fight with Sturmvogel and you still have to ask?"

"Sturmvogel isn't Ashanti Garuda."

"And Ashanti Garuda isn't me."

Jim turned his head to look at Dillon. Dillon's eyes were no longer a sparkling copper. They had darkened to a moody, molten gold.

Jim nodded. "Let's get this done, then."

Slowly they walked toward Shani and she walked to meet them. They met in the middle of the bridge. For a long minute the two men and the one woman sized each other up. She stood in a blatantly insolent manner with one hand on her hip, her smile widening as if in anticipation of a good meal or even better sex. Dillon cracked his knuckles. Jim Anthony rolled his neck and shoulders, working out the kinks.

Dillon lunged forward and Shani's leg whipped upwards in a front kick Dillon blocked with crossed forearms. Shani pulled back the blocked leg and brought it back and up over her head to slam her foot into Dillon's face. He stumbled backwards.

Shani ducked under Jim's roundhouse punch and delivered a side kick into his ribs on his right side. She followed that up with a spinning kick to the side of his head that knocked him to his knees.

Both men staggered to their feet, stunned, just into time to catch both of Shani's feet in their chests thanks to the flying double kick she delivered with stunning force.

Dillon and Jim lay on their backs, pulling air into their lungs as Shani strolled around in a wide circle, straightening her disarrayed sari. She still smiled.

"She's showing off," Jim muttered as he got to his feet, held out a helping hand to Dillon who took it and stood up.

"And doing a damn good job of it, too," Dillon replied. And he came in at her, this time with a front snap kick of his own that Shani blocked with an embarrassing ease. She sent him flying with a short yet powerful jab to his jaw. She turned to meet Jim's attack, sliding under his straight punch and ending up in back of him. Her right elbow landed in the middle of his back, throwing him into Dillon, who had gotten to his feet.

Dillon caught Jim, thrust him to one side and reached out, caught Shani's arm, deflecting the punch she threw at him. He twisted the arm up behind her back, his intention to break it.

Incredibly, Shani flipped up and over and landed behind Dillon, twisting her arm loose as she did so. She gripped the top of his head and yanked it viciously backwards. At the same time she swept his legs out from under him and he hit the ground once more with bone-numbing force.

Shani turned around just in time to catch a hard right from Jim. He back fisted her with the same hand then closed in to get his hands on her neck. All he needed was three seconds to break that slim pale neck-

-which he never got as Shani brought her her arms up and inside Jim's. One of his arms were easily as thick as both of hers put together but the strength in her body was nothing short of astounding. She broke the death grip he had on her neck, seized him by his clothing and threw him to the ground.

Shani dropped a knee into his midsection, driving the air out of his lungs. The world grayed out for a few seconds and when it came back into focus, Jim saw Shani leaning over him, a knife in her hand. The knife sped towards his heart-

-and never found its target due to Dillon's flying kick throwing Shani off of him. The knife clattered away as she rolled over and over.

Dillon reached down, yanked Jim to his feet. "Go! Get Sun Koh!"

"I can't—"

"Dammit, Jim, GO! The point is to stop Sun Koh, right? Then go stop him!"

There was no time to argue and Jim knew that Dillon was right. Shani wasn't even trying to kill them. She wanted them to see **Der Wurmloch** activated and Sun Koh triumphant and *then* she would kill them.

Jim turned and ran.

Dillon grinned at Shani. It was a wide grin full of righteous maliciousness. "Just me and you, sweetness. What say we forget all this silly fighting business and just go for a walk until Jim and Sun Koh finish their beef, okay?"

Shani's answer was a spiteful hiss and she flung her arm in Dillon's direction. The golden bracelet entwined around her left forearm slid off

and straightened out and Dillon realized the bracelet actually was a living snake of some sort that she wore as an ornament.

The snake sped directly at him like a living arrow. Dillon's right hand came up with a speed that made even Shani blink in surprise and then Dillon held the snake at the base of its head between the first two fingers of his hand. With a casual pressure of those fingers he broke the snake's head and flung it at Shani's feet.

"I guess this means we can't hold hands during that walk, huh?"

Shani screamed and came at Dillon so quickly he had no time to get out of the way or even adequately block her blows. Stunned, he staggered backwards. Shani grabbed his arm and gave it a wrench and Dillon bellowed as he felt his shoulder dislocate with excruciating agony. Shani pounded a series of rapid punches into his chest while holding onto the dislocated arm, agony flooding Dillon's entire chest.

Barely able to see through the blinding pain he snapped his head forward, smashing Shani in the face. She yowled in unexpected shock. Dillon promptly head-butted her again. And again. She let go of his arm.

Shani staggered around and around in a small circle, tears running freely down her face. Dillon had broken men's noses with a single head-butt but Shani's cute snub of a nose remained unbroken and indeed, except for some redness looked as if it had suffered no damage at all.

What is this woman made out of? Dillon wondered. He seized his wrist and yanked his shoulder back into the socket with a dull, meaty pop. The pain was still there but long ago Dillon had been taught how to use pain or ignore it.

But he couldn't ignore the slim daggers that came flying his way while he had been putting his shoulder back in place. One sank half its length into the meaty part of his right thigh while the other bit deep into his right side. He felt the wickedly sharp blade scrape his ribs.

And then Shani came at him again with a spinning tornado kick that lifted him completely off of the ground. He twirled in mid-air and came down on the ground hard. He rolled, got up on one knee just in time to catch a front kick right in his face. He rolled again, tried to put more distance between the two of them so that he could have some time to regroup.

Another blistering fast and powerful kick that made his already throbbing head feel as if it were exploding from within. Blood burst from his nostrils as he skidded along the rough concrete, losing skin on his arms in the process.

He could feel blood running down his leg inside his pant leg and down his side. If he didn't get himself together quick and defend himself he would soon lose too much blood to be-

-Shani's slim leg flickered out again like a snake's tongue and once more Dillon arced through the air, propelled by her kick. Again he tried to get up but Shani was having none of it. She danced around him, hips wiggling in a manner that in another setting would have been sensual. Again Dillon tried to get up and again she kicked him viciously in the face. Dillon hit the ground hard this time and he felt something inside of him break. *This bitch is going to kick me to death,* he thought, dimly.

That very thought brought a volcano of pure roaring rage to life inside of him. Dillon rolled over on his back and lunged to his knee in time to catch Shani's leg. Her mouth sagged open in disbelief. She looked deep into Dillon's eyes which were now raging golden swirls of fury.

He punched her in the stomach so hard that he felt tissue and muscle fibers in her body rip and tear. Shani shrieked and staggered away, doubled over, gasping in great heaving whoops as she fought to get air back in her lungs.. Dillon wobbled to his feet, dragging the leg with the dagger in it as he got into a defensive stance.

Shani recovered and came at him again, feinting toward his head with her left hand and too late Dillon saw the trick and fell for it. With her free hand she went for the knife in Dillon's side and shoved it in all the way.

But at the same time Dillon reached down, ripped out the dagger in his leg and brought it up and around, bright drops of his own blood flying in the warm air. Jim had told him that Shani's saris were all woven from spider silk and could stop a bullet or a knife.

That's if you stabbed her where she was protected by the spider silk, that is.

Dillon slammed the knife home right into the armpit of her upraised arm she had used to feint with as it was now the one unprotected spot on her body.

Shani screamed and threw herself backwards. Dillon collapsed to the ground, weak from blood loss and the brutal battering he had taken.

Shani's face was no longer beautiful. It was now a demonic mask of hate. "You *dare...!*" she hissed. Her trembling hand went up, tore the knife loose. Blood freely dribbled down her side, splashing on the ground.

Lightly she ran at Dillon, the bloody dagger held high and her intention was plain. She meant to bury it in his chest, carve out his heart and eat it raw in front of his dying eyes. And there was nothing he could do to stop her. He had nothing left. But at least he'd held her here, he'd gotten Jim through and Dillon had no doubt Jim would stop Sun Koh. This was not a good death, no. But at least it was not a wasted one. Dillon looked Shani defiantly in the eyes as she drew back the dagger with both hands.

The sounds of the rifle shots reverberated through the air a few seconds after the bullets slammed into Shani's chest, knocking her back and away from Dillon. She threw up her arms to protect her exposed head as more bullets battered into her, coming fast and furious, the sounds of the shots echoing and reechoing through Ultima Thule. She was driven further away from Dillon, the impact of the bullets like sledgehammer blows to her body.

Shani turned to run but she had misjudged how far back the barrage of bullets had forced her. Normally she had perfect spatial awareness at all times. But the shock of being stabbed, of having a weapon pierce her flesh in all these years…! It had completely and totally disoriented her. She slammed into the balustrade of the bridge and flipped over.

Dillon dimly heard her fading scream of frustrated hatred as Ashanti Garuda fell into the gorge under the bridge. Weakly he smiled and lay down on the cool concrete. Even smiling hurt.

He heard footsteps approaching him and then something wet on his face. He opened his eyes to see that one of the sled dogs stood there, licking his face, whining in anxiety. Dillon turned his head to see that all the surviving sled dogs were there. And they hadn't come alone. "What the hell are you doing here?" Dillon demanded in an angry whisper.

"Savin' your black ass it looks like to me," Alaska Jim Hoover replied. He put his still smoking Henry rifle down on the ground next to him. He pulled Dillon's shirt up to look at the the knife still embedded in his side. "But I'll say this for you; Anthony picked good when he picked you to side him. If'n I hadn't seen you take on ol' Shani I never would have believed it."

"You coulda shot her sooner, y'know."

"You were doin' jus' fine until she stuck you. If she hadn't I do believe you'd'a took her. C'mon, let me get to tendin' to them wounds. You done lost a fearful lotta blood. Where's Anthony?"

"Went after Sun Koh."

Alaska Jim nodded, unsheathed his Bowie knife and began cutting Dillon's shirt off of him. "Think I should see about keeping you alive in case he manages to stop th' end of th' world?"

"I'd appreciate that greatly."

He heard footsteps approaching him and then something wet on his face.

7.

The passage Jim Anthony had been following for the past ten minutes had no lighting but he could see a light far ahead of him that provided not only enough illumination for him to see where he was going but also gave him a destination. He paused to remove what remained of his clothing and stood garbed only in linen pants. Around his waist were two belts. One was his indispensable main weapon-the belt woven of fibers from a rare South American plant. The other greatly resembled a money belt with a number of reinforced pouches.

Having divested himself of the encumbering garments, Jim seemed to undergo a transformation. Even at his age he was still a big man with muscles of impressive proportions. The dull ache in his limbs faded away as the old fire seemed to infuse every nerve and muscles with renewed energy. Jim proceeded, feeling how right this was. If this was to truly be his final battle, he would rather go out no other way than this.

He continued down the passage, having about another forty feet to go before coming to the end. Jim's skin tingled and he reached out a hand to feel the nearest wall. It was warm to the touch, like a human body. And he could feel something he could not identify in the very air itself.

And then Jim came to the circular entrance and stepped into a chamber of dizzying size. Before him he could see a horseshoe-shaped control center. Made of some black metal, Jim could see that the touch sensitive surface had no numbers or alphabet he was familiar with. Instead there were what he supposed to be geometric shapes and glyphs that might have been the Atlantean language.

Behind the control center, some sixty feet in the air, a swirling ball of Vril energy floated serenely, held in check by three black crystal rings rotating slowly around the ball. The rings themselves were attached to pillars of silver blue crystal that pulsed from within, suffused as they were with arcane energies. The entire room seemed to be rhythmically pulsating in time with the throbbing ball of Vril energy.

And all across Ultima Thule, no matter what they were doing, the people stopped. They stopped cooking. They stopped reading. They stopped swimming. They stopped sculpting. They stopped writing. They stopped making love. They stopped all their activity. They turned in the direction of **Der Wurmloch** and began a soft, slow chant that quietly, steadily grew in volume.

"Vril-Ya…Vril-Ya…Vril-Ya…"

Jan Mayen capered madly at the control center, dashing back and forth, manipulating the controls like a demented organist. Jim could hardly believe the change in the man. Once upon a time Jan Mayen had been an extraordinarily dashing and handsome man. He moved through high society like a prince, causing women to swoon whenever he entered a ballroom. And his reputation as a scientist had been impressive. Many compared him to Tesla himself. But now…this Jan Mayen looked as if he hadn't slept or eaten in weeks. And even from here Jim's sensitive nose told him that he certainly hadn't washed.

"Dear God, Mayen…what's he done to you?"

Mayen looked up, his huge eyes staring wildly at Jim. He laughed, a ragged bark. "Anthony! Good of you to join us! Sun Koh said you'd be along! Good! Good!"

Jim moved forward, slowly and carefully. *Where the hell was Sun Koh?* "Mayen, shut it down. You don't know what it'll do."

"Of course I know what it'll do!" Mayen pointed up at the sphere. "Here we collect the Vril energy necessary to power **Der Wurmloch** and when it has done so, the world will forever be transformed! We will bring peace and order to the planet at last!"

"Step away from there, Mayen. I mean it. I'd prefer not to hurt you—"

"The only one who will be hurt is you, Anthony." Sun Koh emerged from a side tunnel. He had changed into what looked to Jim to be a lightweight suit of flexible modern material shaped to look like medieval German armor. He walked toward Jim with that unnerving natural graceful majesty. A majesty only amplified by the armor he wore as if born to it. "The Aerash Evocation Drive has been programmed and installed. The Vril energy is being gathered from the very people and city of Ultima Thule. There is nothing you or anyone else can do to prevent the correction of The Great Mistake. Soon, the world as you knew it will be gone and a new world will be born."

"A world with you as its king?"

"I give you a last chance to leave, Anthony. Go be with your friend in these final moments and worship whatever god claims you. Leave me to my destiny."

Jim said not another word. The time for talking was way past. He sprinted toward the control center, his hands going down to his belt with the pouches. Thanks to long years of experience he did not need to look at the pouches to see what he needed.

He performed a somersault over the control center and landed next to Jan Mayen. A simple shove with his brawny shoulder and Mayen went flying. Jim held marble sized colored hard gel capsules in both hands. The combination of the marbles would produce a powerful acid. If they could eat through the controls-

-Sun Koh's fist crashed into the side of his head. The gel marbles scattered in all directions as Jim's hands reflexively opened. "Not this time, Anthony! Not this time!"

In the city, the people lifted their arms, their eyes glowing as the Vril energy that had kept them alive for so many thousands of years slowly left their bodies.

"Vril Ya…Vril Ya…Vril-Ya!"

The crystal rings spun faster as if they had to work harder to contain the ball of swirling Vril energy that grew in size, pulsing faster and darkening to a savage orange-gold.

Jim recovered and set himself in a defensive stance as Sun Koh charged at him. They exchanged a dizzyingly rapid series of strikes and blocks, neither man able to get past the other's defenses or land an effective blow.

Jan Mayen shakily got to his feet, pushing his dirty, greasy hair out of his eyes. He stumbled back to the control center, his eyes anxiously scanning the enigmatic symbols that even after all this time made his eyes ache if he looked at them for too long. He had to regulate the Vril energy carefully or it would become unstable. He'd blown up one *Der Wurmloch* and he did not think that Sun Koh would look upon him with favor if he blew up another.

Jim twisted out of the way of a roundhouse kick, rolled and came back up on his feet. He whipped his belt off of his waist, the fibers stretching easily as Jim whirled it around his arms and up around his shoulders like a makeshift nunchaku.

Sun Koh came back at him again and Jim whipped his belt back and forth, the weighed half-buckle striking sparks on the armor. Sun Koh blocked, threw a sidekick that Jim leaped over with an agility a cougar would have envied. He came back to the attack, slamming the belt buckle into Sun Koh's face. Sun Koh stumbled backwards, more surprised than hurt. He reached up one armored hand, looked at his blood on his metal fingers. With a roar he leaped back to the attack.

Underneath the massive sphere of Vril energy, a portal irised open.

Within was a black shaft that led to nowhere but infinity.

Across the city, the people began to fall, their bodies once full of eternal life now desiccated husks, sucked dry of the precious Vril energy that had sustained them. But the ones who were still left chanting ever louder as if urging on their own deaths:

"Vril-Ya! Vril-Ya! VRIL-YA!"

The fountains of Vril energy were now leaving their pools and streaming through the air like ribbons of cosmic fire, pouring into the chamber through pyramidal windows and cascading into the blazing ball of what was now pure Vril of such flawless, undiluted quality that had not been seen on the planet in a million years.

Jim back-flipped away from Sun Koh's sweeping roundhouse punch. He leaned to the right to evade Sun Koh's follow up and slammed a shoulder into his armored side. It was enough to back him up, give Jim enough room to wrap his belt around Sun Koh's wrist and pull, the rippling muscles on Jim's back and shoulder moving like pythons under his scarred, bronzed skin.

His intention was to yank Sun Koh off his feet and get him down on the ground but Sun Koh instead went with the yank, using the momentum to somersault over Jim's head and come down on Jim's other side with a huge Thud! Again his armored fist crashed into the side of Jim's head and Jim felt blood fill his mouth.

Dillon and Alaska Jim looked up at the dozens of blazing strips of Vril energy that writhed through the air toward a tall pyramidal tower. All around them they could hear what sounded like the very city itself chanting;

"Vril-Ya! **VRIL-YA! VRIL-YA!**"

Alaska Jim calmly removed something from a pouch and offered it to Dillon. "Have a chaw?"

Dillon had one arm wrapped around one of the dogs, comforting it. The other dogs huddled together, their eyes fearful as they looked up at the Vril energy filling the sky.

Dillon sniffed, frowned. "What is it?"

"Chewin' tobaccy, a'course." Alaska Jim bit off an impressive hunk and vigorously chewed it.

"That's all you can think to do at a time like this?"

Alaska Jim shrugged. "Ain't got a jug or a woman."

Dillon sighed and wished he hadn't. His entire chest felt as if someone had taken a rusty saw to his ribs. He pulled the dog closer to him and the animal licked his face. Dillon smiled weakly at the dog. "It'll be over soon, girl…one way or the other."

Sun Koh came up off the ground as if levitating, his scissor kick sending Jim flying through the air. Jim slammed up against the control center. Even that was pulsing in time with the sphere as if it were alive and breathing.

"Master! Master! We have done it! At last we have done it! **Der Wurmloch** is primed and ready!"

And so was Jim. He pushed himself to his feet, whirled his belt over his head, the weighed halves of the belt buckle clinking together.

Sun Koh saw what he was going to do and ran to try and stop him. "NO!"

Jim Anthony let fly with the belt, whirled around to meet Sun Koh's charge. Jim fell back on the control panel, whipping his feet up and into Sun Koh's stomach. With every bit of strength and accuracy he could muster, Jim pushed him over and out.

Like a well-returned golden volleyball, Sun Koh flew through the air toward the shaft. He hit the edge of the open portal and rolled into the shaft. One hand went out to grab the edge. He dangled over the black abyss, reaching up with his other hand to try and get a more secure hold on the lip of the portal and haul himself up.

"You don't understand!" Sun Koh bellowed. "None of you ever did! We could have made this world Heaven! We could have been gods!"

The belt hit the sphere of Vril energy and a ripple ran through the sphere as the iron of the belt buckle agitated it. Pure white light burst from the sphere as the control center shuddered and ripped itself apart from the backlash of disrupted energy that ran through it.

The black crystal rings exploded into powder and the sphere of Vril energy, freed of its spinning cage dropped down into the shaft, taking Sun Koh with it.

Jim ran over to the shaft and looked down. He saw Sun Koh, glowing in his armor like a small star at the center of a larger one as he rode the ball of pure Vril energy. And Jim could still hear his voice; "It was our destiny to save the world…"

And then Sun Koh was gone.

Jim bent his head and said a silent prayer for Sun Koh's soul. He walked over to where Jan Mayen lay unconscious. The control center had blown up in his face. Amazingly, the man was still alive. Jim picked him up, threw him over his shoulder in a fireman's carry and left that smoking, ruined chamber.

Alaska Jim helped Jim Anthony lower Jan Mayen to the ground. "Why didn't you leave him?" he wanted to know.

"For the same reason I didn't kill you when I had a chance to back at your cabin."

Alaska Jim nodded. "Fair enuff." He paused to spit a healthy stream of tobacco juice. "Your friend ain't doin' so good."

He didn't have to tell Jim that. He could see for himself, starting with the pool and trail of dried blood. Jim knelt down next to Dillon who had his eyes closed. "Hey."

Dillon opened his eyes. Eyes that were suddenly so old, watery and tired. "Hey. How'd we do?"

"Sun Koh is gone. Where's Shani?"

Dillon was too weak to even gesture with a hand at Alaska Jim. Instead he waggled his head in his direction. "He saved me. Shani got me good with a couple of knives. If he hadn't shot her, I'd be dead."

"Shot her?" Jim frowned. "You know those saris she wears are bulletproof."

"Shot her enough times to knock her back over th' railin', though. She fell into the gorge."

"Then she's dead."

But Alaska Jim shook his head. "Until an' unless I see her body, Ashanti Garuda ain't dead. Not by a damn sight."

"You really think she survived that fall?"

"You really think she didn't?"

Jim didn't answer that. He looked back down at Dillon. "Let's see about getting you out of here, kid." The greyish look of Dillon's skin and that terrible look in his eyes worried him. Jim kept his voice light and joking as he said, "This is no fit place for a man who helped save the world."

Dillon smiled. "You saved the world, Jim…I just kept you company while you did it. And I'm glad I did." His eyes closed and Dillon's head fell limply to the side, resting on his shoulder.

"Dillon!"

SIX MONTHS LATER...

Dillon looked up at the portrait of his mother. Chamberlain Frick had been good enough to provide him with a high resolution jpeg of it which was now the wallpaper on Dillon's cellphone and Frick had promised that when Dillon found a permanent residence he could have the original portrait. Frick had already commissioned an artist to paint a duplicate that would replace it.

The past six months had been truly intense ones as well as interesting on many levels. Jim Anthony had insisted that Dillon take an entire month to properly recover from his extensive injuries. Dillon had given him quite the scare back in Ultima Thule when he passed out as Jim had feared the younger man had succumbed to his wounds and died. Dillon had been too weak to explain to Jim at the time that he was placing his body in a state of induced hibernation to keep himself alive until Jim could get him proper medical attention. It was a technique Dillon had learned during his time training with The Warmasters of Liguria.

The five months after that had been spent at The Pueblo and devoted to Jim teaching Dillon the skill sets of tracking as both art and science, of how to correctly identify sign, of how to constantly refocus between the miniscule data of the track and integrating that into the entire pattern of the quarry's behavior. Of how to anticipate and predict what that quarry would do. And then, after all that, how to apply that to the hunting of men.

Jim had also taught Dillon some Criminology as he considered it essential that Dillon be familiar with the various schools of thought and theories of Criminology. They had stayed up late many nights debating Classical School theory with Sociological Positivism or the Chicago School with the Italian School. In time, Jim had become as impressed with Dillon's mind as he was with his martial arts skills. Dillon had a fine mind and as a result, Jim had asked Dan Fowler for an extraordinary favor and Fowler had granted it.

While Dillon had been training, Jim Anthony had tons of explosives quietly shipped to Antarctica. Alaska Jim Hoover had spent three full months planting explosives all throughout Ultima Thule and wiring the entire city. And then at the end of those three months, he had left with the dogs.

Back in New York, once he had gotten the word from Alaska Jim that he was clear, Jim pressed a button, detonating the tons of explosives and burying the city of Ultima Thule for all time. It was a decision he had agonized over for those three months. The city was one of extraordinary archeological value. But all the Vril-Ya were dead, their life force sucked out of them, stolen by that infernal device. Jim had finally made the decision to bury them and their city and let them rest in peace.

Alaska Jim Hoover had taken the dogs and returned to ("Where else would he go?" Jim had said with a chuckle) Alaska. Dillon had spoken to him several times since then, requesting one of the dogs when he found a permanent residence. Alaska Jim had informed him that two of the dogs were pregnant and anytime he wanted a dog, he'd have his pick of what were sure to be huge litters.

Jan Mayen had spent four months in a private hospital, receiving the best of care, paid for by Jim Anthony. When he was released, Alaska Jim had requested that Jan Mayen be sent to him. Alaska Jim had even somehow managed to contact Ludwig Minx and he had also come to Alaska to live with his old friends. "They'll be good for each other," Jim Anthony had said when he heard this. "They'll heal each other."

As for Rudolf Sturmvogel and Rolf Karsten, there was no sign of them anywhere. Vera Gemini put a staggeringly large bounty on their heads and Jim himself had made a special trip back to Buenos Aires to try and pick up their trail but it was no use. The two men had vanished as if they'd been teleported off the planet. But Jim knew that one day they would return. Especially Sturmvogel. His pride would not allow him to forget that Dillon had effectively bested him. One day he would look to settle that score. But Dillon wasn't worried. If and when he and Sturmvogel fought again, Dillon intended to make sure that The Storm Bird wished he'd just let the whole thing go.

The only thing that gave both Dillon and Jim Anthony cause to worry was their uncertainty over the final fate of Ashanti Garuda.

Dillon had asked Jim one night while they sat next to the grave of Jim's grandfather, just talking; "And Ashanti? You know that Alaska Jim has always maintained she's still alive, even after that fall."

Jim had shrugged. "My head tells me that there's not a human being alive who could have survived that fall. But my experience with Ashanti Garuda tells me to check under my bed and in my closet at night before I go to sleep. But considering all the security systems Vera is building into the new Teepee I don't think I'll have anything to worry about."

Vera Gemini had taken it upon herself to rebuild The Teepee which, she assured her father, would be totally impregnable when she was done with it. Dillon believed her. He also came to believe that he and Vera Gemini would never have a conventional relationship. She simply wasn't a conventional woman. She had a decidedly different path to walk and it wasn't with him. Not in that way. But he knew he had her respect and her friendship and that was far from a small thing.

Dillon turned his head as Frick rounded a corner and came towards him. "Ah, I thought I would find you here. Mr. Anthony has just arrived. Are you all packed?"

In answer, Dillon bent down to pick up a backpack. Frick had had it made for him. Based on the design of the MOLLE backpack it was a modular load bearing backpack that carried far more than one would have guessed from its size. "Yes. All ready to go. I guess you'll be glad to get rid of me freeloading off of you the past couple of days."

Frick reached out both hands to rest them on Dillon's shoulders. "You are always welcome here at The Baltimore Gun Club as my guest, young man. Through fair or foul, we will be here for you. And as I have told you before, if you wish to join both Mr. Anthony and I would be more than honored to sponsor you."

Dillon placed his right hand on Frick's. "One day, Frick. One day. I still have a lot to learn and I have to do a lot to be worthy of her." Dillon looked at the portrait of his mother. "She was magnificent. I could never even come close to what she was. But I'll never stop trying."

"As you wish, Master Dillon. Come."

Frick led the way to the library. Jim sat in the same chair that he had sat in when he and Dillon first met. And, as before, there was a seat for Dillon. He sat down while Jim said to Frick; "Tea, please."

"Of course, sir."

Jim Anthony smiled at Dillon. Dillon could have sworn he was wearing the exact same clothes he had worn when they first met. The only difference was that Jim was now clean-shaven.

"So, we come to the end of our time together. You've been a good student, Dillon."

"I couldn't have asked for a better teacher. And I still can't believe I'm going to train at the FBI Academy," Dillon said. "From everything I've read about it, their requirements are very stringent. And I'm not a citizen of this country. I don't even have a Social Security number! How did you get past all that?"

"Well, it helps to have the Director as one of your best friends. Dan himself will be supervising your training so don't make me look bad. Not after the way I've bragged about you." Jim reached into the inside pocket of his sports jacket and withdrew an envelope. "There's your train ticket, a passport, driver's license and social security card all in the name of Jake Dillon. That'll be your name while you're in Washington D.C. There's some walking around money in there as well. Go straight to FBI headquarters and Dan Fowler's office when you arrive. He'll be waiting. You'll stay the weekend at his house and then Monday morning you'll start your training."

Frick returned with the tea and as he poured the steaming liquid into china cups he said, "So have you decided to become an FBI agent then, Master Dillon?"

"I don't know, Frick. I really don't. But the opportunity for further training is one I can't pass up. And there's still so much about the world I don't know that I have to learn before I decide what to do."

Dillon nodded. Frick left them to see to his other tasks and they drank tea quietly for a few minutes. Then Jim spoke quietly; "There's something I think you should know. I know that you say you don't know what you want to do but I think your course has already been laid out for you."

"What do you mean?"

"All through the world's history there have been men and women of courage and bravery possessing talents, skills and abilities that place them a cut above humanity. I know without a doubt that you are one. Remember that list you showed me when we first met?"

Dillon grinned. "I've still got it."

"One day a young man or young woman will come to you and they will show you just such a list. And your name will be on it. And you know why?"

Dillon shook his head.

Jim put his cup down and leaned forward, hands clasped between his knees. "Because you will remember what Sun Koh forgot. Look out the window. What do you see?"

Dillon looked at the street, at the bustling throngs of men and women going about their daily business, oblivious as to how close they had come to their lives being stolen from them.

"Before he fell into the abyss he had created, Sun Koh said to me that it was our destiny to save the world. 'We' being myself, him, those names on your list and many others besides. But what Sun Koh forgot is that it isn't our destiny to save the world. It's *theirs*." And he pointed at those men and women. "We are just the guardians of this world. We hold it in trust and keep it safe for *them* and it is for them to decide the course they will take. Do you understand what I'm trying to tell you?"

Dillon nodded, copper eyes shining bright with promise and purpose. "Yes, Jim. Yes. I do."

Abruptly Jim stood up and held out his arms. Dillon stood up and the two of them hugged fiercely, bonded together in a friendship forged in blood and fire.

Jim broke the hug and pretended there was something in his eye as he said, "Best be on your way. Your train leaves in ninety minutes. Did Frick arraign a car and driver for you?"

"He wanted to walk, Master Jim." Frick said. He had something draped over one arm. "It's a bit chilly out there, Master Dillon. You should take this." Frick held it out. Dillon took it and almost dropped it in surprise. The dark bronze colored leather jacket was far heavier than he had expected it to be.

"What is this thing made out of? It feels like it weighs a ton!"

"Body armor plates are inserted in the sleeves, the back and the front. The lining is a combination of Kevlar and Fugunaga micromesh fibers which makes the jacket fireproof as well as bulletproof. For all intents and purposes you might as well be wearing wearing body armor." Dillon put it on. Frick adjusted it on his shoulders by tugging on the braided passants.

"That looks really good on you, Dillon," Jim said. "I'm jealous. Where did you get it from, Frick?"

"It used to belong to me, Master Jim. I wore it when I was a much younger man living what I like to call my wild days." Chamberlain Frick smiled. "That jacket saved my life more than once. It would give me great comfort to know that it was keeping you safe, Master Dillon."

Thank you!" Dillon hugged Frick. He bent to pick up his backpack. "The two of you have given me so much. I'll never be able to repay you."

"Be the man your mother would be proud of and that is all the repayment required, Master Dillon," Frick said. "Come, I'll walk you to the door."

"Dillon," Jim said.

Dillon half turned, his backpack slung over one shoulder.

"Thank you. For everything."

Dillon smiled and again followed Frick.

Jim reseated himself in his chair and poured another cup of tea.

Presently, Frick returned. He stood by the chair and they watched as Dillon walked the path leading to the gates and beyond that, Fifth Avenue.

"That's a young man I daresay the world will be hearing a lot of in the coming years, Master Jim."

"I would not dare to dispute your wisdom, Chamberlain Frick."

"It was good of you to thank him, sir."

"And why not, Frick? That young man taught me that I still have a few adventures left in these old bones."

"I never doubted it, sir."

Dillon reached the gates, which opened automatically at his approach. He paused briefly to turn and wave. Jim Anthony lifted his teacup in return. Then Dillon was out the gate and swallowed up by the never-ending parade of humanity going about their business that kept the world eternally turning.

EPILOGUE

Sun Koh opened his eyes to look up into a star-choked sky. He could never remember having seen a night sky with so many stars. It was as if entire galaxies were up there, so clear that he felt he could reach up and take a handful. Slowly he sat up, golden ash sloughing off his skin as he did so. He lay in a field of lush, knee-high grass. The golden armor he had been wearing had turned to powder on his body. Slowly he got to his feet, naked as the day he was born. He stood on thickly muscled legs, a magnificent titan of bronze in the night.

Where was he? Jim Anthony's accursed belt with its metal buckle had disrupted the delicate matrix the crystal rings and pillars had woven around the ball of Vril energy. There was no telling where the Vril energy had taken him. He could be in the past, the future. He looked around, his genetically superior eyes able to see in darkness almost as well as in the daylight. Lush plant life and vegetation grew up all around him. Sun Koh looked back up in the sky at the stars and began doing elaborate and complex calculations in his head based on the constellations he was looking at. They would be able to tell him where he was and, even more importantly, *when* he was. And when he was finished he threw back his head and his booming laugh filled the night air.

By his calculations where he was standing was somewhere in the middle of the Atlantic Ocean. This was ancient Atlantis. But easily a hundred years before the founding of The Atlantean Empire. The irony was far from lost on Sun Koh. As was the inescapable circle of destiny. He had been sent here to give The Atlantean Empire a second chance! With what he knew of the future he could now steer the empire on the proper course, prepare it far in advance of The Ice Age so that it would never fall! His plan had not gone as he had envisioned but he had won! Armed with what he knew he could correct all that was wrong thousands of years before it could happen.

Hearing the low growl from his right, Sun Koh dropped into a crouch. Bulky, malformed man-shaped forms crept towards him, guttural sounds emerging from their throats. Sun Koh counted at least a dozen. He didn't even stop to think about it twice. He turned and ran across the grassy plain.

The beast-men gave chase, howling and hooting as they galloped after

Sun Koh, most of them using their long, apish arms to propel them even faster over the ground.

Before him in the dark, Sun Koh could see a rude, pyramidal altar that the beast-men had built. Sun Koh had no idea who or what they were but he had no intention of dying at their hands. He had an Empire to build.

He scrambled up the rude pyramid, clumsily made from dirt and rocks piled on top of each other and then packed into shape. Sun Koh made it to the top and looked down.

On all sides he could see the beast-men gathering around the base of the altar. More of them had joined the first dozen. The sounds they made were sounds that Sun Koh knew well. They were sounds that animals made before they attacked. He smiled. It was well. He was Sun Koh, Prince of The High House of Thule and heir to The Ocean Throne. And now he knew that it was his almighty destiny to lay the mighty foundations of The Atlantean Empire. And if there was to be a baptism of blood to begin this great work then so be it.

He stood up, hands outstretched. "Come then! Come to me! Come to Sun Koh!"

The beast-men swarmed up the pyramid and the bloody slaughter began. Sun Koh had no reason to hold back and he unleashed his full power on the beast men. Bones were shattered. Jaws were completely torn loose by sledgehammer punches. The screams of the beast men filled the night and mingled with the songs sung by Sun Koh and the uncaring stars above glowed with their pure divine light.

THE END

ABOUT OUR CREATORS

WRITERS –

DERRICK FERGUSONis from Brooklyn, New York where he's lived most of his life. Married for 25 years to the wonderful Patricia Cabbage-stalk-Ferguson who lets him get away with far more than is good for him.

Derrick's interests include old radio shows, classic pulps from the 30's/40's, comic books, fan fiction, Star Trek, pop culture, science fiction, animation, television and movies...oh yeah...movies. He is currently the co-host of the podcast BETTER IN THE DARK http://betterinthedark. podomatic.com where his partner Thomas Deja and he rant and rave about movies on a bi-weekly basis.

Derrick's primary love is reading and writing having written four books to date: Dillon And The Voice of Odin, his love letter to classic pulp action/adventure with a modern flavor. Derrick Ferguson's Movie Review Notebook and its sequel The Return of Derrick Ferguson's Movie Review Notebook. Diamondback Vol I: It Seemed Like A Good Idea At The Time, a spaghetti western disguised as a modern day gangster/crime thriller. For information on how to purchase them, please visit the Pulpwork Press website: http://www.freewebs.com/pulpworkpress/

Anything else you'd like to know about Derrick, check out his Live Journal: http://dferguson.livejournal.com/

JOSHUA REYNOLDS is a professional freelance writer. In addition to his own work, he has written for several media tie-in franchises, including Gold Eagle's Executioner line and Games Workshop's Warhammer Fantasy and Warhammer 40,000 lines. An up-to-date list of his published work can be found at http://joshuamreynolds.wordpress.com/

COVER ARTIST-

ADAM BENET SHAW –Accomplished painter, illustrator, and comics creator, Adam has garnered acclaim across a number of artistic media. After completing studies at the Cleveland Institute of Art in Ohio, the Edinburgh College of Art in Scotland and Watts Atelier in California, Shaw was selected as an emerging American artist to watch by European gallery owners and exhibited in London, England. He has been featured in "New American Painting", selected multiple times for the Arkansas Art Center's Delta Exhibit, and shown at the prestigious "Red Clay Survey" at the Huntsville Museum of Art. His work has also been shown in over 50 group and solo shows in the US and internationally.

His figurative paintings are a prominent part of a 140-foot mural entitled "The History of Cotton" at the National Cotton Exchange Museum, St. Jude's Children's Research Hospital, the National Contact Bridge Museum, and a treasured part of private and corporate collections. He has created storyboards for several motion pictures, including Paramount Pictures' film "Black Snake Moan" directed by Craig Brewer, stage design for operas and corporate events, and character illustrations for the gaming industry. His published graphic novel work includes the series "Dead In Memphis", "Bloodstream" for Image Comics, "David: The Illustrated Novel" from Shepherd King Publishing and "Harpe: America's First Serial Killers" from Cave-in-Rock Publishing. He shares his love of art through teaching and workshops at his studio in the Broad Avenue Arts District in Memphis. Recently he has been painting book covers for pulp publishers Pro Se Productions and Airship 27 Productions.

INTERIOR ILLUSTRATOR –

ROB DAVIS is a freelance artist who, since 1989, has penciled comic books from Malibu, Marvel, DC, and others and is best known for his work on the Star Trek comics from Malibu and DC Comics working on Star Trek, Star Trek The Next Generation, and Star Trek: Deep Space Nine.

Currently Rob is the Art Director, Designer and Illustrator for New Pulp Publisher Airship 27 and self-publisher of comics via his Redbud Studio Comic imprint. For Airship 27 he is the regular interior illustrator on their series of Sherlock Holmes-Consulting Detective books, Robin Hood trilogy, Secret Agent "X" series, and others. For Redbud Studio comics he is the illustrator of Graphic Novels: ROBYN OF SHERWOOD with writer Paul Storrie, and DAUGHTER OF DRACULA with writer Ron Fortier. His online gallery is at: robmdavis.com/gallery